THE NATURE OF THE BEAST

The Dunes and the field were deserted. He withdrew the mask, hands and feet from under his belt, his hands shaking.

Every time he went to don his costume he would tremble like crazy. A plane passed far overhead and he gazed up at the flickering lights, relishing the tingling sensation pulsating through his belly.

The werewolf's time was near.

He slid his hands into the gloves.

His body was twitching and quaking, his muscles shuddering and bulging in a paroxysm of intoxication.

Another minute and the werewolf would be reborn.

He slowly inched the mask downward over his face, adjusting it to align the eye slits and nostrils and ears over his own, his head spinning. Why did his thoughts always whirl this way . . . why was it so difficult fo focus . . .

A taloned foot shuffled forward a pace, followed haltingly by another, than another, each stride gaining in length and strength. He climbed to the rim of the nearest dune, raised his arms skyward and howled.

The werewolf was on the prowl.

THE WERELING

DAVID ROBBINS

LEISURE BOOKS   ∞   NEW YORK CITY

DEDICATED

*To the memory of
the works of the peerless few:
Homer, Poe, Hitchcock,
and
those other weavers of the illusion
known as fear.*

Deception, yes.

But try telling that to your goosebumps.

A LEISURE BOOK

Published by

Dorchester Publishing Co., Inc.
6 East 39th Street
New York, NY 10016

Printed in the United States of America

THE WERELING

PROLOGUE

1881

"QUIET NOW, BOYS," THE BURGOMASTER WHISPERED, "or he'll hear us for sure!"

The twelve villagers and the Englishman stopped in their tracks, their hushed murmurings abruptly fading to complete, attentive silence.

"Can we be sure, Otto?" the priest asked, his pale white skin a stark contrast to his black vestment.

"Is there any doubt in your mind?" the burgomaster responded, pointing at the fresh tracks clearly revealed in the mud at their feet. "Is there any doubt at all?"

The Englishman gaped at the imprints, his mind still reeling from the recent rush of events. Wasn't it only thirty minutes ago they had arrived in this small village on the border of Hungary, stopped to rest and refresh their horses before continuing their journey to Budapest? Hadn't their coachman indicated the Red Boar Tavern and urged them to enjoy themselves for twenty minutes while their team was attended to?

"Are you feeling poorly, sir?" the burgomaster asked the Englishman, gently gripping his arm near the elbow. "Brace yourself. There is more to come."

More? *More?* The Englishman shuddered, vividly recalling the horror of the past half hour. They were only three feet from the door of the tavern when the . . . *thing* . . . swept out of the encroaching twilight and leaped on his wife. Poor Sheila! She had managed a horrified shriek, and then the hairy monstrosity had sunk its fangs in her neck and born her off into the darkness. It had all happened so damn fast! He hadn't even had time to react!

"Would you rather go back?" the priest was asking him.

The Englishman shook his head. Not on your bloody life! He wanted the thing that had abducted his wife! He wanted it *dead*.

"What now, Otto?" one of the villagers, a lean man bearing a pitchfork, asked the burgomaster.

All the men gazed at the ramshackle hut thirty feet in front of them.

"We must go in after it. The beast has taken this man's wife inside. We all know what that means, don't we?"

As one, the rest of the villagers nodded their understanding. The priest crossed himself.

"What is this thing?" The Englishman could feel his initial shock being replaced by a building rage. "What took my wife?"

The priest sadly turned to the Englishman and muttered a word in Hungarian, a term the Englishman did not understand.

"What is it, in English?" For the first time the Englishman noticed the fear apparent in every face.

"I don't think you have a word for it," the priest answered, his hands nervously fingering a large crucifix which was attached to a gold necklace.

"What is it?" the Englishman demanded, clenching his

fists, his blue eyes flashing.

"It is the Man-Wolf, sir," the burgomaster stated, "and there is no word for it in your tongue. But we know of it. And you would, too, if your senses were not dulled by too much civilization."

"What the hell do you mean?" The Englishman was thoroughly confounded. "Make sense, will you?"

"It is the spirit of the wolf using some pitiful soul to wreak vengeance on us mortals," the aged priest replied.

"The spirit of the wolf? What do you mean?"

A piercing howl suddenly rent the night and the villagers whirled, facing the hut.

And the thing.

The Englishman could scarcely credit his swirling senses. There, framed in the doorway of the hut, was something resembling a cross between a man and a beast. It stood as tall as a man and had two arms and two legs, but there any resemblance ended. Hair sprouted all over its face, hands, and feet. There were actually talons on the tips of its fingers. And, worst of all, a coating of blood caked the thing from head to toe.

The priest crossed himself again.

"On him, boys!" the burly burgomaster ordered, and the villagers charged.

The thing in the doorway crouched, snarled, and leaped on the first of the villagers to reach him. Muscular arms swept the screaming villager into the air and tossed him aside. The second villager was grabbed by the throat and contemptuously flung away. The third villager, the tall one with the pitchfork, cursed and lunged, and his pitchfork sliced into the thing, catching it full in the chest.

The Englishman stood stunned, transfixed. He saw the

thing howl and knock the tall villager to the ground. It staggered for a moment, stopped, grabbed the handle of the pitchfork with both hands, and simply yanked the prongs from its chest.

"Lord, give us strength!" the priest shouted.

"Step clear!" the burgomaster yelled, and as they did he drew a large revolver from the pocket of his bulky wool overcoat.

The thing saw the gleam of the gun and started to back off, stumbling, blood oozing from the wounds in its chest.

"Do it now!" the priest directed.

The burgomaster gripped the gun firmly, aimed, and fired.

Amazed, the Englishman watched as the bullet hit the creature squarely in the forehead. The thing flipped backwards and sprawled in the mud. It twitched for a minute and then was still.

"I just wish . . ." the burgomaster began.

"I know," the priest said.

The villagers closed in on the creature in a circle, their clubs, axes, and knives at the ready.

"We got him," one of the villagers gleefully cheered.

"Yes, but not the spirit of the wolf," the priest commented gloomily.

The Englishman stood next to the thing, numb, watching as they turned it over. The facial features were twisted and horrible, coarse and bestial.

"I don't understand . . ." the Englishman began.

"There, there, son." The priest draped his arm over the Englishman's shoulders. "I doubt you ever will. This is part of our way of life, but to you, an outsider, it must remain a puzzle."

"But . . . but what is this abomination? What was that you were saying about the spirit of the wolf?"

"He deserves to know," said the burgomaster, the only other one present who spoke English with any degree of fluency. "It was his wife, after all."

"My wife!" The Englishman roused from his stupor. "Where is my wife?"

Two of the villagers came from the hut, glanced at the priest, and shook their heads.

"What . . . ?" The Englishman started for the hut, but three of the villagers restrained him.

"What the bloody devil do you think you're doing?" the Englishman raved, straining to break their grip.

"It is for your own good, sir," the priest soothed him. "You must understand that."

"I don't understand any of this! Let me go!"

The burgomaster came over and stood in front of the Englishman. "I will try to explain it to you, although I doubt you will ever comprehend. We live with this every day of our lives. You outsiders call it superstition. We know it to be real. This man," he said pointing at the dead creature, "was formerly of our village. Two months ago the spirit of the wolf came on him, changed him, transformed him into what you see. He began attacking us, his former friends and family, and he almost killed his own sister. We tried to track him, but the ground was too dry and he was too clever. Last night it rained and rained. Tonight he attacked your wife. We were able to track him and kill him, but we could not kill the spirit of the wolf. We did not have the silver bullet."

"What is this drivel?" the Englishman fumed. "Let me go this instant!"

"We can not do that, sir, for you would try to see your wife, and that would be bad, very bad." There were tears in the priest's eyes.

"You . . . you mean . . . she's dead?" The Englishman could barely get the words out, although he had known in his heart that she was—dreaded in his soul that she was.

"I am so very, very sorry." The priest lowered his friendly gaze. "But yes, I'm afraid so."

"Dear God!" The Englishman slumped, and if not for the villagers he would have fallen.

"Not God, sir," the burgomaster disagreed. "The evil one. The one who sends the spirit of the wolf to invade a man and take over his soul, to turn that man into a beast with an unending thirst for human blood. The spirit of the wolf has haunted man for ages, since time was first recorded. It will continue to do so until it is recognized for the evil it is and stamped out."

"I still don't see . . ." The Englishman could not go on, the multiple shocks taking their heavy toll on his state of mind.

"It is simple," the burgomaster continued to explain. "The spirit of the wolf can be destroyed, but we did not have the silver bullet necessary. The spirit of the wolf will continue to roam this world, seeking victims, until finally stopped. It passes from human to human, from generation to generation, until someone can stop it with the ordained means. Even then, even when you do use a silver bullet, you only kill a part of the spirit of the wolf, the part which took over that particular human. The spirit lives on, weaker, but enduring. It will linger until we can remove the beast in all men. We—"

"You can stop. He can't hear you," the priest said.

The Englishman had passed out.

"The man . . . such a tragedy . . ." one of the villagers mumbled.

"The tragedy is that it is not over," the priest sighed. "We killed the man but not the wolf in him. It will live on, biding its time, seeking new opportunities, looking for another human receptive to its evil. Maybe not in our lifetime, but you can count on the fact that the spirit of the wolf will find some miserable soul, somewhere, sometime, and satisfy its need for blood and violence."

The burgomaster glanced up at the cloudy sky. "I wonder when?"

It was hungry.

It was thirsty.

It was time.

Hovering undetected over one of the larger land masses on the rotating planet, it searched. There had to be one, at least one, somewhere.

There was always at least one.

It was so very thirsty.

But this time a new method was called for. The vessels were becoming smarter; they possessed more knowledge. True, they were still skeptical when it came to diverse realities, but that was good. They would not be ready. They could not kill an enemy if they did not know what the true enemy was.

Still, caution was called for.

A new way.

Just the mind this time. Leave the body, externally, alone. Besides, the mind was the key. Dominate the mind and the vessel was powerless.

Yes.

The new way would work. Effectively.

Fill the vessel and leave the external to work itself out.

There was always a way.

Always.

It was hungry.

It was thirsty.

And, vibrant with expectancy, it discovered the next vessel.

It was indeed time.

April 10

HARVEY GRIPPED THE EDGES OF HIS pillow and riveted his eyes to the small screen in breathless expectation. The eager band of human hunters closed in on their elusive quarry. The track dogs, straining on their leashes, bayed a chorus of excited yelps and yowls. They knew the killer was nearby.

They didn't know the hunted had turned on the hunters.

He appeared on the rim of a low hill in front of them, silhouetted by the full harvest moon. His piercing howl froze his pursuers, human and canine, where they stood.

Then he was among them.

The first two dogs were torn to bloody shreds with savage swipes of his glistening claws. A deputy, scared and shaking, grabbed for the revolver in his holster . . . too late. His throat was slashed open as the werewolf vented another banshee howl of bloodlust and delight.

This was his favorite part of the picture. Harvey couldn't contain himself.

"Go! Go! Go!"

The werewolf was in full primal stride, tearing and rending and maiming at will. The hunters were panic-stricken, decimated. The werewolf paused, red lining his mouth and streaking his chin, and howled for the third and final time.

Harvey had seen the movie a dozen times. He knew it by heart, and knowing what came next provoked him to groan in desperation.

The minister arrived, hurrying up to the spreading carnage, clutching the cure, the ultimate cure, in his hand.

Shrieking, the werewolf spied the minister and charged, his twitching claws extended.

The minister raised the gun, aimed carefully, and pulled the trigger.

A red circle blossomed on the werewolf's chest and he staggered, surprised and puzzled by the first pain he'd ever known. Another circle appeared as the minister fired again and again. The werewolf twisted and snarled as the silver bullets penetrated his body.

In seconds it was over. The werewolf lay on his back staring lifelessly up at the moon. The minister stood over him and watched as the transformation began.

"I'm sorry, dear brother," the minister said sadly. "There was no other way."

Harvey did not wait for the final scene and the closing credits. In disgust, he jumped from his bed and flicked the television set off.

"Damn them!"

Harvey walked over to his second-floor window and gazed out at the night sky. Why was it always the same? Why did they have to kill him? Why couldn't they just leave him in peace to enjoy the forest and the mountains? He hated it when the werewolf was killed, yet it happened in every movie he saw, in every story he read. *Why?*

"Harvey?" He heard his mother's high, raspy voice yell from downstairs. "Did you call me?"

"No, Mom." Couldn't she leave him alone for five minutes? "It was the TV."

"Well, keep it down. A body can't hear herself think around here with you making such a racket."

"Yes, Mom." Harvey clenched and unclenched his hands as he fumed with suppressed anger.

Damn her! How much longer? He just had to get away from her, from this house, from Ocean City itself. Nowheresville. One day he would leave, simply pack up and head for New York City and a life of adventure, a life of freedom. To be free, at last, of her domination! It was a dream. But how could he do it? On his deathbed his dad had made him promise to take care of her, comfort her, and insure she was never lonely or wanting. Harvey leaned his forehead against the cool glass pane in his window. He'd certainly tried his best for twelve years.

Somewhere in the night a police siren sounded, prompting memories of his dad. Harvey could still vividly recall the thrill he felt when his dad had been dressed in his police uniform for his next shift. The shining badge, the metal buttons, and the gun were all so impressive to a child. How proud he'd been of his father, and how devastated when that escaped convict had gunned his dad down. Harvey clearly remembered the chilling experience of his seven-year-old mind being forced to cope with the staggering reality of his dad lying on a hospital bed, attached to various life support systems, appallingly pale and weak. Why had it happened? *Why?*

Harvey vigorously shook his head to send away the scary recollection of a night he'd prefer to forget. He turned from his window and checked his alarm clock. Eight. Time to get going.

It wouldn't stay dark forever.

Warren was working late in the newsroom, scanning the Associated Press wire for any relevant state news, when the phone lit up on one of the incoming lines. He knew the jock wouldn't bother to answer it and the office and sales staff were usually gone by six. Sighing, he picked up the receiver.

"WREN, Warren Mckeen, news director here." He stifled a yawn. "May I help you?"

"Is this the radio station?" asked an elderly male voice.

"Yes it is. WREN radio, six-ten on your dial."

"Well, is this where I can get fifty dollars for my news tips?"

"News tip?"

"Yeah. There's a fire going on here at the corner of Fifth and Prescott. They took one woman away in an ambulance."

"It figures! The one time I'm not listening to the scanner . . ."

"Beg pardon?"

"Nothing. Did you say Fifth and Prescott?"

"Sure did. Now do I come down there or do you send the fifty bucks to me?"

"Fifty bucks?"

"Sure. Like you say on the radio. Fifty bucks for the best news tip of the week."

"I'm afraid I have good news and bad news for you." Warren was busy scooping up his recorder, journal, and jacket. "The good news is that this is the best news tip I've received in a month . . ."

"And the bad news?" his caller broke in.

"The bad news—" Warren couldn't help but smile— "is that the station which offers the fifty dollars is WGYN, not us."

"Why, you dirty son—" the old man began indignantly.

Warren hung up.

The fire was probably extinguished by now and the injury undoubtedly slight, but he couldn't pass up the chance to be covering a live event. He relished the rare opportunity to actually be at the scene. The news director and sole news department of a second-rate radio station seldom enjoyed such a professional treat.

Warren hurried out the rear station exit and hustled to his '74 Ford. Even as he slid in behind the wheel and started the engine he was mentally calculating the time and distance involved in reaching Fifth and Prescott. For once, he prayed, let me reach the scene before everyone's gone home.

His hasty petition was answered.

Three police cruisers and two fire units were ringing a three-story structure situated on the corner of Fifth and Prescott. Flames were evident in the third-floor windows and on the roof. A small crowd had gathered to watch the firemen douse the flames. The blaze was under control, posing no danger to any homes on nearby lots. Four policemen were clustered together shooting the breeze.

Warren approached the ranking officer, a sergeant, and drew his Atlantic City Police Department press pass from his wallet.

"Hi, Sarge. I'm Warren Mckeen from WREN news. Can you tell me—"

"Warren? Is that you?" the sergeant cut him off.

"Who . . ." The flickering flames prevented Warren from distinguishing the officer's features.

"George Sanders. Remember?"

Warren remembered. Classmates at Atlantic City Central High. George had graduated and gone on to the police academy. He'd always known which career he would pursue.

"The last time I saw you was—what?" George reflected for a moment. "I got it! Four years ago, after you'd returned from the Navy. You're in broadcasting now?"

"Unfortunately."

"What do you mean? We all know radio people make big bucks." George laughed and extended his hand.

"Don't I wish," Warren said. He shook, then pointed at the gutted house. "Anything I can use?"

"Sorry." George chuckled. "Some old lady falls asleep while smoking in bed. She wasn't feeling well and had gone to bed early. A neighbor spotted the fire and got her out in time. She's at Seacrest Hospital by now, suffering from mild smoke inhalation. Not much of a story."

"I know," Warren admitted, "but it's the only one I've got."

Harvey admired his reflection in the full-length mirror attached to the outer panel of his closet door.

Sweat glistened on his body. His finely developed physique, conditioned from seven years of weightlifting on a rigorous regular regimen, pulsed and gleamed with health and vitality. The biceps and triceps in particular displayed the growth characteristic of concentrated attention.

Harvey reveled in his decidedly masculine weightlifter's

20

form. His superb body was his one outstanding accomplishment, the reason none of the kids at school had ever possessed the temerity to mock him or challenge him despite the general consensus that he was weird. Harvey knew they had thought he was strange. Who cared? Who needed them? Besides, he was through with school, with that entire intellectual pansy scene. Who needed it?

The clock on his dresser indicated nine o'clock.

It was time.

Harvey glanced down at the barbells on the floor near his feet. They were, without a doubt, the wisest investment he'd ever made. Even his mother, who had initially scoffed when he'd purchased them, now respected his presence and his power. Oh, she still nagged and carped and criticized. But she hadn't struck him in five years. Not in five years.

It was getting late.

Harvey grabbed his jeans and pulled them on over his jockey shorts. He selected a navy blue tee-shirt and slid it on. Finally he put on his blue sneakers. He was all set for his nightly tonic, his nocturnal prowl.

Harvey turned on his radio to provide his mother with the impression he was still in his room. She knew better than to enter without his express permission. He paused at his door to stare longingly at the posters adorning all four of his bedroom walls. They were carefully organized. On the north wall were his treasured werewolf posters: Lon Chaney Jr. from *The Wolfman*, Michael Landon from *I Was A Teenage Werewolf*, and others. Some were classics, collectors' items. On the east wall were his vampire posters, from Bela Lugosi to the present day. The south wall was covered with posters of different monsters from

21

numerous horror films; *King Kong, Godzilla, The Mummy, The Creature,* and two dozen others. The west wall held only a few posters, and magazine and newspaper clippings.

The north wall arrested his attention again. The werewolves. His favorites.

Harvey cautiously eased his door open and listened. His mom, as usual, was wrapped up in some mindless television program. He could never understand how she could tolerate that juvenile trash. Except for a periodic movie it was all nonsense. At least she would be occupied for several hours.

He shut the door and quickly went down the stairs to the front hallway. The outer door, his gateway to freedom, was inches away. At the far end of the hall sat his mother, her eyes glued to that blasted screen.

The Dunes beckoned.

The moment Harvey stepped into the night, into the sea breeze coming off the Atlantic Ocean, into the clamor and confusion of the resort sounds of Ocean City, his spine tingled and he inhaled deeply. Let others flock to Ocean City for the heat, the sun, and their vacation tans. Give him the cool night winds, the protection and seclusion of enveloping darkness.

Harvey turned left, heading down Avalon toward the boardwalk. Their white frame home was located four blocks from the highlight of Ocean City's scenic attractions—the flashing lights and alluring amusements found on the boardwalk. Let the ignorant tourists be entertained by silly man-made diversions. They didn't know what they were missing.

The Dunes.

One block from the boardwalk Harvey turned south on Surf Avenue. He began jogging. Two miles to go, two miles to the untarnished, isolated, natural splendor of the Dunes. He easily covered the distance, running in blackness once he passed the end of the boardwalk and the last street light. The lack of illumination didn't bother him. His night vision was exceptional.

Sounds filled the air, crickets, night birds, an occasional frog. Once, in the distance, a dog howled. He bore to the left across Surf Avenue and entered a field, following a path he knew by heart, a path he'd taken nearly every night for three years, ever since he'd discovered the Dunes.

Harvey sprinted up a small rise and stopped, thrilled at the sight of the rolling stretch of sand, brush, and gnarled trees. The one place in the world where he felt truly at ease, at home.

The Dunes, as the remote area was called by the locals, was a square mile of sand, dense, almost impenetrable shrub, and widely scattered stands of trees. The eastern edge bordered the Atlantic Ocean. The beach in that area was unusually rocky, unfit for sun bathing and shunned by the tourists. Hunters tended to avoid the Dunes because game was scarce. Only brave romantics ventured into the Dunes, and then not very far.

"Damn!" Harvey whispered in annoyance. A couple was there. Feminine giggling carried to his ears. A man laughed.

Harvey crouched and worked his way around the nearest dune, careful to make use of any cover provided. He hated it when his privacy, his home, was violated by these idiots.

They weren't behind the first dune.

Harvey used a clump of bushes to conceal him from their view as he crawled to the top of the next dune and peered over the rim.

They were there.

The woman was a diminutive blonde, the guy a brunette, both in their twenties. They were lying on a green blanket, their antics displayed in the dim glow of a lantern. The woman was on her back, still giggling, evidently amused by her companion's fumbling attempts to unfasten her bra. He was muttering mild obscenities.

"Blake, if you keep going at this rate," the blonde laughed, "we'll be here all night. Wouldn't my dad just love that?"

"It happens every time!" The guy yanked at the elastic back strap. "Who the hell was the moron who invented these things, anyway?"

"You know, I really don't know," the girl said in mock seriousness. "I really should look that up." She giggled even louder.

Harvey slid backward until the dune shielded him from their view. This sure as hell pissed him off! And it happened too damn often! During the winter months it wasn't so bad, but as soon as spring and summer rolled around they would be back. In July and August twelve nights out of the month could be ruined by these clods!

More laughter from the other side of the dune.

Harvey bit his lower lip in raging frustration.

Not this year, damn them! *Not this year!*

But what to do?

He pondered a moment. If he wanted the Dunes to himself—and he wanted nothing more—then he had to think of something, come up with some way to insure that the yokels kept their distance. But how could he do it? Countless times in the past he'd arrived at the Dunes prepared to relish a night of peace and solitude, only to discover his retreat occupied by cuddling couples. Countless times he'd repressed an urge to grab them and toss them out on their ears or some more appropriate portion of their anatomy. Something was called for, something effective . . .

Harvey grinned.

It was simple. It would be effective. It was freaking *brilliant*! Why hadn't he thought of this before?

Harvey cautiously inched his way to the bottom of the dune, stood up, and quietly walked deeper into the Dune, circling the pair of snickering lovers. He hid himself in a large thicket, almost laughing aloud at the thought of what he was going to do. He was thirty feet from the young twosome, their continuing banter clearly reaching his ears.

"Finally! Honestly, Blake, I think you should take lessons."

"That's enough, Lucy! Do you want to spoil the mood?"

"What mood?" Lucy retorted.

Harvey grinned. Well, you two banana-brains, he thought, let's see how this mood strikes you. He cupped his hands around his mouth and, in the finest werewolf tradition, howled.

There was a momentary silence.

"What the hell was that?" he heard Lucy ask.

"Sounded like a dog to me."

"That was no dog."

"Sure it was."

"Blake, that was not a dog! Go and see."

"What?"

"You heard me. Are you scared?"

"Of course not." Blake did not sound convincing.

"Then go and see what it was."

"Oh, Jesus! Women! All right!"

Harvey saw Blake appear at the edge of their dune. He nervously glanced in every direction.

"There's nothing out here," Blake stated.

Now Harvey knew. He howled again, slowly, eerily.

"There it is again!" Lucy yelled. "Do you see anything?"

"Nothing. Maybe it's some kids playing around," Blake suggested.

"Out here? At this time of night? Are you crazy? We're getting out of here, now!"

"Well, if you insist . . ."

Harvey saw Blake disappear behind their dune. A moment later he came into view carrying the lantern and the blanket. Lucy was right behind him, pulling on her top.

"We're never, ever coming here again," she said.

"Fine by me," Blake agreed.

"This place gives me the creeps."

"Should we tell anyone what we heard?"

"Are you serious? And have our parents hear about it? Sometimes, Blake, I don't think you use your head."

"Just thought I'd ask."

"Boy, I never heard anything . . ."

They passed out of hearing range. Harvey stood and watched as they crossed the field to Surf Avenue and began walking towards Ocean City.

Damn! It worked!

Harvey stretched, grinning. He'd discovered the perfect technique for preserving the Dunes for his exclusive personal use. This was fantastic! He walked from the thicket and climbed to the top of the nearest dune. Their dune. Their ex-dune. The crisp sea breeze ruffled his black hair. Quiet had descended on the Dunes again. It was exquisite. He stared out at the ocean and caught sight of the incoming waves rolling onto the rocky beach. Something white flashed in the corner of his eye and he glanced down.

Harvey laughed.

At the bottom of the dune, evidently discarded in haste, partially covered with sand, was the proper trophy to commemorate this historic occasion.

Lucy's bra.

April 11

"ALLAN!" THE BIG MAN'S VOICE BOOMED across the verdant, tree-covered valley. "Allan! We're leaving in twenty minutes!"

Allan Baxter lifted his eyes from the tracks he was following, sighed, and shook his head. He'd never find the fox now. He stood and gazed at the lush forest surrounding him. There would be another time, another fox. Maybe next year, if his dad elected to come to the Pocono Mountains again next spring. He invariably did. After eighteen years with the mill in Bethlehem he was eligible for four weeks of vacation each year. Two weeks in the spring the Baxter family would spend at a resort in the Pocono range. In the fall two more weeks, the two Allan hated, would be spent at a point along the Jersey shore. This year, Allan knew, his parents planned two weeks in Ocean City.

Allan headed back to the Baxter cabin. This vacation had been terrific, providing more than ample opportunities to cultivate his hobby, tracking. His mind strayed to his earlier years, to his childhood fascination with the tracks all creatures made, to his intense interest in learning what animals made which tracks, to his dedication to proving his belief that it was possible to track anything, anywhere, anytime, provided the tracker was proficient at his craft. Over the years he'd practiced and practiced, waiting for the chance to prove himself, and two years ago, thanks to the Klien girl, everyone in Bethlehem knew how good he was. The Klien girl . . .

It was the day after his twentieth birthday, March 10, a date etched in his memory. While showering that morning he'd heard a report on a local radio station's news concerning a four-year-old girl from Bethlehem who was missing and feared lost in the Nockamixol State Park, a rugged area twelve miles southeast of Bethlehem. Her father was a park ranger. He'd taken her on his rounds, left her unattended in his jeep at one point, and became frantic when he discovered she'd wandered into the woods. The rangers scoured the immediate vicinity with no success. Dogs were called in, to no avail. The ground was still damp from a recent freezing rain and they weren't able to follow the scent. A helicopter arrived and searched from the air. Again, no luck.

Allan rushed downstairs and informed his dad of the critical situation and his intention to help. His father agreed, a bit reluctantly, to drive him down to Nockamixol State Park. On the way down they heard an update detailing the general fear that the small child, if not located before dark, might freeze to death before morning. March nights in the park were frigid and harsh.

They had no difficulty locating the focal point of the search. Police, reporters, rangers, and a crowd of onlookers had gathered around a large tent pitched at the point where the girl had strayed into the trees. Allan and his dad introduced themselves and asked to speak with the girl's father.

A heavyset ranger with a distraught expression came over to them.

"I'm Dan Klien. They tell me you can help." He was wringing his hands and couldn't stand still.

"I'd like to try," Allan said. "I think I can find her."

"How? With a crystal ball?" Klien snapped sarcastically.

"No, sir," Allan answered politely.

Dan Klien seemed to soften a bit.

"I'm sorry, really sorry. But we've tried everything. Dogs. 'Copter. The works. Thirty minutes ago there was some kook here who claimed he could locate Beth psychically for the paltry sum of five thousand dollars. Are you a kook?"

"No, sir. And I won't charge you, either."

"Really?" Klien gripped Allan's shoulder. "Just what are you, son?"

"I'm a tracker."

Klien looked at Allan's dad, who simply nodded in agreement.

"We've tried tracking her, son. We lost the trail. You think you can do better than professional rangers?"

"Would it hurt if I tried?"

Klien reflected a bit.

"Nope. Guess not." He stared up at the sun. "And we don't have more than three hours before nightfall. Come on."

Klien led Allan into the woods, hurrying, acutely conscious of the lack of time. Allan opened the buttons of his wool coat, the exertion of keeping up with Klien warming him, making him hot despite the forty-degree temperature.

"We have four dozen people, rangers, hunters, and others, still out searching. They're scattered over the countryside." Klien jumped over a fallen tree. "Our best hope is prayer."

"Where did you lose the trail?" Allan asked.

"Not much farther," Klien said. "Say, I don't think I caught your name."

"Allan Baxter. My dad's name is Don."

"Tell me, Allan, what do you do when you're not tracking?"

"I'm majoring in engineering in college."

Klien stopped and stared at Allan.

"No lie?"

"No lie."

"Shit." Klien resumed walking at a faster clip.

They emerged from the trees into a clearing. Ahead was a small stream and a large hill.

"We lost her tracks at the stream." Klien stopped at the edge of the creek, a small tributary of Lake Nockamixol. "We went up and down the stream and no go. No tracks exiting from the water anywhere."

Allan knelt close to the hard ground.

Despite the recent rain the earth was like granite, frozen and unyielding. There were plenty of tracks near the stream, the tracks of all the searchers who'd passed that way, not to mention the dog tracks everywhere.

Allan stood up.

"Giving up already?" Klien asked. "I don't blame you."

"I need clear prints," Allan stated.

"What?"

"I need a set of her tracks that haven't been mucked up

by all the searchers."

"Oh."

Allan backtracked the trail of prints, scanning the ground for just one unmarred set of the girl's. Twenty feet from the stream he found them. They stood out because of their small, dainty size. Beth had paused at a large bush, leaving her impressions in the relatively softer earth at the base of the shrub. Allan knelt again and studied them intently.

"Well, you've found them," Klien said impatiently. "Now what?"

"Just checking."

"Checking?"

"Beth is, let me see, somewhere between three feet and three feet four . . ."

"She's three feet, one inch tall. But how the hell can you tell that?" Klien leaned over to stare at the footprints.

"And she weighs about forty pounds?"

"Yes, but how . . ."

"I told you, Mr. Klien." Allan walked to the stream. "I'm a tracker."

"You're also a saint if you can find Beth."

Allan watched the clear, obviously cold water flow past them. Cold? He bent over and touched the water. Freezing would be more like it. Would a four-year-old girl enter a stream of ice water? No way. What, then? He turned and scoured the clearing.

"You say her tracks stopped here?" Allan inquired.

"Sure did." Klien nodded. "I saw them myself. They came right up to the edge of the water and stopped. This creek is only a foot deep, maximum. She'd have no trouble crossing."

But would she, Allan wondered? Klien had said they'd looked upstream and downstream and found no footprints. It was doubtful that Beth could remain in the icy water for any length of time. Allan stepped back from the stream, then stopped, staring at his own feet. Of course! Why not? He'd done it often enough as a kid.

"Mr. Klien, does Beth have an imagination?"

"Sure does." Klien smiled, proud. "She can draw real well for a girl her age. Why?"

Allan slowly backed from the stream, carefully placing his feet, one after the other, in the exact tracks he'd made approaching it.

"I might have something."

"What are you doing?"

How far would she go? A four-year-old? Not far, he decided. Maybe back to the end of the clearing.

Allan crouched and studied the soil.

"What are you doing?" Klien demanded again.

Allan pointed.

There, distinctly visible at the base of a tree, was another set of Beth's footprints. This pair was heading away from the clearing, moving east.

"I don't understand . . ." Klien began, confused.

"Your daughter's quite a girl, Mr. Klien." Allan grinned. "She knew she'd done wrong by going so far from the jeep. She came through the woods, all right, to the stream. But she didn't cross it. No little girl would. That's why your search teams couldn't find sign of her across the stream or up the hill."

"Then what did she do?" Klien was still gaping at the new set of tracks.

"She played a game kids often do."

33

"A game?"

"Sure. She backtracked herself. Didn't you do it when you were a boy? Step backward in the same tracks you'd just made? She walked backward to this treeline. You and the other hunters missed noticing it because you were upset. You probably rushed your first tracking because you were so alarmed she was gone. You followed her footprints to the stream and assumed she'd crossed over. After you summoned assistance and the search teams arrived on the scene all the tracks between the timberline and the water were obliterated. Beth must have realized she better get back to you. Unfortunately, she's going in the wrong direction."

"But surely she'd notice the helicopter or hear us calling?"

Allan didn't answer. That point bothered him.

"Mr. Klien, can you lend me your walkie-talkie?"

"Sure." Klien unclipped it from his utility belt and handed it to Allan.

"Thanks. I can move faster alone. Go back to camp and get a doctor and stretcher ready, just in case."

"You don't think . . ."

"We can't know, yet. Best to play it safe."

"I'm on my way. Call me if . . . *when* you find her." Klien broke into a run.

Allan leaned down and began following the tracks as quickly as the spoor permitted. It was tough. Every couple of yards he'd come across a partial footprint. In between would be smudges, scuffs, and random bent twigs. Complete prints were few and far between. As he tracked he considered Beth's lack of response to all the men searching for her. In the earlier stages of the hunt those men had called her name over and over. She couldn't have wandered that far from the clearing. Beth would hear those searchers, unless . . .

Allan straightened. He'd gone maybe a quarter mile from the clearing. The trees were beginning to thin. Through them he could see the outline of a large wooden structure. What?

A cabin. An ancient, dilapidated log cabin, standing in silent testimony to the hardiness of the rugged outdoorsman who'd constructed it decades ago. The roof had long since collapsed. Only three of the walls were standing. The cabin yard was overgrown with weeds and bushes.

Allan glanced up at the setting sun. He'd been tracking longer than he'd realized. Less than an hour till nightfall. He'd better hurry. Kneeling, he examined the ground, carefully considering every impression and smear, seeking any indication that Beth had passed this way. The area was rocky, the soil and sign extremely difficult to read. He grinned when he found a partial indentation made by her left heel. She had been here.

There was a rustling in a shrub near the cabin and a large red squirrel darted into the open, spied Allan, whirled, and ran up the nearest tree. It paused in the fork of two branches to stare at him and chatter in irritation.

"Don't blame me," Allan chuckled. "You're the one out of hibernation early."

Allan decided to cross the small clearing where the cabin was situated and attempt to pick up Beth's trail at the point where she would have entered the trees again. He took several full strides, then froze, a new sound reaching his ears.

A brief, low whine or whimper.

Where?

Allan listened attentively, but the noise was not repeated. He surveyed the surrounding forest. No sign of movement, no crackling in the brush.

The cabin.

Allan approached it slowly, vigilant for any hint of life or another utterance.

The three walls still standing were in abject disrepair, covered with plant growth, the logs rotting and sagging in sections. The fourth wall had fallen outward, spreading over a wide area. Covering the former floor were the shattered remains of the roof. Broken logs were piled and stacked in grotesque positions. Allan stood at the edge of the floor where the fourth wall had once withstood the natural elements and studied the ruins.

"Beth?" he said aloud.

No response.

"Beth?" he repeated.

It was useless. He turned to walk away.

"Daddy, is that you?"

Her voice came from within the jumble of roof logs.

"Beth," he called, excited, "this is a friend. Where are you?"

"I want my daddy."

"And he wants you. I can take you to him if you'll tell me where you are. I don't see you."

"I . . . came in here 'cause I got real scared. I fell in this big hole . . ."

Allan was climbing over the logs, pushing some aside, eager to catch sight of her.

"Big hole? I don't see any . . ."

"Down here, mister. Look down."

He did. She was standing in ankle-deep water. Her yellow dress was torn and caked with mud. She smiled, revealing a row of even white teeth.

"I'm real happy you came for me, mister. I was scared."

Allan braced his legs against one of the logs and dropped his arms. Her "big hole" was a five-foot deep, four-foot square pit, at one time probably the cabin's root cellar.

"Grab my arms, Beth. Are you hurt?"

"Nope." She reached up and he placed his hands under her armpits. "But I'm awful dirty. Think my daddy will be mad at me?"

Allan pulled her from the root cellar and hugged her.

"I doubt it, Beth. I doubt it very much."

She grinned, and her eyes gazed fearlessly into his, and at that moment the importance of what he had done hit him, the fact that his skill was responsible for the preservation of a human life—the life of this precious little girl.

"Allan, will you get the lead out?" his dad yelled. "We're waiting on you."

Allan snapped out of his reverie and waved to his parents. They were standing arm in arm next to the family station wagon, watching him approach.

A crow cawed behind him and he turned and watched it glide through the air, envious of the fact that it could remain in the forest but he had to leave. He might be able to return after graduation. This would be his last free summer. In September he'd begin work with an engineering firm in Scranton. And in August . . .

"Come on, Allan," his mother shouted. They were getting into the wagon, and Allan still had a hundred yards of field to cover.

He sighed. In August his parents would drag him to Ocean City for one last family fling. Two weeks of scorching sand, smelly ocean water, and boring nights spent indulging in childish amusements. Give him the woods, the wildlife, the mountains any day. Ocean City. Detestable. There was no excitement, nothing to hunt. When was the last time anyone tracked a fish?

Harvey tossed the comic aside and picked up the latest issue of *Chilling Creatures*. He still had an hour to kill before his evening exercise period. Before reading the illustrated stories he paged through the classified section in the back of the magazine. Sometimes he came across rare posters for sale.

Tonight it was an advertisement for something else that caught his eye.

In the midst of the classifieds, taking up half a page, was a full-color ad for a werewolf mask. He'd seen countless similar ads before and knew from experience that the mask invariably was constructed of plastic and fashioned in ludicrous style. But this one appeared to be different. If the photograph was accurate, the mask displayed incredible detail. He skimmed the three paragraphs below the snarling visage. The mask was constructed of a pliable synthetic and guaranteed to snugly fit the facial contours of any wearer. It was touted as grimly realistic and frightening. He smiled. Weren't they all? Then he saw the price. Seventy bucks! They had to be kidding! Who could afford it? His job at the deli didn't pay all that much. It would deplete his meager savings to purchase this mask, wipe out months of scrimping, and delay his eventural departure for New York City or other parts unknown. Nope. No way.

He read the final paragraph.

Not only did the buyer receive the mask, but they would also get a set of werewolf hands and feet as lifelike as the mask. And, incredibly, the hair on mask, hands, and feet was not plastic, wool, cotton, nor any other man-made fiber or animal hair. It was the real thing, genuine wolf hair.

Wolf hair!

Harvey's hands trembled. Could it be possible? Where would they obtain it? Real wolf hair! Fantastic!

He slid off his bed and grabbed his checkbook from the top of his dresser. He opened it to his current balance.

One hundred and sixty-four dollars.

He giggled, delighted. He could do it! Sure, it might delay his getaway for a while. But, hell, he could take off anytime. This was the chance of a lifetime! If he had to stick around and tend to his alcoholic mother, the least he could do was enjoy himself.

Harvey stood in front of his mirror and envisioned himself in the werewolf outfit. Fabulous. It would be freaking *fabulous!* But what good would it do him? Should he spend seventy dollars just to admire himself in the mirror? Maybe it wasn't such a dandy idea after all. Where could he wear it except in his bedroom? Where but the . . .

The Dunes!

No one came there except the damned lovey-dovies and even they wouldn't bother him if they feared the Dunes. He'd learned that lesson last night. He laughed. This would be perfect! If the werewolf outfit was all the manu-facturers cracked it up to be, his prayers were answered.

He could insure his privacy and scare off all intruders. Once the word spread that the Dunes were haunted by a werewolf he'd have them to himself every night. And what harm would it do? He'd only frighten the fools, not hurt them.

It would be terrific!

Harvey sat down at his desk to write out the check.

This would be the smartest move he'd ever made.

"I think it's the dumbest idea I've heard this week."

"The captain says we do it, we do it."

"It's asinine."

"Is that your esteemed opinion?"

"There's more. Want to hear it?"

"No, Patterson, I don't," Lieutenant Gilson said wearily. "It's out of our hands, anyway. There's nothing we can do about it."

"Request permission to see the captain."

Lieutenant Russ Gilson slammed his fist on his desk. "No, dammit! Now drop the subject, Earl."

"But Russ . . ." Earl began to protest again.

Russ rose from his chair, his massive hulk towering over the slim, blonde, agitated sergeant. He leaned on his knuckles and glared into Earl's blue eyes.

"Earl, you listen, and you listen good. I agree with you one hundred percent. I told the captain, in so many explicit words, that he was a fucking idiot. And—are you paying attention, Earl?—he agreed with me. But he doesn't have any choice. The word comes from higher up. Do you understand now? If we're told to pair off the female officers, we pair off the female officers."

Earl glowered at Russ, unwilling to give an inch.

"Just like that? Don't get me wrong. I'm not saying the girls can't handle themselves. They can. But what if a 10—92 or a 10—95 comes up? We've got the tourist season coming up. You know how damn hectic it gets. Besides, it's standard procedure to pair a female officer with a male officer. So . . ."

"That policy is being superseded," Russ interrupted.

"Why, for God's sake?"

"Because, as you just mentioned, we've got the busiest part of the year coming up and we're short staffed and the city budget was cut back this year and I could go on and on and on, but I'm tired and disgusted and not at all in the mood for any more crap from you. So—" Russ held up his hand as Earl started to speak—"unless you want to pull desk duty for the next two weeks, I'd suggest you leave it be for now. Get your ass on home. Your sister Gloria probably has supper waiting for you."

Earl wheeled on his heel and stalked from Russ's office.

Russ wearily sank into his chair. Christ! It'd been a long day. Earl had been one more aggravation to add to the list. Funny, though. He couldn't blame Earl for being pissed off. It was only four years ago that Earl had been on stakeout with Officer Clayton and she'd been blown away. What a mess that'd been! The press on the department's back. The politicians on the scent of a career booster. And poor Earl, blaming himself where no blame was due, chiding himself to this very day.

Time to go home. Russ leaned back and stretched his tired muscles. It would feel good to stand under a hot shower for fifteen minutes. After that, steak and potatoes and . . .

Oh, shit! Gretchen! He'd forgotten Gretchen. She'd

called yesterday afternoon and asked him to stop by. Why the hell had he agreed? What did she want this time? Why wouldn't she leave him alone?

Russ rubbed his eyes with the palms of his hands. He knew the answer to that one.

"I guess," he said aloud, staring out his window at the traffic on Meridian Avenue, "we all have a cross to bear."

"Are you paying attention, sonny?" the shipping clerk asked his temporary replacement. "I don't want to find this all screwed up when I get back from vacation."

"Sure, man, sure." The part-timer, a long-haired kid in his late teens, nodded. "I'm payin' attention. Don't worry. I need the bucks. I'm cool. I won't blow it."

Bet my ass you will, the shipping clerk thought. Bet my ass you fuck up the entire operation just like the asshole they brought in here last year.

"Listen." The clerk pointed at the shipping clerk. "I'm going through this one more time just to be sure. Now"— he tapped one of the cubbyholes in the top of the maple desk—"you get your mailing labels out of here. In this next slot you find your reinforced tape and scissors. This ledger here is to keep track of your shipping costs. Leave that alone!"

The kid was fiddling with one of the masks.

"These are really spooky." He lifted one up. "What would anyone want with something like this?"

"Oh, you know." The clerk snatched the mask and placed it back on a wall shelf. "Parties, costume affairs, stuff like that."

"Wouldn't catch me dead in one of them," the kid stated.

"It'd be an improvement, the clerk grinned to himself.

"I think I'm all set to start." The kid glanced around the shipping and receiving department. "I think I've got it down pat."

"Oh, yeah?" The clerk picked up a pink sheet from the center of the desk. "What do you do with this after you send the merchandise?"

"Let me see . . ." The kid's forehead furrowed. "That's called a purchase order. I'm supposed to . . . supposed to . . . include it in the box!"

"No, not quite." The clerk rolled his eyes toward the ceiling. Where did the front office get these fruitloops? "The packing slip goes in the box. This"—he held one up—"white sheet is the packing slip. It lists the contents of the box you send out."

"Then what's the pink thing for?" the kid asked.

"That pink thing," the clerk sighed, "is the purchase order. I can see I'd better go through the procedure again. First, an order arrives at the front office. They type it up on a purchase order . . ."

"This!" The kid touched the pink sheet.

"Yeah. Now, we make out our mailing label using the information provided on the purchase order. Next, we fill out the packing slip, again using the purchase order to list the merchandise the customer wants. Then—and here comes the important part—we place the *packing slip* in the *box* with the merchandise to be shipped out. Finally, we . . ."

"I know!" The kid snapped his fingers. "I fill out the 'shipment sent' section and turn it in at the front office."

"You got it." The clerk smiled.

"What happens if I accidentally send the purchase order

instead of the packing slip?"

"Should that occur," the clerk said, glaring at the kid, "we would have no record of who ordered the merchandise."

"That's a big deal?"

"A very big deal. We're required by law to keep track of who we send our merchandise to."

"Well, don't you worry about me. I won't screw things up."

Bet my ass.

Russ arrived at the Painter home at eight forty-five. He rapped on the door three times. A minute passed and his knock was still unanswered. He toyed with the idea of departing before someone came to the door. A hurried ride home, a relaxing drink, a thick, juicy steak, Sinatra on the stereo. Ahhhhhh. He savored the thought. Maybe she was asleep.

No such luck.

The door opened inward, the sudden glare of the hallway light causing him to shade his eyes with his hand.

"Russ!" she exclaimed, her breath almost gagging him. "You came!"

"You know I'll come any time you need me, Gretchen," he said, moving past her as she beckoned him inside and closed the door.

"It's sweet of you to cater to the whims of an old lady."

"You're no older than I am," Russ said. He leaned over and kissed her on the cheek. "You're better-looking, though."

"That's right," Gretchen sighed. "We were all born in the same year. You. Me. And Brian."

I'm not here two minutes, he thought, gritting his teeth, and already she starts with the morbid memories.

"Won't you come in and have a seat in the living room?" she asked.

"Sure."

"Oh, wait." She stopped and glanced up at a closed door at the top of the stairs. "I should let Harvey know you're here."

"I hope he's home," Russ lied, hoping the boy wasn't home, hoping he wouldn't need to again face the living reminder of his stupidity, praying he could suppress his ever-present sense of misery and guilt.

"Harvey!" Gretchen called. "There's someone here to see you."

Russ nervously picked at a loose thread on his jacket.

"Harvey, did you hear me?" Gretchen practically screamed.

"I heard you, Mother."

Russ flinched. Christ, the kid was growing! He stood over six feet tall and had the body of a boxer.

"Hi, Harvey," Russ greeted him. "How's it going?"

"Fine, Uncle Russ, fine." Harvey was dripping perspiration.

"Come on down and visit with us a bit," Gretchen suggested.

"I'd like to, Mom." Harvey grinned. "But I'm in the middle of my workout. I can't stop now."

"Those silly weights!" Gretchen snapped. "What are you ever going to get out of them?"

"This." Harvey smiled and flexed his arms. The muscles bulged.

"But what good will it do you?" Gretchen persisted.

"You wouldn't understand, Mother. You never do. Nice seeing you, Uncle Russ."

The door closed and Gretchen stamped her foot in apparent anger.

"The boy's got no manners," she declared.

"It's all right, Gretchen," Russ assured her. "I understand." For twelve years he'd harbored the burning suspicion that Harvey blamed him for Brian's death.

"Well, come on in to the parlor." Gretchen motioned him along. "I won't keep you long."

I certainly hope not, he reflected.

As they had done hundreds of times over the previous dozen years, he reclined on her worn, garishly patterned sofa and she sat in her favorite chair, a wooden rocker positioned inches from her television set.

"Can I offer you a drink?" Gretchen pointed at a half-empty whiskey bottle on top of a small maple table.

"No, thanks," he answered, studying her haggard features, remembering the exquisite beauty she'd once possessed. Once. Before that fateful night twelve years ago when Brian and he were patrolling the boardwalk. Leave it to Brian. He always was the bright one, the go-getter, the one blessed with an incredible memory for details and events. But was he blessed that muggy June night? Was he blessed when he spotted that escaped con? When he approached his suspect, thinking his partner was right behind him, ready to back him up, not knowing Russ had stopped to flirt with one of the waitresses, not realizing he'd made the biggest mistake of his life when he didn't mention his supposition concerning the pale man eating spaghetti at a table in a far corner of the restaurant. Russ trembled for an instant, recalling the horror he felt when he turned to follow Brian, not believing what he saw, petrified as the pale man pulled a magnum from his waistband and fired twice before Brian could clear leather. The suspect attempted to rise and aim at Russ, but he was hampered by the table; his foot slipped and he was momentarily off balance; he screamed when Russ drew and fired. It only took one neat, clean shot between the eyes. But that reflex action was too little, too late. Brian died two days later.

". . . and I worry about him all the time . . ."

Russ closed his eyes and sighed.

"Are you all right?" Gretchen inquired. "For a while there I thought you weren't listening."

"Of course I was." Russ smiled, staring at the premature wrinkles lining her face, creases caused by years and years of consuming too much booze, a nasty habit she'd developed shortly after Brian passed on. Was he to blame for her condition, too?

"Well," she continued, "what should I do?"

"Do?"

"About Harvey. He's nineteen now. A high school graduate. He can't keep himself locked in his room all his life."

"Does he still have that job at the deli?"

"Sure. But he doesn't make much. We barely got by all these years on the pension and insurance benefits. I was grateful when he went to work part time in junior high school. When he graduated I thought for sure he would get a bigger and better job. But no! He's still working at the deli, full time. What'll I do, Russ?"

"He's young, Gretchen. Give him time."

"Time, hell! He's had all the time he needs. He doesn't know if he wants a career job, and he doesn't know if he wants to go to college or one of them technical schools, and he doesn't know if he wants to go into the service. He doesn't know spit! He'd never do what I want him to do." She bit her lower lip and gave the whiskey bottle a longing glance.

"What's that?" he asked, anticipating her response.

"Follow in his father's footsteps," she stated softly, moisture brimming in her eyes.

"You can't mold Harvey in Brian's image," Russ said gently.

"But it would be for his own good!" Gretchen persisted.

"Would it? You can't force the boy to do anything he doesn't feel like doing. That would do more harm than good in the long run."

"I suppose you're right." Gretchen wiped at the corners of her eyes with her hand.

"I know I'm right," Russ said emphatically.

Gretchen eyed the whiskey bottle again.

"Believe me," Russ continued, "the boy will decide, sooner or later, what he wants to do with his life. Allow him some breathing space, Gretchen."

"Okay. I'll try. Are you sure I can't get you something to eat or drink?"

"No. Really. I can't stay too long."

"Oh." The disappointment showed clearly on her face. "But I promise I'll come again, real soon."

"I know you will." She brushed at some stray wisps of her stringy brown hair. "I look forward to your visits. They're the sunshine in my gloomy life."

"You know—" Russ sat forward and locked his eyes on hers—"you talk about Harvey, about him locking himself in his room all the time. You're no better, Gretchen. You

48

keep yourself isolated in your house. You never go out and enjoy yourself. When was the last time you went out with friends? When was the last time you caught a movie? When?"

She didn't answer.

"I thought so. It's not good for anyone to be alone. We're not made that way. Maybe, if you were to socialize more, Harvey would follow your example. Did you ever think of that?"

"I . . . I don't know." She averted her eyes from his stare. "I just don't feel the need to mix and mingle. I'm happy the way I am. Ever since Brian . . . I just haven't felt the need."

Russ began to speak, then changed his mind. They'd covered this territory again and again. It was useless. Countless times he'd attempted to persuade her to change her lifestyle, to quit the hard stuff before she drank herself to an early grave. He might as well have been banging his head against a brick wall for all the good his entreaties had accomplished. He sighed, weary from fatigue and frustration.

"I've got to go." He stood up.

"Thank you for coming." She escorted him to the front door. "I'm glad you could make the time."

"No problem."

"I'll tell Harvey you're leaving."

"No need to . . ." he started to protest.

"Harvey!" she called. "Harvey! Uncle Russ is leaving!"

"Really, Gretchen . . ."

"Don't be silly! The least he could do is say goodbye. Harvey! Come down here this instant!"

Russ could hear music coming from Harvey's room.

"Maybe he's asleep," he suggested.

"At this time of the night? Nonsense! He's reading those comic books of his again. They're as big a waste as his weights. Harvey! Harvey! Do you hear me?"

"Please, Gretchen, leave him alone."

"He's got no manners whatsoever."

Russ opened the front door.

"Russ." She gripped his arm. "Maybe we could take a stroll on the boardwalk sometime soon. The three of us could make an evening of it. What do you say?"

"I say it sounds great." Russ kissed her on the cheek for the second time that night. "We'll do it soon."

"You'll call?"

"I'll call."

"Take care." She stood in the doorway and watched him walk to the curb.

"I will." He waved goodbye and got into his unmarked car. Christ! What a lousy evening! Every visit he made served to remind him of his guilt, his profound sense of moral shame. Would it ever end? Gretchen and Harvey were like a milestone hanging from his neck, constantly dragging him down to a personal hell of emotional torment.

Christ!

What would it take to get them off his back?

May 2

"OH, COME ON, PRETTY BIRD, LET'S you and me go under the boardwalk and cuddle. How 'bout it?"

Officer Leta Ballinger tried her pet technique for dealing with drunken bastards when they got her goat. She counted, slowly, to ten.

"What say, sweets?" The portly sailor draped his arm across her shoulders. "You'd enjoy the treat!"

"For the final time," she said softly, a grim edge to her voice, "I'm asking you to come along peacefully."

"And if I don't?" He laughed and pinched her thigh with his free hand. "What's a dainty girl like you going to do about it?"

"Will you take your arm off me?"

"I don't think so." The sailor chuckled.

"I think so," Leta said.

"Oh?"

She went into action quickly, efficiently, catching the drunk by complete surprise, She whirled around and her right foot swept back, knocking him off balance, enabling her to grab his left wrist with both her hands and heave. The momentum carried him over her shoulder. He grunted when he slammed into the sand, and to her amazement he lay there laughing, waving a finger at her and cackling like crazy.

"What so hilarious?" she demanded, cautious, expecting a trick.

"I knew you was the delicate type the second I laid eyes on you!" he giggled inanely.

The sailor's inebriated mirth was contagious. Leta burst into laughter.

"You married?" He tittered a bit. "I sure hope not 'cause I think I'm in love!"

"You're crazy, sucker." Leta unhooked her hand cuffs from her belt.

"Sure am." He nodded his head in agreement. "Ya gotta be crazy to love a cop!"

Leta grinned.

"Can I join this party or is it an exclusive affair?"

Officer Charlene Winslow positioned herself on the other side of the sailor, her right hand resting on the butt of her service revolver.

"Oh, join us, please," the sailor urged, his speech slow and slurred. "The more the merrier!"

Leta cuffed him.

"This wasn't necessary." He waved his manacled arms in the air. "I'd follow you anywhere!" He winked at Leta.

"You certainly attract the cream of the crop," Charlene commented sarcastically.

"Hey." Leta grinned. "I saw the last guy you were out with, remember? You've got no room to talk."

"Was he better lookin' than me?" the sailor asked.

"Honey"—Leta grabbed his left elbow, Charlene his right, and they yanked him erect—"nobody, but nobody, is a bigger hunk than you."

"Hell." The sailor beamed, pleased. "I knew that."

"Handsome, and with brains to boot," Charlene snapped. "Which is more than I can say for you." She glared at Leta.

"What's bugging you?" Leta inquired, anticipating the answer.

"What's bugging me?" Charlene angrily mimicked Leta. "Oh, nothing! Nothing at all! My partner just wanders off while I'm in the ladies and decides to collar a drunk all by her little lonesome. What could possibly be bugging me? Is it the fact that we're a team? Is it the fact you didn't follow procedure? Is it the fact you left the boardwalk and came down to the beach by yourself? Is it the fact that if it had been anyone else but lover-boy here, your fucking head might be split wide open right now that bothers me? What the hell do you *think* is bugging me?"

"You always make such a big deal out of things. I saw some poor inebriated slob . . ."

"Who's a slob?" the sailor interrupted in a hurt tone.

". . . Who might keel over into the water at any second and drown his ass, and I didn't want to bother you when nature called, so I decided . . ."

"To play heroine," Charlene finished for her.

"Who's a slob?" the sailor demanded again.

"Really, Char, you're sounding like an old mother hen—or worse, like Earl."

"Earl loves you. He knows what a hardhead you are. He's just watching out for you when he chews you out for doing some bonehead stunt like this."

"I always thought I was kinda spiffy," the drunk said.

"I suppose," Leta said. "Sometimes, though, I think it goes deeper than that, like there's something he's not telling me."

"Like what?"

"My momma raised me neat and proper," the sailor threw in.

"I'm not sure." Leta frowned, her brow furrowed. "I've heard some rumors, though."

"What kind of rumors?" Charlene asked.

"I change my socks every day." The sailor was weaving, trying to keep his footing.

"Now's not the time." Leta nodded at the drunk. "You have the right to . . ."

May 30

HARVEY'S EAGERLY EXPECTED PACKAGE ARRIVED. HE'D listed his return address falsely. The box arrived at the New Wave Deli, his place of employment, to prevent the possibility of his nosy mother opening the parcel before he got home. His employer, Mr. Salisbury, handed him the carton when he walked into the deli punctually at three.

"This got here in the noon mail," Salisbury said, reaching under the meat counter to pick up the box. "You didn't tell me you were having something sent to you here."

"Sorry. I hope you don't mind." Harvey took the carton and breathlessly stared at the return address. *MONSTER MADNESS*, San Francisco, California.

"Not at all. Just wait until you get home to open it. We've got a lot of work to do. There's a dance we're catering tonight at seven, and you've got to get the meat, cheese, and loaves sliced. Hop to it."

Harvey placed his package in the employees' clothing closet in the kitchen area and went to work. It was the hardest shift, the longest eight hours, he ever put in. He kept glancing at the closet whenever he was near it, yearning to open the carton, impatient at the delay.

Finally, eleven o'clock rolled around.

"I've never seen you move so fast." Mr. Salisbury walked up as Harvey was untying his apron. "What's in the box, anyway? Gold?"

"Something more valuable," Harvey answered, folding his apron.

"I bet I know what it is," Mr. Salisbury said knowingly.

"Oh?" Harvey felt his insides turn to ice, dreading the chance that Mr. Salisbury really did know, that he'd managed, somehow, to guess the contents. His plans would all be ruined, his investment all for nothing if anyone knew he owned . . .

"I bet"—Salisbury grinned, poking Harvey in the ribs—"it's some of those X-rated comics. You know, the gory, kinky kind. I saw the return address."

Harvey laughed.

"What's so funny?"

Harvey opened the closet and retrieved his package. "I never thought of myself as kinky."

"What else could it be? Why have it sent here unless you don't want your mom to know that it is?"

"It's not what you think." Harvey visibly stiffened, suddenly defensive.

"Hey, son, it's okay!" Mr. Salisbury placed his arm on Harvey's shoulders and assumed a fatherly attitude. "I was young once, myself. I went through the phase you're going through now. It's perfectly normal, Harvey. Sooner or later boys wake up to the fascinating fact that there's an opposite sex. It's one of the major discoveries in life. Don't be ashamed to be normal."

"I'm not ashamed of myself."

"Good." Mr. Salisbury scratched his graying temple. "You go home and enjoy yourself. I hope Gretchen doesn't catch you. I know what a pain in the ass she can be at times."

"You've got that right," Harvey chuckled. Pain in the ass was an understatement.

"See you tomorrow." Mr. Salisbury turned his attention to cleaning the kitchen counter.

Harvey hesitated, suppressing an urge to request the next day off. He was afraid Mr. Salisbury might become suspicious if he did.

"Anything else?" Salisbury asked him.

"No. Nothing." Harvey nodded and departed.

There was a full moon shining in the night heavens, but for once Harvey hardly noticed. He hurried home, covering the eight blocks in record time. His emotions were in upheaval. He was thrilled to finally possess the werewolf costume, worried that his mom might spot him entering the house with it, and fuming that it should arrive on the one day in six months when he worked the evening shift at the deli.

The living room light was on, gleaming through the cracks in the blinds. Of course. His mother and her damn television. She should be thoroughly plastered by this time. At least he hoped so. It would be easier to get inside and up to his room undetected.

Harvey tried the front doorknob.

Damn!

The door was locked. Why? She never locked the stinking door! Why had she done it tonight? Did the old biddy forget he was at work? Damn!

Harvey checked his jeans and found his key in the pocket. He could get in, but he could do it without her noticing? He tucked the carton under his right arm and inserted the key in the lock. Carefully, slowly, he twisted the key and gingerly pushed the door open. He peeked inside.

His mom was seated in the rocker, dozing, her chin on her chest.

Harvey stepped inside, quietly closed the door, and hastened upstairs. When he shut his bedroom door behind him, he grinned and breathed a sigh of relief. He'd done it! Damn!

He turned on his light, braced his chair against the door to prevent any unwarranted interruption, and set his box in the center of his bed. He sat beside it and stared at the labels. It was here! Actually here! He could scarcely believe it.

Harvey walked over to his dresser and rummaged through it until he found his penknife. He pried the largest blade free, sat on his bed again, and cautiously sliced apart the reinforced tape securing the top of the carton. It was within reach! His skin tingled! He dropped the knife on the bedspread and stretched the box flaps apart. A lining of white Styrofoam covered the contents, shielding them, protecting them from mistreatment by the postal service. He lifted the Styrofoam panel and threw it aside.

There they were! Cushioned by the Styrofoam, folded neatly, one against the other—the mask, the hands, the feet! A large pink sheet of paper practically obscured the merchandise. He gave it a cursory examination, noted it was called a purchase order with his name on the deli address, and tossed it onto the floor. The paper wasn't important.

Harvey paused, relishing the moment, admiring the detailed craftmanship on the costume. They did appear to be strikingly realistic. Nervously, haltingly, he reached in and lifted the mask.

Damn!

The werewolf mask was amazing. The hair was soft and neatly groomed, the synthetic-weave backing pliable and resilient to the touch. The features were accurately gruesome. He stroked the wolf hair, marveling at the soft texture, delighted and pleased with the workmanship.

It was a dream come true!

Harvey picked up the werewolf hands and feet and compared them to the mask. They were of the same high quality.

Fantastic!

He stooped over and removed his sneakers and socks. An urgency was building inside him, an overwhelming need to see how he looked in the costume.

The order form in the monster magazine had requested his shoe size. He noticed *size 11* imprinted on the inside sole of the werewolf feet.

Would they fit, though?

Harvey slid the false feet on over his own and stood up. They were a perfect fit, roomy and comfortable. The mesh weave backing allowed air to flow through the costume, not around it, and would enable him to wear it for extended stretches without discomfort.

Next he tried on the werewolf hands. They clung to his fingers as nicely as any gloves he had ever owned. The nails, constructed from a hard plastic, were long, red, and tapered into points.

The piece de résistance remained.

He pulled the mask on over his head, tucking the

lengthy neck border under his shirt. The mask was snug, the eye slits aligned properly with his own eyes, the ear holes parallel with his ears.

It felt good, but how did he look?

Harvey took a step toward the mirror on his closet door, then hesitated, apprehensive, worried the costume would appear ridiculous on him, concerned that maybe, just maybe, it was childish for a grown man to garb himself in a monster costume. He took a deep breath and stepped in front of the mirror.

"Damn!" The exclamation shot from his lips.

Incredible!

All the movies, all the posters in the world could not have prepared him for the reality, the extraordinary sight he presented.

Harvey knew he made a terrifying werewolf. The mask, hands, and feet completely covered his skin, conveying the impression that the wolf hair was actually his own. His height and build lent a massive dimension, an imposing aspect, to the image. He radiated strength and vitality.

Harvey glanced at the werewolf posters adorning his north wall. The werewolves in them were grim, bestial, even striking, but they couldn't begin to compare with him. He was . . . awesome! Anyone who saw him would piss in their pants! With the costume on he was, for all intents and purposes, a werewolf—a real werewolf. He could go where he wanted, do whatever he wanted, whenever he wanted, without anyone being able to stop him or even knowing who he was. He could do anything! Anything! And the first thing he wanted to do was insure that the Dunes were his and his alone. It would be so easy! Nothing could stop him!

Tomorrow he would work his normal, shift at the deli, from eight in the morning until five in the afternoon, so he'd be free tomorrow night. Free!

Look out, world! The werewolf would be on the prowl!

May 31

CHARLIE MURDOCK WAS FURIOUS. IF HE could get his hands on his brother-in-law he'd throttle him! Why the hell had he listened to him? Every time he did, every time he let Kay convince him to follow Greg's advice, he would up royally screwed. When would he ever learn?

That bastard Greg!

So your outboard broke down, Greg had said, and you want to spend an afternoon trolling. No problem, Greg had said. I can help you out. I know someone who has a used outboard motor for sale, the bastard had butted in. Cheap. Of course Charlie had tactfully told dear brother-in-law Greg what he could do with his suggestion. And of course Kay had to interfere, to say she felt buying the used outboard would be a terrific idea and save them a bundle. Greg couldn't steer them wrong! Not sweet, lovable Greg! Oh, no!

Why, Charlie asked himself, why did he let those two birdbrains talk him into purchasing the motor? From a friend of *Greg's*, no less!

How fucking stupid could one person be?

Then, to compound his own insanity, he actually *used* the damn thing this afternoon! He shouldn't have been so surprised when the outboard sputtered and died. He shouldn't have flown into a rage and cursed his brother-in-law a blue streak as he drifted for over four hours under a blazing sun. Nope. He should count his blessings and give thanks that the current had carried his small boat to ground on the Point and not out into oblivion on the Atlantic Ocean.

That damn bastard Greg!

So what if the boat didn't ground until after dark? So what if the Point was almost eight miles from Ocean City? So what if too many lazy afternoons watching the tube and too many brews had resulted in a gut a woman in her ninth month would be happy with? So what if he was out of shape?

At least he was alive.

Besides, only two more miles of wilderness and he'd be back in Ocean City. He'd call a taxi, ride home, feast and drink and bathe. Then he'd call Greg, invite him over for cards, and strangle the son-of-a-bitch!

Just two more miles.

Charlie had been walking for the past hour without paying particular attention to his surroundings. He was preoccupied, considering various means of avenging himself on Greg. Only when his feet suddenly sank in sand and he stumbled, nearly falling, did he bother to stop and fix his bearings.

Sand? He wasn't near the beach. He was making a bee-line cross-country, adhering to the straightest course. There shouldn't be any sand . . .

The Dunes!

Charlie nervously glanced around, aware of where he was and not liking it. Since his childhood he'd avoided the

63

Dunes. He could still recall the scary stories his grandfather had told him when he was a tyke. Tales of evil, flesh-craving creatures lurking in the Dunes, waiting to pounce on the unwary and the young. Nonsense, sure. But those fictions had scared him silly.

Charlie forged on. He was a mature male. Fairy tales couldn't frighten him. And after all, the shortest route to town was through the Dunes, smack dab through the center of the rugged, uninhabited wasteland.

Fortunately, there was a full moon. The Dunes were faintly illuminated, sufficient to permit him to distinguish the jumbled rocks, shrubs, and intermittent trees dotting the harsh landscape. Charlie estimated he had a half mile or so to go and he'd reach Surf Avenue. That would carry him right into Ocean City.

And home, sweet home!

Charlie's legs were beginning to ache. This activity was the most exercise his fifty-year-old body had undergone in ages and the strain was starting to show. He made a mental note to develop a mild routine of regular calisthenics, or maybe jogging or tennis would be good. An insurance salesman simply wasn't afforded the opportunity to keep slim and trim, not unless he strenuously worked at it. Charlie only worked at it when the mood hit him.

There was an abrupt snapping of twigs in some underbrush to his right and Charlie froze. He waited, breath bated, for a repeat of the sound. What could it have been? A dog, perhaps? There wasn't too much in the way of wildlife in this remote area.

Several minutes elapsed and Charlie resumed his trek at a more hurried pace. He continually glanced over his shoulder. This place sure gave him the creeps! He had the distinct feeling that someone . . . or something . . . was shadowing him.

More time passed.

Charlie relaxed a bit, certain he was nearing the edge of the Dunes not far from Surf Avenue. He was climbing up an immense dune when he heard the soft, stealthy pad of feet somewhere behind him. His scalp tingled as he whirled, one foot slipping out from under him, and he fell on his arm with a sharp pain knifing along his elbow. He ignored the ache and hastily scrambled to his feet.

Something growled.

Charlie reached the rim of the dune and, although posed for frantic flight, he couldn't resist scanning the nearby brush and rocks for the source of the snarl.

He saw it, and the sight chilled him to the marrow.

The head was huge, hairy, wolfish. The . . . thing . . . was staring at him from the cover of some small trees twenty feet away. The eyes gleamed, reflecting the moonlight.

It growled again.

Charlie fled, plunging down the slope and across the field bordering the Dunes, the field that separated the Dunes from Surf Avenue. He reached Surf Avenue and turned toward Ocean City.

He looked back once.

At the top of the last dune, looming, black, menacing, was the figure of the . . . *thing*.

Charlie ran for all he was worth, forgetting, for the moment, Greg and Kay and the outboard motor.

"Ocean City Police Department. Sergeant Bean here. May I help you?"

"Uhhhh, Sarge, this is Charlie Murdock."

"Yes, Mr. Murdock. What can we do for you?"

"Well, I don't know how to put this . . ."

"Beg your pardon?"

"It sounds so dumb . . ."

"Let me be the judge of that, sir. You have something to report?"

"I'm not sure."

"Why don't you tell me about it?"

"Maybe I imagined the whole thing."

"Imagined what, sir?"

"Well, I was out fishing today and the motor conked out."

"Yes."

"And I drifted in down near the Point. I walked into town . . ."

"That's quite a walk."

"You're telling me! Anyway, I cut through the Dunes on my way back, and . . ."

"And what, Mr. Murdock?"

"I saw something, Sarge."

"What, exactly?"

"I'm not sure. It was big and hairy . . ."

"A dog?"

"No, I don't think so. I swear this thing stood on two legs."

"Did it attack you?"

"No."

"What did it do?"

"It growled."

"It growled?"

"Growled."

66

"Mr. Murdock, I don't quite understand what you're reporting. It sounds like a large dog. We get reports of them running wild from time to time. It didn't attack you, but if you feel it's dangerous we'll send a car by the Dunes and see if we can spot it."

"No, never mind. I knew it was stupid to bother you . . ."

"It's no bother, Mr. Murdock. It's what we're here for."

"It's my wife, you see. She said I should report it."

"Thank her for us. Anything else?"

"Nope."

"Thank you for calling, Mr. Murdock."

"Yeah. 'Bye."

June 4

LEON AND JOYCE TAUGNER WERE THRILLED with the matching ten-speed bicycles their son had bought them for their golden wedding anniversary. The bright red bikes were presented to them two days before they departed from Pittsburgh for their annual two-week vacation at their summer cottage in Ocean City. They arrived in Ocean City Sunday evening. Wednesday night at nine o'clock Leon suggested they take their first extended bike ride on their new gifts.

"Sounds super!" Joyce responded.

They rode west from the cottage along Mentor Avenue until they reached Harrison. They crossed Harrison and stopped at Surf Avenue.

"Which way?" Joyce asked.

"It doesn't matter. Let's try that way." Leon pointed south.

They pedaled slowly, enjoying the breeze and the night sounds. The expensive bikes were equipped with headlights and rear reflectors, insuring illumination ahead and protection behind.

"You know, Joyce," Leon said, "I had my doubts about Mark's choice of gifts, but these are great. They'll keep us in shape."

"Sure will," Joyce agreed, "if we can find the time to ride them." She pulled in front of Leon.

The automobile and truck traffic become progressively more sparse as they traveled farther south. Eventually even the homes and businesses lining Surf Avenue gave way to fields and shrubs.

Leon and Joyce rode in silence except for the swishing sound of the ocean breaking on the beach to their left and the recurrent clamor of the insect world.

"It's so beautiful here at this time of the year," Joyce commented.

"And peaceful," Leon added.

"What's that?" Joyce applied her brakes too quickly, her bike swerving and the brakes screeching.

"Watch it!" Leon sharply turned his own bike and narrowly missed colliding with his wife. He stopped several feet past her and shifted his body so he could glare at her. "Why did you do that, Joyce? We almost had an accident out here in the middle of nowhere!"

"What's that?" Joyce ignored his angry outburst and pointed at something up ahead.

"What's what?" Leon gazed in the direction she indicated.

"See it? In the middle of the road. Some kind of animal?"

"I don't see . . . wait, there is something there." Leon saw it too, thirty yards in front of them, squatting in the center of the highway. The features were indistinct, but Leon could make out gleaming eyes and hairy limbs.

"It's just a dog," Leon stated.

The "dog" reared up on two legs.

"Oh, my Lord!" Joyce exclaimed, wheeling her bike.

The "dog" was lumbering towards them.

"It's a bear!" Joyce screamed, racing north on Surf Avenue. "Run, Leon!"

Leon was trying. He spun his bike and started pumping his pedals as vigorously as he could. Joyce was fifty yards ahead of him. He was catching up, putting distance between himself and the bear, when the pain hit.

The bike wobbled as he struggled to regain steering control.

A lancing spasm racked his left side again.

Oh, Sweet Jesus, he prayed, please don't let it be my heart! Not again!

Eleven months ago he'd undergone a physical, his first in five years. The doctor had been puzzled by some results and ordered more comprehensive tests. Leon was surprised to discover he might have experienced a mild stroke some six months before the exam. He vaguely recalled suffering slight aches in his chest cavity some time back. But a stroke? Not likely. He could remember laughing and ribbing his physician, sarcastically criticizing modern medicine.

Now, as a third pang pierced his torso, he knew those tests had been accurate. Deadly accurate.

Leon concentrated on controlling his surging fear, on diminishing the surge of blood. The agony was subsiding. He managed to cast a look over his shoulder.

There was no sign of the bear.

Joyce was at least a hundred yards in front of him and showed no indication of abating her speed. Leon gritted his teeth and hunched over his handlebars. If he took it real easy . . .

"Ocean City Police Department. Sergeant Bean here. May I help you?"

"Sergeant Bean?"

"Yes?"

"This is Doctor Brannon, over on Eisenhower Drive. I require an escort to rush a patient up to Seacrest."

"The house number, sir?"

"Seven sixty-three."

"One moment, Doctor."

Doctor Brannon waited, listening to the desk sergeant dispatching a car.

"Will you require an ambulance?" Sergeant Bean asked.

"Negative. The patient is not critical, but speed is crucial."

"What is the nature of your patient's illness?"

"Possible heart problem. He's not a regular. His name is Leon Taugner, a tourist from Pennsylvania. He was out riding a bike when some chest pains developed. I was the first physician listed in the yellow pages. His wife drove him over."

"A car will be there in a matter of minutes."

"Thank you. I appreciate it."

"Anything else you need?"

"No, although I might have some information for you, for what it's worth."

"How do you mean?"

"Well, Mr. and Mrs. Taugner swear the condition was aggravated by a bear."

"By a *what?*"

"A bear."

"Are they crazy?"

71

"No." Doctor Brannon chuckled. "And they're not inebriated, either. They appear to be respectable and thoroughly sane."

"But where in the world did they see this bear? The nearest zoo with bears that I know of is in Philadelphia."

"They told me they were riding south on Surf Avenue."

"Surf Avenue . . ."

"Yes, why? You sound like it rings a bell."

"Well, maybe I've had this damned night shift too long, but I vaguely remember a call over the weekend, something about a big dog or a large hairy animal."

"Where was this creature reportedly seen?"

"The Dunes."

"And the nearest artery to the Dunes is . . ."

"Surf Avenue," Sergeant Bean completed the statement.

10–57," Earl Patterson requested, certain the monotony and the double shift were producing hallucinations.

"You heard me correctly, Earl." Beanie sounded irate. "Drive by the Dunes and see if you can spot a bear."

"A bear?" Earl laughed into the mike.

"10–4." Earl heard a surge of static as Beanie switched to another frequency.

"Touchy, aren't we?" Earl asked aloud.

What had he done recently to get Beanie so pissed off at him? Why'd Beanie send him on this wild goose chase? Maybe it was because he already was on Surf Avenue, heading north.

Oh, hell, Earl sighed, making a tight U-turn, he'd sweep by the damn Dunes and call it a night. His swing shift ended at midnight. Gloria would have a fit, but he intended to spend the night with Leta. He gunned the engine, eager to get off duty. Let Gloria blow her stack. His sister had no business butting into his love life. Besides, it was time she got used to the idea of living by herself. She certainly couldn't expect him to live with her forever.

Earl estimated he was three miles from the Dunes.

Funny how quickly time could fly. A year ago when Gloria divorced that bastard Duncan he'd agreed to move in with her for only a couple of months, to protect her if that sadistic prick should try to beat up on her again. And, Earl mused, it had been a wise move, although he'd had plenty of reservations at first. But that night Duncan had tried to break into the apartment, the night Earl got to punch that sucker out but good, justified the idea of moving in temporarily with Gloria. Duncan had moved to the west coast three months ago. It was high time Gloria accepted the fact he couldn't stay with her any longer. Older sisters! What a nuisance they could be.

A skunk was crossing Surf Avenue, visible at the perimeter of his headlights. Earl instinctively slowed, dreading an impact, detesting the scent of skunk, and recalling how annoyed the boys in the motor pool had been the last time he hit one.

The polecat ambled off the tarmac and into the brush on the side of the road.

Earl speeded up. He should be nearing the Dunes by. . .

What the hell was *that?*

Earl slammed his foot on the brake pedal, his patrol car careening to a grating, lurching stop with the front end in the opposite lane, effectively blocking the highway.

What the hell had it *been?*

Earl reached under the seat and scooped out the unit's searchlight. He swiftly plugged the jack into the accessory

73

outlet on the dash, switched the light on, and swept the high-intensity beam over the surrounding area, seeking another glimpse of . . . what?

The view he'd had was too fleeting, too ambiguous. A large, hairy animal had darted across Surf Avenue just beyond his headlight range. He didn't know what he had seen, but he was certain of one thing—it wasn't a bear. Not that lean, that quick.

What, then?

He scanned the field separating Surf Avenue from the Dunes, his beam clearly revealing everything it touched. There was grass and brush and some small rocks, but no creature. His light was able to reach the first row of dunes, the sand glistening, barren, presenting a barrier between his beam and the wilderness beyond.

Whatever he had spotted had raced across the field and into the Dunes before he could stop the cruiser and whip out the searchlight. That feat would require terrific speed.

Earl leaned against the car and pondered the wisdom of leaving his vehicle unattended and venturing into the Dunes to find the animal. He might have imagined the entire incident. If he called for a backup and they scoured the Dunes and found nothing he'd become the laughingstock of the force. On the other hand, if a wild animal was hiding in the Dunes, sooner or later it could hurt someone and he'd be . . .

"903," his radio blared to life. "903!"

Earl recognized an excited tone in Beanie's voice. He snatched his mike and pressed the ENGAGE button.

"903 here."

"10-92 at Harrington and Berkshire. Handle code three."

"But Beanie, I saw . . ." Earl began.

"Earl, forget the stupid bear report."

"But—"

"*Sergeant*, this is a code three."

"I know, but—"

"Earl, unless you want to find yourself on report, move your—wait a minute, there's a 10–32 in progress—move it, Earl!"

Earl jumped into the cruiser, threw the searchlight on the floor, shut his door, and executed his second U-turn of the night. His attention was glued to his monitor as he followed the account of the chase. He turned on his red lights and siren, concerned that one of his fellow officers might be injured by the fleeing robbers, and relegated his peculiar sighting to the back of his mind, convinced that he suffered from a hyperactive imagination. With his peers in jeopardy how could he waste precious time dwelling on someone's escaped dog? What else could it have been?

"Suspect has turned east on Broadway," the radio crackled.

A man had to have a sense of priorities.

Two joggers heard the police siren shatter the nighttime stillness and they slowed their pace a bit, listening, wondering, their sneakered feet pounding the beach sand in muffled rhythm. As the shrill shriek faded in the distance the two joggers picked up speed again, their strides increasing as they settled into their ordinary gait.

"Wonder what that was all about?" the petite redhead inquired between breaths.

"Beats me," her running mate replied. "Sounded real close there, for a minute. But now it sounds like they're

75

heading into town."

"Probably just a fire or something," the girl guessed.

"Probably. How you holding up?"

"No problem. We've only done, what, two miles so far?"

"About that."

"We've never come this way before."

"Yeah. It's quiet out here. We can run our hearts out without being disturbed."

"Yep. Nice," she commented.

"I bet we take the state meet," her tall, skinny companion predicted.

"You're always so confident, Sandy."

"The power of positive thinking, Faye, the power of positive thinking."

"Sometimes I wonder about you."

"How so?"

"I wonder if you're confusing positive thinking with ego."

"What? Are you serious?"

"How long have we been going together now?" Faye asked.

"Oh, about seven months. Why?"

The lights of Ocean City were far behind them. The beach was becoming dotted with more and more rocks the farther they went.

"Well, I think I've come to know you pretty good." Faye was breathing heavily.

"So?"

"So I think that for a junior at Oceanview High School you've got an unusually high opinion of yourself."

"And I keep telling you—" Sandy slowed to a walk—

"it's positive thinking. It's how we got together in the first place."

Faye pressed her hands against her sides, inhaling deeply, catching her breath and gathering her energy for the return run as she strolled alongside Sandy.

"What do you mean?" She tried to read his eyes in the dark.

"Simple." He halted and gazed out over the ocean. "That first time I saw you, that very first meet of the season, I knew you would be my girl."

"Oh, you did, did you?" She laughed.

"Absolutely. I never even paid any attention to the girls' track team until I laid eyes on you. What a fox!"

Sandy grabbed her by the waist and kissed her on the neck.

"Cut that out!" She giggled.

"Oh, really?"

Sandy swept her off her feet, lifted her in his arms, and carried her to the incoming waves, the surf lapping over his ankles, covering his sneakers.

"What do you think you're doing?" Faye demanded, wrapping her fingers around his neck.

"Shhhh."

"Try dunking me and I'll throttle you."

"Quiet."

"You let go of me and I'll scream . . ."

"Faye, shut the hell up!"

Sandy released her legs, dropping her feet into the swirling salt water.

"What . . ."

Sandy clamped his left hand over her mouth, placed his right hand on her shoulder, and forced her to squat. The incoming tide touched the hem of her shorts.

Faye grabbed his wrist and tried to pry his hand from her lips.

"Stop struggling," he whispered. "Look!"

Sandy pointed with his left hand.

She squinted, alarmed at his insistence, forgetting his gag, focusing on the object of his anxiety.

Some . . . *thing* . . . was coming up the beach towards them.

The sky was moonless, gloomy, and obscuring the terrain in their immediate proximity. Faye's vision was gravely impaired by the darkness, preventing her from ascertaining exactly what the approaching apparition was.

Sandy released his grip on her mouth.

The . . . *thing* . . . was running their way. It was thirty yards away, moving in a stooped, lopsided, lunging sort of motion. Faye marveled at its speed. If she could race that fast she could easily win every race she—

The . . . *thing* . . . was ten yards from their position, and for the first time several features stood out. Massive size . . . lanky limbs . . . hair—lots and lots of hair.

Fay tensed, frightened that the . . . *thing* . . . had seen them. Maybe it was attacking!

The . . . *thing* . . . came abreast of their inadequate, exposed hiding place and stopped.

Faye gripped Sandy's arm and held her breath.

The . . . *thing* . . . glanced back down the beach.

Faye felt certain they had been seen. It was only eight feet away, hunched over, making sniffing noises. How could it miss spotting them? What *was* it?

The . . . *thing* . . . grunted and resumed its headlong sprint, leaving the beach, cutting across the bordering field. Within a minute it was lost to view.

Sandy slowly stood, helping Faye to rise.

"Whew!" Sandy extended his hand. It was trembling. "What the hell *was* that thing?"

"Sandy, let's get out of here!" Faye urged.

"Did you see it?" Sandy stepped onto the beach and gestured excitedly in the direction the thing had taken. "Did you see it?"

"How could I miss it?" Faye stood beside him and shook the excess water from her sneakers.

"It was incredible!"

"Let's get out of here."

"Like some kind of . . . of . . . monster! Part man, part animal!"

"I really believe we should leave."

"And how about all that hair! You know, it reminded me of something, but I can't put my finger on it."

"*Sandy*, let's split!"

"I got it! I got it!"

"Got what?"

"What did it remind you of?"

"My worst nightmare," Faye responded.

"No! No! Be serious."

"I am *completely* serious."

"A werewolf!"

"A *what?*"

"Don't you realize what it was?" Sandy nervously paced back and forth as he spoke.

"You tell me."

"It was a werewolf."

"You're crazy."

"What else could it have been? That hair! The way it

79

moved!"

"It was just some old hermit, or else a wandering tramp or a hobo."

"No. I tell you, it was a werewolf!"

"Sandy?"

"What?"

"There's no full moon. Not even a quarter moon. Besides, everyone knows that werewolves don't exist."

"But it sure looked like one," Sandy insisted.

"Does it matter?"

"Wow! A werewolf! Wait until I tell Bert!"

"Do you expect your older brother to believe you?"

"Bert doesn't have a closed mind, unlike *some* people I know."

"I can't believe you're acting this way." Faye shook her head. "Why is it you men get so excited over the stupidest things?"

"You're full of questions tonight, aren't you?"

"I only have one more."

"What is it?" he demanded, irritated.

"What do we do if this werewolf of your comes back here?"

"Oh. I hadn't thought of that." Sandy gazed over the field nearest the beach.

"And now?"

"I think we should get the hell out of here."

"You know, that's the best idea you've had all night."

June 5

WARREN WAS ON HIS WAY OUT the front door when the secretary answered an incoming call.

"Warren!" she called after him.

He caught the door before it could close and came back into the reception area.

"What is it?" He sat on the edge of her desk.

"Call for you on line seven. It's Craig Stevens from Seacrest Hospital."

"Thanks, Marcy."

Warren walked into his office, shut his door, and lifted the receiver.

"Craig, this is Warren. How's the intern business?"

"Just fine. Did I catch you at a bad moment?"

"Nope. I'm on my way to Ocean City to get some actualities on the liquor store robbery and the high speed chase they had down there last night."

"Good. You're going to the right place."

"What?"

"I've got a freebie for you."

"It won't cost me the usual ten spot?" Warren asked, slightly surprised.

"Nope."

"What's the catch?"

"None. It's just that I'm not too sure about this tip, and considering all the dough I've made off you in the past . . ."

"Enough to put your kid through law school," Warren interjected.

"I think you deserve this one gratis."

"I'm all choked up. What have you got?"

"A bear."

"A what?"

"A bear. You know, as in Smokey."

"What is this bullshit, Craig?"

"I'm not scamming you, man. I thought you'd like to know that a tourist was admitted here last night for observation. Heart palpitations. He was telling everyone who would listen that the attack was caused by a bear. His wife swears the same thing."

"Were they drinking?"

"Not a drop. The guy is a butcher. Conservative type."

"What's the name?" Warren opened his desk drawer and extracted a tablet.

"Leon Taugner. Wife's name is Joyce."

"And where'd they see this bear again?"

"Ocean City. Some drag called Surf Avenue."

"What's the official line?"

"The report isn't concrete. The police suppose they were scared by a large dog or some other kind of animal."

"Some other kind of animal . . ." Warren repeated, musing, his new instincts stirred by this story.

"Like I said, not much to it. But I thought I would pass it on to you anyway."

"Thanks, buddy. I appreciate it. Say hi to Ethel for me."

"Will do. Take care, Warren."

"Yeah. 'Bye." Warren hung up, tore the top tablet sheet off, folded it, and placed it in his jacket pocket. He hurried toward the front door.

"I'll be in Ocean City for several hours, Marcy," Warren said as he passed her desk.

"Got it," she replied, not bothering to look up from the letter she was typing.

Warren started his car and pulled from the station parking lot. If traffic wasn't heavy the ride to Ocean City would encompass twenty to thirty minutes. The robbery and chase was the bigger story, the purported reason for his trip, but he found himself speculating on the Taugner incident. If the Taugners were respectable, as Craig maintained—and he hadn't been wrong yet—then they had seen something that scared the hell out of them. What? Butchers dealt in blood and guts each and every day. Admittedly, they were carving up animals. Still, Warren had never heard of a squeamish butcher.

Warren cursed as he sped up to pass a slowpoke in a pickup.

And if the Taugners had seen a bear, so what? The story wouldn't be worth much, except as a light feature. Warren unconsciously bit his lower lip as he analyzed his reaction to this tip. There was an indefinable premonition disturbing him, a foreboding that he was on the verge of a story of immense proportions and staggering implications, the scoop of his life. But that was ridiculous. Granted, a bear in Ocean City would be unusual; they rarely traveled this far south from their haunts in the Appalachian Mountains in Pennsylvania. Such a news item would be unique, but not exceptional, and definitely not worthy of the concern he was giving it.

So why did he feel this way?

Damn!

Harvey sat crosslegged at the foot of his bed, grinning, staring in enraptured fascination at the werewolf mask, hands, and feet draped across the top of his pillow.

Damn! They were beautiful!

Harvey checked the time. Eight forty-five. Soon, very soon, it would be time for the werewolf to prowl. He'd never expected in his entire life to feel such intense delight as he felt when he donned the werewolf garb and roamed the Dunes and the outlying areas.

Damn!

Harvey laughed, recalling the panicked expression on the fat man's face that night he'd frightened the intruder from the Dunes. How dare that slob violate his territory! And then there'd been the two bikers. The stupid old woman had thought he was a bear! A bear!

"How dumb could you get?" he asked aloud.

Harvey rocked on his haunches, snickering, remembering the way the old man's bike wobbled as he frantically sped away.

"They're just like sheep," he said to the werewolf mask, "and they flee at the sight of the big, bad wolf."

Harvey chuckled, relishing his sense of power and the control he could exercise over those frightened fools who ventured into the Dunes. Sooner or later, he knew, the word would get out that there was a monster dwelling in the Dunes and people would shun his sanctuary, never enter his refuge, and provide him with the privacy he craved. Maybe, he hoped, maybe the word was already being spread. Why else would the cop have been cruising Surf Avenue?

It had been close with the cop.

Harvey had seen the car approaching and, before he realized exactly what type of vehicle it was, he'd charged from cover and prepared to leap directly into the headlight beams. Fortunately, at the last instant before he would've been clearly illuminated, he'd spotted the overhead light rack.

Still, it had been so damn close!

That cop had stopped his patrol car on a dime and whipped out that searchlight so stinking fast! Harvey barely managed to duck beyond the first dune when the beam knifed through the night air, sweeping over the ridge.

If he'd been a second slower crossing that field . . .

The cop must have been there for a reason. Cops never came by the Dunes. But then, the police were never around when you needed them. Look at his Uncle Russ. That fucking hypocrite! Russ hated to visit them. Harvey knew that. And Harvey had a good idea why. Russ knew it was his fault that Brian Painter had died. It must have been Russ's fault! Brian Painter was an excellent policeman, too professional to let a cheap hoodlum get the drop on him. Russ Gilson was to blame, all right, and the entire police department must have backed him up and covered up the facts surrounding the shooting. Why else wasn't Russ kicked of the force? Why else—

"Harvey!"

Damn.

"Harvey! Come to your door!"

Doubledamn.

"Harvey!" his mother shrieked. "Do it this very instant!"

Harvey went to his door, sighed, and stepped out to the top of the stairs.

"Yes, Mom?"

She was leaning against the wall at the base of the steps, her knees slightly bent, her chin drooping. She did not respond to his question.

"Mom?" Harvey recognized the symptoms; glazed eyes, weaving stance, and sluggish reflexes. The bitch was drunk again.

"Harvey?" His mom glanced up at him, squinting.

"I'm here, Mother."

"Come down here and watch some television with me."

"No, thanks."

"I insist." She weakly stamped her foot. "I *insist*."

"I'd rather not."

"Why not?" She fumbled with one of the buttons on her pink blouse. "We hardly ever see one another anymore."

"I'm busy working."

"We still could see more of each other. We don't talk together like we used to."

"There's just not time."

"You can't make time for your own mother?" Her blue eyes pleaded with him.

"I'm sorry, Mom, but I'm busy." Harvey tore his eyes from her begging expression. Sometimes, when she looked at him like that, he felt uneasy and uncertain, stirred by the spectacle of her loneliness and her alcoholism. When that occurred, he would take a firm mental grip on his surging emotions and rein them in, determined to maintain his control. "I'm really sorry."

"I don't think so," she snapped, drawing herself up to her full stature.

"No?"

"No! I think you deliberately avoid me!"

Why shouldn't I, he thought? Look at the miserable shape you're in. You're disgusting.

"Mom, you're imagining things."

"I don't think so. I don't think you like me." She took several steps toward the living room, towards her rocking chair and her comforts.

"Mom . . ."

"Who needs you?" she rattled on. "Who needs you and your silly weights and your waste of a job."

"Mom, please . . ."

"I don't need you, that's for sure! Works at a deli!" she crossed over the living room threshold, still mumbling. "He'll never amount to anything, never follow in his father's footsteps . . ."

Harvey couldn't stand to hear anymore. He whirled, stormed into his room, and slammed the door. Damn her to hell! His body shook with a raging fury.

"I hate her!" he hissed. "I hate her guts!"

It was past nine.

Harvey picked up his werewolf costume.

"Why does she do this to me?"

He tucked the mask, hands, and feet under his thin brown belt and pulled his blue tee-shirt over them to conceal them from sight in case someone should spot him before he put them on.

"Why?"

He was halfway down the stairs when he heard her, still prattling, still ranting.

". . . I've tried, Lord. I've tried. You're my witness."

Harvey leaned over the oak railing and peeked into the living room.

"He's hopeless! That's what it is! He's a hopeless case." She lifted her whiskey bottle and sipped.

Harvey reached the front door undetected.

"He'll never amount to a hill of beans. He's not like his father, not at all. Doesn't have it in him. Wastes his time piddling around at a deli. A deli!" She cackled and took another swallow.

Harvey opened the door.

"Where did I go wrong, God? Where? I did the best I could with him. Maybe he's a bad seed. That would explain it. But where did he get it from? Not from *my* side of the family!"

Harvey shut the door and stood on their small concrete porch, trembling. He needed the Dunes tonight more than any night in his life! And no one, but *no one*, had better desecrate his domain . . . *or else.*

Warren spent his afternoon collecting information and actualities. He stopped at the Ocean City police station and gathered the background names, times, and addresses. Next, to flesh out his report, he visited the liquor store which had been robbed, talked with several of the officers involved in the high speed pursuit of the robbery suspects, and finally he checked on the condition of an innocent bystander who'd been clipped by the robber's car during the course of the chase. The victim, a young male pharmacist, was resting at his home, nursing a fractured leg and, Warren suspected during the interview, enjoying his sudden, newfound notoriety.

At five o'clock Warren decided to eat at a drive-in burger joint. He ordered, then settled back in his seat, debating his next move. Logically, he should head back to Atlantic City and prepare his report for the next scheduled newscast. Logically. But he was still bothered by the bear report, still nagged by the feeling he should take the time to check it out.

A roly-poly carhop interrupted his reverie.

"Here you go, sir," she grinned, reciting from memory. "You ordered one deluxe with the works, a large fry, and a large chocolate shake. That'll be three twenty-four."

Warren smiled, marveling at the machine-gun rate with which she chomped on her gum. "At the rate things are going up, pretty soon we won't be able to afford to eat."

"Hahaha," she dryly replied, casting her gaze over his midriff. "You look like you could go a year without food and still not starve."

"Touchy, aren't we?"

"You want sympathy, see a psychiatrist." She swayed off.

Warren slowly consumed his meal, watching the other customers pull in, order, or leave. Life sure was a monumental bore at times, he reflected, nibbling on a cold french fry.

Wasn't a newsman's life supposed to be exciting?

Allan Baxter was walking the family's husky on its evening jaunt through Harmon Park in Bethlehem, retaining a tight grip on his end of the leash. Their massive dog, Napoleon, was in his prime and as powerful as corded steel. Allan would slip whenever Napolean strained after a new object of his canine curiousity. The dog wanted to play with everyone and everything. Allan could keep his footing only with the greatest difficulty.

"There should be a law," Allan said to his animal charge, "preventing people in cities from owning any pets larger than a beagle. Some creatures weren't intended to be cooped up in the confines of an apartment or a small yard. I know dad thought he would please me by buying you, Napolean, but honestly, sometimes I wish he hadn't."

Napoleon saw a red squirrel dart from one tree to another and he leapt after it, dragging Allen along at a rapid shuffle.

"At least we could have sent you to obedience school."

The squirrel noticed the approaching twosome, stopped on the lowest branch in the tree, and chittered a taunting challenge.

Napoleon howled and pawed at the base of the tree.

"Come on, Napoleon!" Allan yanked on the leash but the dog didn't budge. This was turning into the longest summer of his life! And he still had August and Ocean City to survive. B-O-R-I-N-G!

Warren did some late evening shopping on the boardwalk, watching the surf, the surfers, the sea gulls, and the women in their bathing suits. Especially the women in their bathing suits. He was in no particular hurry to return to Atlantic City. Earlier that day, while studying the police log and reviewing the report of the robbery and chase, he'd also read the police report concerning Leon Taugner and the bear. The incident had occurred near some area called the Dunes.

At eight that evening Warren slowly drove south on

Surf Avenue toward the Dunes. The sun was setting, tinting the atmosphere a reddish hue. Gulls whirled and spiraled above the beach, searching for that last morsel of food before night descended. Warren whistled along with a pop tune on his radio. The ocean could, at times, appear mysterious and beautiful, he mused.

A couple of miles from Ocean City, as the fading light was rapidly waning, he spotted a wide expanse of sand dunes to his left, stretching beyond his sight to the sea. Warren braked and pulled his car onto the shoulder of the road. There weren't any signs, but this had to be the Dunes.

Warren locked his car and crossed the road, then a field. He climbed to the top of the first row of dunes and scanned the countryside. It certainly was desolate. How, he wondered, would a bear survive in terrain like this? He began to seriously question his intuition that there was a story involved here. From somehwere in the Dunes a peculiar, sharp bird call sounded. He trudged through the sand, determined to cover the area and confirm that there was, indeed, no bear.

For forty-five minutes Warren crisscrossed the Dunes, listening, scouring, hoping. Finally, he had to concede that he was on a wild goose chase. The Dunes were uninhabited by man or beast, and there wasn't enough sustenance for a billy goat, let alone an animal as large as a bear. So much for his prized intuition! He started to return to his car.

That was when he heard the bikes. Motorcycles, several of them, shattering the night stillness with their roaring engines.

Warren hurried now, alarmed that a motorcycle gang

could be nearby, concerned that they might vandalize his car. He couldn't afford to buy a new one on his current salary, not unless he took out a considerable loan. The interest payments alone would be astronomical . . .

". . . come out, come out, wherever you are!"

Warren stopped, puzzled, not certain he'd heard correctly. The bike engines were turned off now, and he could hear laughter and rough voices.

"Yoohoo! Come on out!" someone called in a loud, whining voice. Others laughed.

Warren was worried. Were they calling him? Why?

"Come on out here, chicken-ass!" another person yelled.

"Yeah, or we'll come in and get you!"

Warren trembled, positive he was about to be mugged, and looked for the best available cover.

"Come on, monster! Afraid?"

"You tell 'im, Bert."

Monster? Bert?

"Bert, I think Sandy was full of shit."

Warren inched his way to the top of the final row of dunes.

"Say that again and I'll bust your face."

Warren peeked over the rim of the dune he stood on.

"Ahhh, come on, Bert," a husky, leather-garbed biker was saying to the largest member of the group. "Maybe your brother was pulling your leg."

There were four men and two women clustered near their idle bikes, which were parked in the center of the field.

"Nope." The tallest one shook his blond head. "Sandy was serious. He saw something weird out here and we're

92

stayin' until we find out what it was."

"Fat chance of that happening," muttered the husky one.

Warren had difficulty distinguishing their features in the gloomy darkness.

"There's no fucking monster out here," one of the bikers stated.

Maybe, Warren thought, he could sneak by them if he kept behind the dunes.

"A werewolf, the twerp said!" one of the men laughed. "What a laugh!"

Warren turned—and abruptly froze, spotting a shadowy, huge . . . *thing* . . . perched on the peak of a dune ten feet away.

"There ain't no such thing as a werewolf!" another said.

The eerie form growled, a low, guttural hissing noise that only Warren could hear.

The group in the field laughed and made fun of the one they called Bert.

Warren held his breath, waiting expectantly, sensing that the creature was preparing to charge the bikers, knowing the thing had not spotted him—yet. What in the world would he do if it did?

"I told you not to make fun of Sandy," Bert was saying angrily, "and I *meant* it. If he says there's a werewolf out here, then there *is* a damned werewolf out here!"

"Bullshit!"

Warren kept his eyes riveted on the . . . *thing*. Was *it* their "werewolf"?

Whatever it was—with a banshee howl it charged!

He had spent five minutes standing on their porch, fuming, enraged at the bitch and her nagging insinuations. God, how he hated her! And his hate grew with each passing year. She was revolting! Despicable! Why had he been cursed with her for a mother? She wanted to manipulate him, direct his life, prevent him from doing what he liked to do, stop him from living his life the way he wanted. Well, the bitch wouldn't get the chance! No way! He would leave the drunken cow the first opportunity he had, leave her and her stench far, far behind.

Harvey shook his head, feeling a soft breeze on his brow, realizing he was wasting precious time.

The Dunes were calling him.

He began jogging down Avalon, then went south on Surf Avenue, his mind oblivious to all thoughts except one: he wanted the Dunes, needed the soothing natural tranquility the area offered, and he repeated his mental image of them over and over and over again.

He ran in silence, except for the cushioned pad of his sneakers on the tarmac and the muted sounds of the incoming tide two hundred yards distant. Usually, no matter how agitated his mother would make him before he left for the Dunes, by the time he reached his retreat his mind would be composed, his emotions at ease. Tonight was a different story.

Harvey's blood was boiling, his temples throbbing. He knew his departure from Ocean City was long overdue. The bitch would drive him insane any day now! At last count, he'd saved about a hundred dollars in his account. If he was extremely frugal for the remainder of the summer he might be able to leave by September. Freedom! His dream come true! No more spiteful accusations, no more drunken condemnation.

No more Dunes?

He stopped jogging, surprised at the obvious, disturbed. No more Dunes? Funny. He'd never given the matter any thought. Could he leave the Dunes? Forsake the one spot in the world that was his and his alone? The idea was upsetting, one he'd have to consider at length later.

Tonight, the Dunes were still his.

Harvey resumed his running, pacing himself, eagerly anticipating the hours of solitude ahead, determined to enjoy them at any cost. He'd see to it that no one ruined his sanctuary! Not quite true, he reflected. The *werewolf* would see to it.

The werewolf.

Harvey was now alongside the field bordering the Dunes. He ran across it and up to the top of the first row of dunes, pausing to scan the surrounding area and verify that he was alone. The Dunes and the field were deserted. He withdrew the mask, hands, and feet from under his belt, his hands shaking.

Damn!

Every time he went to don his costume he would tremble like crazy. Was it the excitement? He removed his sneakers and pulled on his hairy feet. He moved a short distance into the Dunes and hid his sneakers behind a small bush. A plane passed far overhead and he gazed up at the flickering lights, relishing the tingling sensation pulsating through his body.

The werewolf's time was near.

Harvey slid his hands into the gloves.

Damn!

His body was twitching and quaking, his muscles shuddering and bulging in a paroxysm of intoxication.

Another minute and the werewolf would be reborn.

He slowly inched the mask downward over his face, adjusting it to align the eye slits and nostrils and ears over his own. The quivering was subsiding. He tucked the mask under his shirt, his head spinning. Why did his thoughts always whirl this way . . . why was it so difficult to focus . . .

A taloned foot shuffled forward a pace, followed haltingly by another, then another, each stride gaining length and strength. He climbed to the rim of the nearest dune, raised his arms skyward, and howled.

The werewolf was on the prowl.

The werewolf wheeled and raced deeper into the barren Dunes, delighting in the serenity, reveling in his unlimited freedom and his exclusive domain. He bore to the left and followed a small ridge of rocks to the beach, one of his favorite spots, the immensity of the ocean staggering his bestial senses. The cool sea breeze was gaining in intensity. He loped slowly along the beach, noisily sniffing the air, attempting to distinguish the myriad scents filling his flared olfactory organ.

One of the incoming waves rolled farther up the beach than any of the others, the icy water covering his frolicking feet and matting the fur.

The werewolf leaped into the air, joyous, playful.

The wave receded, leaving moist sand and small puddles of salt water behind.

The werewolf splashed with his feet in the pools, sweeping his legs in wide arcs, amused by the spray of water.

A crab shell attracted his attention.

The werewolf crouched and flicked the shell with his

hand, watching warily as the empty shell flipped several yards and landed on its back.

No life here.

He lost interest and shuffled farther south on the beach.

A raucous mechanical roar split the night, coming from the north, approaching the Dunes.

His dunes.

What?

The strident whine was nearer, maybe *in* the Dunes.

The werewolf bounded into the concealing cover of the dunes, ears pricked, racing in the direction of the uproar. It kept low, hunched over, bending itself with the inky shadows.

The clamor ceased.

Puzzled, the werewolf paused, waiting for the hubbub to resume. Faintly, almost inaudible voices reached it, wafted on the wind.

So!

The werewolf growled, annoyed. Its territory was being intruded upon. Again. When would they leave it alone? They'd learn. Oh, how they'd learn! It made a beeline for the voices, still growling, its fury at their intrusion mounting the closer it came to them.

Their voices were distinct now, mocking, laughing. The words had no meaning for it, but it recognized the arrogant tone.

The werewolf cautiously crept to the top of the last row of dunes and eyed its quarry. Six of them. In the middle of the field. Some of them were grinning and snickering.

The werewolf shook with suppressed rage, its breath hissing between its parted lips. Two of the group were arguing, polluting its home with their words, their invective, their very presence.

The werewolf felt its senses surging, its bestial instincts overwhelming it, its blood pounding in its temples. It reared up, howled its challenge, and attacked.

Warren, transfixed, fascinated, watched as the creature leaped over the ridge of dunes and rushed at the bikers. They had whirled at the sound of its shriek, and they stood motionless as it bore down on them. Warren wondered why they didn't move, get out of there, before it hit them. As the thing crossed the field he realized they'd never have the time; it was that incredibly swift.

The creature—it certainly *looked* like a werewolf, but that was patently impossible—was on the bikers in a flash, its arms flailing, snarling and snapping. The women screamed and scrambled for safety.

Warren stood up to get a better view. The darkness, distance, and speed of the attacker prevented him from following the sequence of events. Two of the bikers were already sprawled on the ground. The . . . *werewolf?* . . . lifted one of the men completely over its head and brutally dashed him, head first, into the earth. The remaining male biker was sprinting away, towards Surf Avenue, following the retreating figures of the women.

The werewolf started to chase them, then inexplicably stopped, changed direction, and ran for cover, towards the Dunes, straight toward—him!

Warren froze, shocked. Had the thing seen him? Was it after his blood now?

The creature was thirty feet from his hiding place.

What should he do?

Twenty-five feet and closing.

Warren threw himself to one side, into the narrow space between the two nearest dunes. He kept his body immobile and glanced over at the rim of the dune he'd been standing behind just in time to see the creature hurtle over it. The thing landed lightly on the sand, surprising considering its bulk. Warren held his breath, fearing it would spot him. Instead, the hairy figure plunged into the enshrouding darkness of the barren Dunes and was quickly out of sight and beyond hearing.

Warren waited several minutes to insure that the thing was definitely gone. He heard someone moaning and gurgling hideously. Slowly, with repeated backward glances, he stood and nervously walked to the edge of the field. The three bikers were still prone on the grass, two of them evidently unconscious and the third twitching and groaning.

What should he do? Help the injured ones? Of course.

He began to shuffle towards them, his pace uneven, his nerves still frayed.

Maybe he could render some emergency medical assistance . . .

Warren stopped, troubled by a thought.

What if he did take the time to aid them? Then what? The police would be here soon. They'd detain him for questioning, maybe even prevent him from airing his story. There was no telling with them, sometimes. If they didn't want a report made public they had a subtle way of making life miserable for the idiot who did so anyway. They could be downright nasty, if they put their minds to it. At the very least they'd delay him, giving other news media the opportunity to scoop him while he was occupied answering countless trivial questions. No! He couldn't permit that to happen. He had no other option.

Warren turned and ran to his car.

The story was the vital issue here. It took priority over his altruistic feelings concerning those the creature had assaulted. If the thing he'd seen had also jumped Leon and Joyce Taugner, then that made it two attacks within a week, maybe more. The police must know about it. Were they already covering up this mystery stalker?

Warren was puffing when he opened his car door and slid in behind the wheel.

The story first. Absolutely. What he'd witnessed tonight was every newsman's dream, the story of a lifetime. A legitimate, prize-winning scoop. It'd make all the wire services. Every station on the coast would be calling him for actualities. He'd be noticed, known, respected.

The story came first!

Russ Gilson visibly flinched as he slammed his car door and watched the ambulance crew loading one of the injured onto a stretcher. His instincts were agitated and he knew, even before Earl ran over to him, that he wasn't going to like this one bit. He hoped he wouldn't need to call the captain. Christ! That'd be all he'd need.

"Glad to see you," Earl greeted him.

"What went down?" Russ morosely stared at the scene: the ambulance crew lifting another stretcher, some of his boys scouring the field, and several uniforms perched on one of the highest dunes searching for . . . what?

"You're not gonna believe it."

Russ gave Earl an impatient glare.

"What's wrong?" Earl asked.

"Nothing." Russ heard the ambulance door slam. "Just

a bad day, I guess."

"You seem to be having a lot of them lately," Earl observed.

"Christ! Don't I know it. Now, what's been going down?"

"We've got to back up a bit first."

"How do you mean?" The ambulance engine roared into operation, followed seconds later by the siren. The driver gunned the motor and carefully drove from the field onto Surf Avenue. "Where to?" Russ laconically inquired.

"Seacrest. They're closest. One of the victims is critical. Possibly a snapped spinal column. This thing must be incredibly strong."

"What do you mean?" Russ didn't like the sound of this. If he had to call the captain . . .

"I'm getting ahead of myself. It's a good thing Beanie and I were on duty tonight when this went down."

"Beanie?" Russ interrupted.

"He's on dispatch."

"What do you two have to do with what happened here?"

"Personally, nothing. Let me explain. A week ago Beanie received a call from a local whose outboard conked out while he was fishing. His boat drifted in on the Point and he walked home. Enroute he passed through the Dunes. He called the station to report a large dog . . ."

"A what?"

"Bear with me. This dog hadn't attacked him and he declined to file a formal report, but Beanie remembered the incident when that couple reported the bear attack last night . . ."

"Bear attack?" Russ wheeled on Earl, forgetting the sight of the ambulance disappearing in the distance. "What the hell is this about a bear attack? Why the hell wasn't I told about it?"

"Sorry, Lieutenant," Earl replied, reverting to formality. "But since when has it been policy to inform upstairs about every chickenshit report that comes along?"

"But a fucking *bear* attack?"

"First of all, the couple, a pair of tourists, thought the thing they saw last night might have been a bear, but they weren't thoroughly certain. That's how it was filed. I was sent out here to check on it. I thought I spotted something, but before I could verify what it was that 10–32 went down."

"What about this couple who said they saw a bear?"

"They never got close enough for a positive make. They hauled ass when they spotted the thing, and the guy almost suffered a heart attack. He was sent to Seacrest."

"Well, how does all of this tie in with whatever occurred here tonight?"

"Be patient just a minute longer, Lieutenant," Russ answered. He waved to a group standing nearby in the field. "Bring them over here, Doyle."

Two officers escorted three civilians across the intervening space and up to Russ. Two were young women, similarly attired in shorts and lightweight blouses, and the third was a lean, cocky male.

"What have we got here?" Russ demanded.

"Tell the lieutenant exactly what you told me," Earl directed them.

"He ain't gonna believe it," the young man stated.

"You let me be the judge of that," Russ snapped,

102

peeved.

"Okay. Okay. Don't get hostile, man. I'll tell you exactly what happened."

"You should've seen the thing!" the taller of the two women commented.

"What thing?" Russ urged.

"First things first." The biker held up his hand and the woman lowered her head.

"Tell the lieutenant," Earl ordered.

"Sure. Sure. We came down here tonight to find Sandy's werewolf . . ."

"Werewolf!" Russ exploded. "First a dog, then a bear, and now a *werewolf!* What is this nonsense?"

"Hey, man, be cool." The biker smiled. "I'm only tellin' you what I was told by Bert . . ."

"And who the hell is Bert?" Russ asked angrily.

"Bert Jackson," Earl informed him while consulting a notebook. "Age twenty-three, local, leader of the Packrats. This—" Earl pointed at the biker—"is Sherman Douglas . . ."

"My friends call me Bruiser." Sherman beamed proudly.

". . . and the tall blonde is Martha Nickerson, the brunette Carol Elder," Earl concluded his introductions.

"And who's Sandy?" Russ demanded, restraining his boiling annoyance.

"Bert's little brother," Sherman answered. "He goes to Oceanview. He was out here jogging with his fox last night and they saw a werewolf. At least, that's what Sandy thought it was. He told Bert. Tonight, after we had a barbeque at Tom's and had pretty well polished off a keg, Bert figured he'd bring us out here to see this werewolf for ourselves. We all thought it was a stupid-ass idea,

103

but, hell, Bert's our head, and he can be one mean mother-fucker when he's pissed off. So out we came, and we weren't here five minutes when this fucking thing hit us." He stopped and nervously glanced over his shoulder at the Dunes.

"What was it?" Russ mellowed a bit, noticing Serman's poorly concealed fear.

"I don't know, I tell you." Sherman fidgeted with the large silver buckle on his leather belt. "It was like nothin' I ever saw before."

The women, Russ noted, were equally apprehensive. "Can you tell me exactly what happened?" he asked Sherman.

"Well." Sherman ran his right hand through his shaggy, unkempt brown hair. "It'll be hard. Everything happened so fast, ya see. One second we were arguing with Bert because we wanted to go back to town. The next second this thing comes chargin' over the Dunes, howlin' and snarlin' and tearin' into us like we were matchsticks. It clobbered Bruno and Scully with a sweep of its arms, and then . . . and then . . ."

"Go on," Russ said quietly.

"Well, it picked up poor Bert and slammed him . . ."

"How do you mean, it picked him up? How?" Russ broke in.

"Just the way I said it. This thing—God! You should've *seen* it . . . lifted Bert over its head like he was a pillow or somethin', like he was nothin', and it just smashed him into the ground and I saw his head split open and I heard this awful crackin' sound and I couldn't take any more and . . ."

"It's all right," Russ said. "I know this upsets you. But

there is one thing I've go to know."

"What's that?" Sherman gazed back at the Dunes again.

"What attacked you? What was it?"

"You won't believe me."

"Why?"

"It was a werewolf."

"You can't be—" Russ began.

"I mean it!" Sherman almost whined. "I ain't never been one for religion, ya know, but I swear to God that if there ever was such a thing as a werewolf, then that's what came at us tonight. A werewolf."

Russ looked at the two women and they silently nodded in confirmation.

"Doyle," Earl directed one of the officers, "take these three back to the station and give them some coffee, let them relax, and get their statements."

Doyle and the other officer led the three to a patrol car.

"What do you think?" Earl asked.

"I think," Russ stated, mentally cursing his luck, "I'd better call the captain." He watched the patrol car race towards Ocean City. "Christ!"

June 6

DAMN!

He opened his eyes, squinting in the morning sunshine streaming through his bedroom window, and the pain hit him like a sledgehammer blow to his head.

Damn!

He propped himself up on his elbows and glanced around, amazed that he was in his room, in his bed, because he could not recall coming back last night. Why? He couldn't remember much of anything, except a hazy recollection of the Dunes, the ocean, the night, and—was it real or only a vague dream?—a fight of some kind.

Damn!

Why were the nights becoming increasingly more difficult to call to mind the next morning? What was happening to him?

Harvey sat up, wobbly, struggling to gather his strength. Maybe it was a good thing he was working from three until eleven tonight. He wouldn't be able to visit the Dunes.

What time was it? He focused on his clock. Twelve-thirty? Impossible! He couldn't have slept that late.

Harvey stood and walked over to his mirror, the headache beginning to subside. What he saw reflected there shocked him, jarred awake his sluggish senses.

No!

He was still wearing the werewolf costume! It couldn't be! Trembling racked his muscular body and he leaned on the door for support. This was incredible—and unbelievably, undeniably, dumb. What if someone had spotted him returning while he was still wearing it?

What if—the very thought chilled him—his *mother* had seen him?

The reflection goaded him to action. He removed his mask, the hands and the feet, and placed them under his mattress. His hair was tousled so he took the time to comb it before venturing to the top of the stairs. The house was exceptionally quiet; not even the raucous television was on.

Strange. Where was his mom?

Harvey went downstairs to the living room. There was no sign of his mother. Where on earth, he wondered, would she be? Then he spotted the empty whiskey bottle on top of the table.

That explained it! He chuckled. She was restocking her precious whiskey, one of the few reasons that could induce her to leave their home.

Good! He'd have an hour or so of peace and quiet.

Harvey ran up the stairs to his room, debating with himself as to whether he should have a late breakfast, lunch, or an early supper. His eyes fell on her door and he stopped, surprised.

Her door was open.

Harvey felt a momentary elation. She seldom left her door unlocked, much less wide open. Must have been in one hell of a hurry. Good. That meant he could examine the chest again. He hadn't had a chance to do that in years. Just to play it safe he knocked on the doorframe before looking inside.

"Mom?"

As he expected, there was no answer. He slowly walked into her room and gazed around. It was exactly as he remembered it. Wall-to-wall carpeting, heavy blue drapes, knickknacks everywhere, everything neat and tidy. In the corner near the solitary window was the oak chest, the treasure trove containing all of his dad's possessions, all the mementos his mother had saved. Once, years ago, she'd left her room unattended and he'd examined it and came across the huge chest. His mother had returned before he could inspect all the contents. He recalled that his dad's uniform was on top, and he flipped the unsecured latch up, lifted the ponderous lid, and sure enough, there it was, carefully perserved and folded.

Harvey knelt and ran his fingers over the fabric, delighted. Vivid memories of his dad in uniform came back to him and his eyes moistened. Why, God, why did he have to die? He shook himself and moved the uniform to one side. Underneath were more clothes. He raised each piece in turn and studied them. Shirts. Pants. Underwear. Socks. Then he halted, puzzled by the next garment. It was a vest, but an unusual vest, bulky but lightweight, dark blue in color, constructed of a thick, peculiar weave. He'd never seen his dad wearing a vest. This one was in excellent condition. Maybe it was his mom's. There was a label attached to the inner edge of the collarless neckline. He peered at it closely, reading the fine print.

An electric charge shot through his body.

Damn!

The implications were staggering. He read the label aloud, not believing it, flabbergasted.

"Police issue number three hundred sixty-seven, size large. Bulletproof vest." He repeated the last three words again, thrilled. "Bulletproof vest!"

It was too good to be true!

Harvey stood and tried the vest for fit. Snug. Tight. Just perfect. This was the supreme discovery. If he wore the vest under his shirt he could evict all intruders from the Dunes without fear of being mortally wounded.

A bulletproof vest!

He'd be damn near indestructible!

Afraid of nothing!

There was the faintest scratching of a key in the door downstairs and he moved, a blur as he scooped up the clothes and replaced them in the chest.

"Harvey!"

He closed the lid and lowered the latch.

"Harvey!"

He hurried to her door and listened. If she came upstairs he was dead!

"That boy will sleep his life away," he heard her mutter as she walked toward the living room.

Good.

He slid from her room and ran to his, closing his door and locking it.

Whew! That was close! He laughed, overjoyed with his prize. It was doubtful she'd ever miss it. He didn't think she opened the chest very often anymore. Even if she did notice it was gone, he'd deny he had it. No way was she going to get it back. He had as much right to the vest as she did, maybe even more.

Harvey admired himself in the mirror.

Tomorrow night the werewolf would prowl again, and nothing would stand in its way!

"So what's that leave us with?" Captain Grout asked, probing for ideas.

Russ Gilson fidgeted in his seat. There were five of them seated around the circular table in the staff room: Captain Grout, Chief James Watson, Mayor Bob Perkins, Lieutenant Pierce, and himself. Lieutenant Petrie, the final officer on the small Ocean City police force, was on vacation. The five had spent the morning hours reviewing all the information they had concerning the sighting reports of the thing in the Dunes and the attack on the bikers the previous night.

"Russ, what do you think?" Captain Grout prodded.

"I believe—" Russ selected his words carefully— "we're dealing with a nutcase or a prankster."

"Would a prankster assault those bikers?" Perkins inquired. "He'd be running a good risk of getting his ass kicked, to say the least."

"Good point," Chief Watson commented. "Scaring that couple and the guy whose boat stranded him on the Point could have been the work of some idiot who never outgrew trick-or-treating. But the savage attack lends a new dimension to this entire affair. If this guy, and I take it we all have eliminated the possibility that we're dealing with a *real* werewolf . . ."

"Maybe it was the tooth fairy," cracked Perkins, always the joker.

Everyone smiled.

". . . was nuts enough to go after the bikers," Chief Watson continued, "then we can assume we have a mental case on the loose. I suggest we call in a consulting psychiatrist and prepare a psychological profile."

"Do you think there will be another attack?" Perkins raised the question uppermost in their minds.

"Why not?" Captain Grout answered. "So far we have three reported incidents. There could be some we don't know about."

"And we've got to stop this kook before there are any more," Chief Watson stated. He ran his fingers through his graying hair.

"How do we do that?" Perkins lit a cigarette, his fleshy jowls twitching.

"We post a stakeout in the Dunes," Chief Watson replied, "and wait for the bastard to make another move. So far he's restricted himself to the Dunes. Let's hope he continues to do so. We'll collar him the next time he shows his hairy face."

"Speaking of which," interjected Lieutenant Pierce, the youngest present. "Do we assume this was a big guy with a lot of facial hair, or was he wearing some sort of costume?"

"Good point," Chief Watson said, reflecting. "The descriptions we've received all indicate excessively hairy features, too hairy for only a beard and mustache. I opt for the costume theory." He gazed at the others and they all nodded in agreement.

"I can run a check," Russ volunteered. "There can't be all that many stores in this area selling werewolf costumes."

"What if he didn't purchase it locally?" Captain Grout

was toying with a pencil, rolling it around and around in his fingers.

Shit! Russ mentally cursed himself. Why the hell had he opened his big mouth?

"If he didn't obtain this outfit locally," Chief Watson responded, "then we've got our hands full tracking it down. Russ, since you thought of it, I'll let you handle that end of our investigation."

Christ! Overtime, here I come.

"We don't know yet whether we have a tourist or a local here," Chief Watson went on. "Personally, I think it's a tourist, and that means trouble, big trouble. A local would be easier to trace. Regardless, I want it completely understood that this is a priority item. I don't care how understaffed we currently are, we bust butts until we nail the turkey or he moves on and gets caught somewhere else. We don't want any more assaults, nothing that the media would pick up on and sensationalize. We've got enough problems."

"Say, Chief . . ." Perkins began, his interest quickened by the mention of the media, "exactly what do you intend to tell the press? We're approaching the height of our summer season and the Chamber would not relish any adverse publicity."

"We don't tell the press a damn thing, for now," Chief Watson said. "If we're questioned about the bikers we'll say we don't have any concrete leads and suspect gang rivalry."

"Good idea." Perkins was pleased, dreading any repercussions to his reelection.

"Then we're all agreed?" Chief Watson scanned the assembled faces with his gaze. "We keep this one from

112

the media."

"Fine by me," Perkins assented.

"Sure," Captain Grout agreed.

Lieutenant Pierce and Russ nodded.

There was a loud pounding on the staff room door.

"Damn!" Chief Watson snapped. "I gave orders that we weren't to be disturbed."

Earl Patterson walked into the room, carrying a small transistor radio held next to his ear, the volume low.

"What is it, Sergeant?" Chief Watson asked irritably. "This meeting is for officers only."

"I'm aware of that, sir." Earl stopped alongside Russ. "But this is very important."

"It better be," Captain Grout said.

"Sir, about twenty minutes ago I was told something by a fellow officer that has a bearing on your discussion, I believe."

"What is it?" Russ inquired.

"Well, Officer Winslow told me she'd heard a certain item on the hourly news of an Atlantic City radio station. The news on the next hour is coming up and I suspected you'd want to hear it."

"Why?" Chief Watson asked.

Each of them sensed what was coming and they visibly tensed.

Earl turned up the volume on his radio.

". . . brought to you by Carrier Rentals. I'm Warren Mckeen for WREN. The top story this hour is a bizarre attack which occurred near Ocean City last night around nine-thirty. A group of six bikers, four men and two women, were assaulted near an area called the Dunes, south of Ocean City. Their assailant is described as a huge, hairy man or creature possessing enormous strength. The bikers were attacked for no apparent reason. Three of the victims are in Seacrest Hospital, one listed in critical condition. Their identities have not been released yet. Reports reveal this was not the first such attack. Ocean City police are investigating. In other news, the legislature . . ."

Earl turned the radio off.

"Son-of-a-bitch!" Chief Watson exploded.

"The shit has hit the fan," Perkins said, fuming.

"Christ!" Russ added, glaring at Earl when he saw that the sergeant was grinning.

"Grout!" Chief Watson barked, his face a fiery red. "Get that bastard here, in my office, by four this afternoon. Tell him we'd just like to ask some questions. If he gives you any lip, stuff the fucking son-of-a-bitch in your trunk!"

"Yes, sir." Captain Grout was up and out the door.

"I suggest, Mayor," Chief Watson whirled on Perkins, "that you hurry over to your office and issue a statement for the media, sticking to the story we devised."

"Yes . . . I . . . guess I'd better." Perkins was sweating, wringing his hands together. He ran from the room.

The Chief eyed Russ and Lieutenant Pierce.

"Well, what the hell are you two waiting for? Go get our fucking werewolf!" he bellowed.

The officers hastened from the staff room. Chief Watson pounded his right fist on the table, rose stiffly, and departed, muttering obscenities.

Earl Patterson, still standing near the table, forgotten by his superiors, started laughing.

Oh, Sweet Jesus, I love it! I just love it!

He threw back his head and laughed and laughed.

114

She was watching her favorite afternoon soap when the phone rang. Oh no, she thought, not today.

The ringing was persistent. Ten times. Fifteen.

Only one reason the phone would be ringing that many times. Not even Earl would keep it going like that. Sighing, she forced herself to rise from her sofa and pick up the receiver.

"Hello?" She knew who would be calling. She just knew it. And on her first day off in two weeks.

"Officer Ballinger?"

"Yes?"

"Lieutenant Gilson wants you in his office within an hour."

"But this is my day off!" she protested.

"Leta, this is Doyle. Do you think they'd have me ruin your off time if it wasn't important?"

"Is it?"

"You better believe it, lady. A lot has gone down since you went off duty yesterday afternoon. You'll be briefed when you arrive. You've landed a special assignment."

"Must be my lucky day," she said sarcastically.

"I knew you'd take it the right way." Doyle chuckled and hung up.

"Why do I stay in this crazy line of work?" she asked aloud. Sighing, she replaced the receiver.

Leta quickly dressed in her uniform, drank a hurried coffee, locked her apartment, hopped into her Datsun and drove to the station, speculating the entire time on the possible special assignment and wondering what could have happened. She tried different stations on her car radio on her way to work. Not one offered a clue.

Thirty minutes from the moment she answered her phone she was sitting next to Charlene Winslow in Lieutenant Gilson's office, nervous, intently watching his every move and expression. He appeared extremely fatigued; his green eyes were bloodshot, his broad shoulders slumped, and he continually suppressed yawns. He must have been up all night, she realized.

"Officer Winslow and Officer Ballinger." He looked up at them and smiled thinly. "I'm happy you could come in on short notice, especially on your day off."

"We're just your ordinary dedicated professionals," Charlene wisecracked.

Leta noticed that Russ didn't laugh. God, it must be serious!

"Ladies," Russ resumed, "you're here because you're the best pair of female officers I've got, and you're exactly what the doctor ordered in this particular case."

"What case is this we're talking about?" Leta inquired.

"The case of the raging werewolf."

"Come again?" Leta laughed, thinking his comment was a joke.

"You heard me correctly the first time. The case of the raging werewolf. While you were enjoying an evening off, doing whatever dedicated professionals do with their leisure hours—" Russ managed a weak grin— "a werewolf attacked six bikers near the Dunes . . ."

"A werewolf?" Charlene broke in. "You can't mean a real, honest to goodness werewolf?"

"Of course not, but close enough for all intents and purposes." Russ stretched. "You'll be briefed on all the details in our reports in just a minute. Suffice it to say we need a stakeout team and I think you two are the best qualified."

"We'll be staking out the Dunes?" Leta asked.

"You're catching on."

"Why women? I get the distinct impression this . . . werewolf . . . is slightly dangerous." Charlene was no longer in a humorous mood.

"More than slightly, as you'll find out in a moment. Don't worry. We'll have six of our own within earshot. I'll lay it on the line. I think you two, in civvies, would be a better target, one this freak isn't likely to resist. You're the bait to draw him out into the open. Once you attract him then we'll do the rest. Read the reports, take some time to talk it over, and give me your answer by six this evening. I don't want to rush you."

"I don't need time to think it over," Leta stated. "I'll do it."

"Are you always this impetuous?" Russ arched his eyebrows.

"This was one of her slower deliberations," Charlene said. "And, as always, where my partner goes I go."

"You haven't even read the reports," Russ mentioned. "You don't know exactly what you're getting into."

"Do we ever?" Leta smiled reassuringly. "Not to worry, Lieutenant. We can take care of ourselves."

"I never doubted it for a minute. Sergeant Patterson is waiting for you in the staff room. He's got all the material for your briefing. I'll see you when you're done."

Leta and Charlene rose and left his office.

"Tell me something," Charlene said as they walked towards the staff room. "Why the hell did you accept this assignment so readily?"

"I get bored when I have time to myself."

"Seriously."

"Seriously?" Leta said, looking thoughtful.

"Seriously," Charlene repeated.

"I honestly can't say. You know me, Char. When something has to be done, I do it."

"Don't I know it. But I'm not worried. After all, I'll be there to babysit you."

"Gee, Mom, how'd I ever manage before you came along?"

"Beats the hell out of me."

Charlene gave Leta's elbow an affectionate squeeze.

June 7

SHE KNEW A MAJORITY OF HER fellow officers detested stakeouts and she didn't understand why. She enjoyed them. A stakeout sometimes with hours and hours of waiting for absolutely nothing to happen, provided her with an opportunity for cherished reflection, a rare chance to reach within herself and commune with her spirit. Tonight was no exception.

They had walked for hours, crisscrossing the Dunes, finding, as she expected, nothing out of the ordinary. Now they were resting, sitting on the slope of one of the larger dunes bordering the rocky beach. Charlene was depressed and Leta couldn't blame her. Charlene had agreed to come only because her partner had volunteered. Some friend I've got here, Leta thought. The best one I've got.

Earl came to mind, his concern at their briefing, his futile attempt to talk them out of this assignment, and later his delight when Lieutenant Gilson selected him as one of the backup officers. Lieutenant Gilson. The poor man had been so exhausted. She and Charlene had been in his office reviewing the plan when Captain Grout stormed in, raving about not being able to locate some reporter. He left just as quickly, still cursing a blue streak. Who, she wondered, was this newsman they were so anxious to talk with?

The sound of the incoming waves broke into her reverie. She gazed at her surroundings, searching, knowing there were six officers in hiding nearby. There was no moon tonight. She couldn't see more than a few feet in any one direction. There was no sign of her protectors.

Charlene shifted her position and placed her chin on her knee, encircling her ankles with her arms. "This is boring me shitless," she commented. "Where's our werewolf tonight?"

Leta grinned, then wondered the same thing. Where was this thing? More to the point, *what* was this thing they were waiting for? No one knew; not any of the top brass, not Captain Grout or Lieutenant Gilson or Earl. They were guessing it was a nut, some bozo parading around in a werewolf costume. But why? What purpose did it serve? Why scare that couple, why jump the bikers? It made no sense at all.

"What time is it, Leta?" Charlene asked.

Leta glanced at the luminous dial on her watch.

"Almost two."

"Damn." Charlene kicked at a small rock. "What a way to spend a day off."

"I wasn't doing very much anyway."

"Yeah, me neither, but this is pointless." Charlene unclipped her walkie-talkie from her belt. "Let's nag Earl to let us go home now."

"We can't." Leta shook her head. "We've got a job to do."

"Oh, come on. Nothing is going to happen tonight."

A low, guttural growl coming from somewhere behind

them silenced Leta's reply even as she opened her mouth to speak. The growl was repeated, louder, harsher. They stared at one another, gathering their nerve. A bush rustled. As one, they slowly turned.

It was no more than five feet away, peering at them over the top of a small shrub, the head huge, the outline unmistakable.

Leta remained motionless, hoping Charlene would do the same, wanting the thing to come closer, to move clear of the bush. Her right hand gripped the butt of her revolver. If only Charlene wouldn't make any noise and scare it off . . .

She did.

Charlene pressed the SEND button on her walkie-talkie and yelled into it.

"He's here! He's here!"

The thing whirled and ran.

Leta was on her feet, her revolver drawn, cursing Charlene under her breath. Why'd she even bother using the walkie-talkie? They'd hear her shout in Ocean City!

"He's heading due west!" Charlene screamed, jumping up, joining the chase.

Leta grabbed the flashlight she'd tucked under her belt earlier and attempted to fix the beam on their quarry. The other officers were closing in as planned, their beams covering the ground in frantic sweeps, none of them wanting the thing to escape.

"Leta, are you okay?" someone bellowed. Earl.

Leta didn't bother to answer. She thought she saw a flash of dark fur race through her flashlight beam.

"There it is!" one of the other men shouted. "It's bearing north now!"

All the lights swung in that direction and for a brief instant their beams found it as it turned at bay and snarled a challenge. In that moment Leta recognized what it was and she knew it wasn't what they were looking for. One of the other officers yelled, "Don't shoot!"—but too late. A gunshot shattered the night. Leta saw the object of their pursuit spin around and stagger sideways, then drop.

"Oh, shit," someone said.

They gathered in a small circle around their fallen quarry.

"Who was the idiot with the itchy trigger finger?" Earl demanded.

Charlene sheepishly took a step forward.

"Great!" Earl snapped. "Just great!"

"I'm sorry. I'm really sorry. I didn't see it clearly. I thought it was getting ready to attack us." Charlene walked away, dejected, her shoulders slumping.

"What happens now?" one of the other men asked.

"We call it in," Earl answered, "and get our asses reamed."

"Christ!" another muttered. "It's even got a tag."

Leta holstered her revolver, watching the blood trickle from the gaping neck wound. Poor animal! Once it must have been beautiful, she thought. A terrific pet. And now?

"I don't think Lieutenant Gilson is going to appreciate this one bit," another male officer stated.

"Why should he?" Earl snapped angrily. "We're sent out here to collar some jerk with a trick-or-treat complex and we end up blowing away a German shepherd. Fuck!"

Leta spotted Charlene leaning against a small tree and she went over to her.

"Hey, you okay?"

Charlene shook her head and sniffled. "I like animals. I thought it was going for you. I didn't mean to . . ."

Leta placed her arm around Charlene's shoulders and hugged her gently. "It's all right. I understand."

"I don't understand it. I just don't understand it." Lieutenant Gilson was pacing back and forth in front of them, his hands folded together behind his back, the fingers nervously gripping and regripping one another. "I send you after a man, spelled m-a-n, and you ninnies shoot a dog, d-o-g. Weren't my instructions explicit?"

They were lined up in a row in front of the desk in his office. Earl, the senior stakeout officer, assumed responsibility.

"Your orders were clear, sir."

"Evidently not clear enough!" Lieutenant Gilson stopped pacing and stretched. "Christ, I'm tired!" He gave them all a glance of disapproval and sat down in his chair. "Well, what's done is done. Sergeant Patterson, you will call the owners of the German shepherd and inform them that their dog was struck by a truck and killed. Do you understand?"

"Yes, sir."

"Am I clear enough for you?"

"Yes, sir."

"Fine. It's now four forty-five. Go on home and get some rest. Be back in my office by five this afternoon. I'm feeling generous. I'm going to give you fuckups another chance. Tonight you'll stake out the Dunes again and, hopefully, be luckier than you were tonight. No dead dogs this time. Not even dead crab. That will be all."

123

They left his office without a word, depressed, fatigued, and subdued.

Russ leaned back and closed his eyes. He'd better get on home, too. If he didn't catch some shut-eye he'd be of no use to anyone. And he'd need to be alert, awake. This case was turning into a real buster!

Without a doubt, the past twenty-four hours had been some of the best in his entire life. Maybe *the* best. He tossed his small suitcase onto the back seat, climbed in behind the wheel, and took off for Atlantic City. What a day it'd been! He reviewed the events, relishing them, knowing that, at last, he was on his way up the ladder of success.

Warren laughed, happy, at peace with himself and the world. Everything was looking up!

There'd been the speedy, reckless drive back to the station to get his story on the air. WREN was a daytimer, and he wanted his exclusive on the first morning news report at six A.M. The report had been aired at six, and thereafter every hour on the hour. He'd notified the Associated Press and United Press International so they could carry it on their wire services and audio feeds. He'd fed his scoop to the State Information Network, closing it with the phrase that would be heard on a dozen major stations in a dozen major markets: " . . . reporting for the State Information Network, this is Warren Mckeen in Atlantic City." Then there'd been the actualities, calling all the large stations in Philadelphia, New York City, and Trenton, offering his story, promising an update as more information became available. This exclusive could be his ticket to a dream come true, a position with a major market station or a first-rate newspaper. Why not? It'd happened to dozens of reporters before. The coattail effect, it was called. This werewolf thing was going to be his coattail, his alone.

Warren chuckled.

Oh, it feels good to be alive! Especially now, after the phone call and his interview. The phone call came in yesterday afternoon from the *Brotherly Bulletin*, from Samuel Fontaine, the managing editor himself. The *Brotherly Bulletin* was a monthly Philadelphia-based news and entertainment magazine. One of the best. It was noted for its exposés and aggressive reporting.

Thank heaven he'd sent those résumés! Warren braked at a stop sign, smiled at a foxy jogger as she ran in front of him through the crosswalk, and turned on his car radio.

Months ago, maybe six or seven, he'd mailed a dozen résumés to leading papers and several of the larger radio stations, not really expecting any replies, but hoping. Praying. He recognized that the odds were stacked against him. Getting ahead in this business, or any business for that matter, depended on who you knew. It was rigged against the average person unless you were fortunate enough to get a lucky break.

His lucky break had arrived!

Fontaine had called, related how the *Bulletin* was in need of a new reporter, how he'd been reviewing the résumés that morning when he'd noticed Warren's and recalled hearing the biker actuality on a Philadelphia station as he rode to the office that morning. Fontaine considered it an omen.

Warren laughed aloud, remembering how hard it'd been for him to suppress a sarcastic response when Fontaine revealed his superstitious nature. Superstition in a reporter had always struck him as remarkably inconsistent. Reporting required objectivity, adherence to facts and truth. Superstition was a belief in the unverified, in illusion and myth. Warren mentally catalogued Fontaine's inclination, knowing he could play off it in the future.

Was Warren still seeking another job, Fontaine had asked. Would he be interested in the position open at the *Bulletin?* Could he come to Philadelphia that evening for an interview? Maybe they could dine together.

Warren turned onto the Atlantic City Expressway.

Casually, coolly, he'd agreed to meet Fontaine, realizing the trip to Philadelphia would delay his follow-up, but not too concerned because he knew the Ocean City police were stonewalling the story and it was extremely unlikely any other reporter would get the jump on him. Besides, his career came first. Funny. The night before last he'd said the same thing about the story. Relativity, that was the key.

At three yesterday afternoon, his overnight bag packed in case the meeting extended into the wee hours, he departed for Philadelphia, instructing the station secretary he'd be unavailable for the next twenty-four hours. Come six o'clock he was seated next to Fontaine in the plush, swank Two Hundred Club, savoring an inch-thick sirloin, invigorated by the emotional stimulation of impending success.

"So tell me, Warren," Fontaine said between bites of succulent, fresh lobster, "what motivated you to send a résumé to the *Bulletin?*"

"Simple, Mr. Fontaine," Warren answered, sipping at his wine to stall, wary, choosing his words carefully. "I'd be honored to be employed by any magazine as reputable as the *Bulletin*. Upward mobility, Mr. Fontaine. That's what I'm after, and I'll keep at it until I achieve my goal."

"Yes, I believe you will." Fontaine eyed Warren critically, measuring him. "I admire initiative and respect a man who knows what he wants from life. Indecision is the reason too many talented young people flounder in this day and age."

"I agree," Warren replied, waiting.

"Warren, let's lay our cards on the table, shall we?" Fontaine set down his fork.

"Fine by me." Warren did likewise.

"I need a go-getter like yourself," Fontaine stated, and Warren's pulse surged. "But I need to be honest with you. You have a definite liability, one considerable enough to prevent me from hiring you right now, on the spot."

"What . . ." Warren felt his throat constrict and his mouth suddenly went dry. "What might that be?"

"Let's face it, son." Fontaine smiled, his craggy, lined features friendly. "You lack experience. You received your journalism training in the service, right?"

"In the Navy. Yes, sir."

"And you've been in broadcasting how long?"

"Four years," Warren responded, inwardly uneasy, certain he'd blown his chance.

"All four years at WREN?"

"Yes."

"Don't look so gloomy." Fontaine grinned. "It's not the end of the world. I didn't say you were completely eliminated from the running."

"Then what . . . ?"

"I'm simply saying you lack experience in print journalism. That doesn't mean you lack talent, Warren. Your service record and the college transcript from the school the Navy put you through indicate you have considerable ability."

"Sufficient to qualify me for the *Bulletin* post?"

"Yes, and if . . ."

"What?" Warren asked, genuinely confused.

"Yes, the job is yours." Fontaine beamed. "If you can pass a little test I have in mind."

"What type of test?" Warren reached for his glass of water and gulped.

"How does this sound?" Fontaine proposed. "I'd like to see exactly how well you can deliver a written report. Cover this incident in Ocean City. File daily written reports to me. If this story is as big as you've indicated you suspect it is, then I'll be able to accurately gauge your journalistic capability. If I'm satisfied—and I've no reason to expect I won't be—then the post is yours. Sound fair to you?"

Warren thought for a moment. The offer was more than fair. Did Fontaine have an ulterior motive? Like maybe receiving daily reports free from the scene of a choice story? Reports that could be incorporated in the next issue of the *Bulletin*. Like maybe hiring untrained skill at a minimum salary?

"Certainly, Mr. Fontaine," he said. "I accept."

"Good." Fontaine swallowed some wine, content with his skillful negotiating.

Good, your ass! Warren snickered and turned his car off at his exit. Fontaine wasn't fooling anyone. Still, the meeting had turned out far better than he had reason to expect. They had talked for hours. Fontaine evidently loved the sound of his own voice. Warren had decided to spend the night in a motel on the outskirts of Philadelphia, reviewing the evening, contemplating the future, planning his course of action.

Now, as he pulled into the station parking lot, he was elated, feeling important, thrilled by the prospect of being able at long last to climb out of the dung hole he was stuck in. There was light at the end of the tunnel.

Yes, sir, there was no stopping him now!

Warren got out of his car, picked up his suitcase, and started to move toward the station door.

"Mr. Mckeen?"

He glanced up and saw two men in suits, well groomed, approaching.

"Yes?"

"Are you Warren Mckeen, news director at WREN?" the taller stranger inquired. He was husky, brunette, and wore glasses.

"Yes, I am. Why?"

"Good. We've been waiting for you since early this morning." The tall one reached into his coat pocket, extracted something Warren couldn't quite see, and flicked it open to flash a badge.

"Police?"

"Yes, sir. Ocean City Police Department. We're the second shift that's been waiting for you."

"What have I done?" Warren kicked himself mentally for such stupidity. Why hadn't he called the station first? This should have been expected.

"Oh, you're not under arrest, Mr. Mckeen," the spokesman said. "Our superiors would like to ask you some questions. You can decline to come, if you wish, but you know we'll be back. Maybe with a warrant. Will you

129

come along with us?"

Warren delayed a minute, considering. He knew they were bluffing. But why *did* they want to see him? His story? It had to be! Why not go? He might learn some more about the attacker. The "werewolf."

"Sure. Is it all right if I follow you in my car? I'll need to return as soon as possible."

"No problem. We'll wait out here for you if you want to drop anything off inside. Do you have an urgent appointment we might be interfering with?"

My, my, my, such politeness! "No, I've got nothing pressing," Warren said. "Let me tell my boss where I'll be and we can get this over with."

"Okay. We'll wait outside for you, by your car."

The better to prevent me from escaping? Warren smiled and headed for the station door.

"So much for my terrific day . . ." he muttered to himself.

The tracks were located in his mother's flower garden in their back yard. They crossed through the center of the floral arrangement, clearly imprinted in the soft, cultivated soil. They were tiny, evenly spaced, and puzzling because they were unfamiliar. That made them exceptionally interesting. They presented a challenge.

Allan knelt over the tracks and examined them, studying the contours, the depth of the imprint, and the length of the gait. He searched his memory, sorting through his mental catalogue of prints, comparing them to this one.

The track was made by a mammal, a rodent to be exact. But which one? It was too small to be a squirrel, too large to be a mouse. The footprints resembled a rat's, but the toes on the rear foot were narrower than a rat's. The front prints were almost handlike in proportion.

Allan was positive he'd never encountered this type of print before. He followed the tracks easily until they ran onto the grass. He crawled on his hand and knees, spotting a print here, one there, aligned with a faintly detectable line of bent blades. The trail wound across the lawn, ending in a cluster of weeds and rocks in the far corner of their yard.

Allan stood up and scrutinized the tumble of stones and plants. He spotted a set of prints between two of the larger rocks and crouched next to them. He sensed his quarry was close at hand and he proceeded slowly. The next set of tracks was positioned at the base of a small pile of stones. He leaned down, examining the pile. Then he saw it.

The hole was about the size of his fist, situated on the western edge of the stones. The tracks went into the hole.

Allan laid on his stomach, ignoring the rocks and dirt, and peered into the hole.

Eureka!

It was asleep, curled up in the hole, breathing regularly. The fur was tan and white. Small golden tufts descended from behind the ears and from the buttocks.

Allan reached in, grabbed it by the loose skin on the back of its neck, and lifted it out. The movement woke it up, the bright sun causing it to squint. It kicked, feebly, and its whiskers twitched as it sought to catch his scent.

"Don't worry, little hamster," Allan said softly, gently stroking it with his other hand. "I'm not about to hurt you. How in the world did you get out here? Did you belong to someone and they let you go? Or did you run away from home? I'll have to check with the neighbors and see if one of them lost you."

The hamster, a female, was calm now, sitting upright on the palm of his left hand.

"You must be famished, little critter," Allan soothed. "Let's go inside and we'll find you some nuts or lettuce. How would you like that?"

The hamster, still weary, was trying to curl up on his hand.

"What shall I call you?" Allan asked as he walked towards his back door. "How about Tiny? No, too mundane. Martha? Nope, you don't look like a Martha. I've got it! Fifi! That's perfect. Dainty and different. What do you think of Fifi?"

Fifi yawned.

"Then you won't reveal your source?" Chief Watson demanded while filling his pipe bowl with his favorite tobacco.

"That's right."

"We can get a court order," Captain Grout snapped, tired from a lack of sleep the night before and irritated by the lack of cooperation they were getting from the damn reporter.

"Go ahead and get one and see what good it does you," Warren said, equally annoyed, fed up with the three hours of questioning he'd been subjected to.

"Don't get smart with me!" Captain Grout hissed. "We could get you on an obstructing justice charge. You won't be feeling so smug in prison."

"Go to . . ." Warren began, rising from his chair next to the table in the staff room.

"Calm down, both of you!" Chief Watson ordered.

"Captain Grout, go get yourself a coffee."

"I'm not thirsty." Grout glared at Warren.

"I don't recall asking if you were," Chief Watson stated. "So go get that coffee anyway. Now."

Grout left reluctantly.

Warren settled in his chair again and warily eyed Chief Watson and the other one, the big man who never spoke a word. What was his name again? Oh, yes. Gilson.

Chief Watson was contentedly puffing on his pipe, filling the staff room with a fragrant aroma.

"Well, what next? You can't keep me here all day. If you're going to charge me, charge me and get it over with."

"Who said you would be charged with anything?" Chief Watson asked.

"Captain Grout just said . . ."

"Captain Grout is impetuous. He gets easily carried away. Please accept my apology for his behavior."

What now, Warren wondered. Why this sudden reversal of tactics? First Watson sicked Grout on him, then, after hours of interrogation, he calls his bloodhound off. "I accept your apology. And now, unless you want me to call an attorney, I'm leaving. Any objections?"

"No."

"No?" Warren responded, surprised.

"None. My main concern was that, somehow, in some way, you might know more about the attack than you revealed in your newscast. I'm convinced you don't. From what you've told us, I strongly suspect you were at the scene of the assault, but I can't prove it. What does it matter, anyway? If there's a connection between the attacker and you, we'll find it sooner or later. Our methods might

133

be slow, but we're effective. I might also add that, initially, we were alarmed because the story was leaked before we wanted it to get out. We were hoping the attacker might strike again. By preventing a premature leak, we were confident we could lay a trap and augment our chances of capturing this nut. As it is now, the harm's already been done. No use crying over spilt milk."

"Then I can leave. Now. Just like that?"

"Just like that," Chief Watson said, a bit impatiently.

Warren stood up and stretched his cramped muscles. He'd hurry back to the station, do some filing, and return to the Dunes by nightfall.

"One final item," Chief Watson stated as Warren reached for the doorknob.

Warren hesitated, uneasy.

"We'll never know for certain, mind you," Chief Watson paused and blew a smoke ring in the air, "but I suspect you might have caused the attacker to lay low for a while. You might be responsible for delaying our arrest and, accordingly, you're also responsible, at least morally, if anyone else is harmed before we can nail this guy. Think about that, Mr. Mckeen."

Warren opened the door.

"Good night, Mr. Mckeen." The parting words were sour and contemptuous.

Warren was glad when he closed the staff room behind him. Glad, and a bit disturbed.

Was it possible Watson was right?

He glanced at his clock, noticed the time was ten minutes till nine, and buried his aching head in his pillow.

What was with these damn headaches? They were becoming more frequent and, worse, more severe. Why? Maybe he should see a doctor. Oh, sure! Despite his pain, he laughed. He could see it now: *"What seems to be your problem, Harvey?"*

"Well, Doctor, I'm getting these severe headaches and nothing I take seems to help."

"I see. Are there any other symptoms associated with these headaches?"

"Yes."

"What are they?"

"Well, I experience this almost irrestitible impulse to don a werewolf costume and go traipsing around the country-side."

Harvey laughed, and the laughing hurt him more. Damn! Maybe there was some connection between these headaches and that lightheaded feeling he felt right before he put on his werewolf costume. Ohhhh, his head hurt! He was thankful his mother was dozing in her rocker in the living room. He'd have a difficult time tolerating her carping tonight.

The clock indicated nine o'clock.

Was he going to the Dunes tonight? Odd. He didn't want to. Not with this blasted headache, anyway. He could stay home and enjoy a quiet evening watching television if a good movie was on.

Harvey gazed at his werewolf costume spread out across the top of his dresser. Folded next to it was the vest. He recalled the newscast he'd heard earlier, about an attack on some bikers near the Dunes, and the thrilling, tingling sensation when he realized the story was about him. Or, precisely, about the werewolf. So it hadn't been a dream after all! The werewolf had protected the Dunes

135

from invading bikers! Fantastic! The werewolf was all that he'd hoped it would be and more!

Nine-ten.

Harvey yawned. Maybe a catnap would help his poor head. Would the police, he wondered, be keeping an eye on the Dunes after what had happened? He doubted it. Who cared what happened to a bunch of sleazy bikers? The police couldn't be bothered. They were only concerned when respectable citizens were robbed or injured. It'd be safe to visit the Dunes again. Besides, even if the police were on the lookout, what could they do against the werewolf?

He chuckled.

Nothing, was the answer! Absolutely nothing.

After all, the werewolf was indestructible.

Indestructible!

"But I don't want to go."

"Your mother wants you to go."

"She'll understand."

"I want you to."

"It's just not fair, Dad."

They were in their living room, watching television. Napoleon was alseep, curled up on the rug at his father's feet.

"This might be the last year we get to do this together, as a family," Don Baxter said, observing the troubled expression on his son's face and not completely sympathizing with the reason for it. "Do it for me. It won't be all that bad."

"I don't think you appreciate how much I don't want to go to Ocean City with you. I always have a lousy time."

136

"Life is what you make it. A vacation is only as enjoyable as you plan it to be."

"Ocean City is boring."

"Will you come with us?"

Allan lowered his eyes, knowing he couldn't refuse his parents, praying the two weeks in August at Ocean City would go by quickly.

"Will you come with us?" his father repeated.

"I'll come along," Allan sighed. "Don't expect me to like it, though."

"I expect you'd like a pizza right about now."

"What?"

"We had a light supper. Your mother should be home from her sister's any minute. What say we go out and grab us a pizza. I'm hungry for one. How about you?"

"I guess I could handle some," Allan said.

"Don't worry about Ocean City. You'll enjoy it."

"Fat chance. I never have."

"You never can tell," his father observed.

June 8

SHE DIDN'T KNOW EXACTLY WHAT TIME it was, but she estimated it was past midnight. This night was colder than the
last, a chill wind tossing and tangling her hair. She tucked
her chin under her jacket collar and buried her hands in
her pockets.

"Sure is cold tonight, isn't it?" she casually asked.

"Now I know why I wasn't born an Eskimo," Charlene
answered. "This sucks."

They were shuffling along in the dark, weaving through
the Dunes, as they had been for hours.

"My feet are killing me," Charlene stated. "How are
you holding up?"

"Okay. But I wish I was home in my soft, comfortable
bed."

"That makes two of us. Wonder where the guys are?"

"They're out there somewhere. Earl assured me they
wouldn't go far." Leta stared at the desolate landscape.

"They'd better not. I think my vocal cords are frozen.
I'd forgotten how cold it can get out here, even in the summer." Charlene pressed her hands over her ears. "I wish
this wind would quit."

"Me too. Think we'll see anything?"

"Are you serious? No self-respecting werewolf would be out on a night like tonight."

"Too cold for him?"

"That, and the fact there's no moon tonight. No moon, no werewolf."

"Listen to the expert on werewolves." Leta grinned.

"I'm no expert. Don't you watch those old monster movies on television?"

"What've they got to do with it?"

"You can learn a lot from them."

"About werewolves?"

"No. About Humphrey Bogart. I think he had sexy lips."

"Sexy lips?" Leta laughed. "Char, you're crazy!"

"I must be, to be in the middle of the Dunes at this time of night. I hope we nail this guy before next Tuesday."

"Why?"

"Sexy lips is on the tube."

Leta thought of Earl, of his lips on her body. How long had it been? Two weeks? First her period, and now this thing. Poor Earl must be feeling frustrated. She giggled.

"What's so funny?" Charlene inquired.

"Life."

"Ain't that the truth."

They walked in silence for several minutes. Charlene abruptly stopped and grabbed Leta's arm.

"Did you see that?"

"See what?"

"Something moved." Charlene pointed at a dune in the distance. "Over there."

Leta looked. "I don't see anything. It was probably your imagination."

"I tell you I saw something. Big."

"Maybe just another dog," Leta suggested.

"I hope not. I'd never live down the shame if we blow away another poor pooch."

"Forget it. It was nothing."

"I guess you're right." Charlene resumed walking, then suddenly stopped and pointed again. "Look, there it is!"

This time Leta caught a glimpse of movement, an ebony shadow flitting across the lighter surface of the sandy dune.

"Must be some kind of animal," Charlene said. "Just the same, we'd best check it out."

"We should notify Earl," Leta mentioned.

"What? And be the laughingstock of the force if it's only a dog or a raccoon? No way. We can handle it."

"I don't know . . ."

"Look who's getting cautious in her old age! You circle around on the right and I'll take the left."

"I don't like this, Char . . ." Leta began, but Charlene was already moving away. "Be careful."

Charlene didn't bother to answer. She hurried toward the far side of the dune.

Leta shrugged and bore to the right, picking her way around bushes and rocks, trying to approach the dune as silently as possible. She lost sight of Char. On the far side of the dune were several trees and large boulders. She stopped and examined them, studying the shadows for any hint of life, of motion. There was none. She waited, expecting Char to come around her end of the dune at any second.

A minute elapsed.

Charlene did not appear.

Two minutes.

"Char?" Leta kept her hand on her service revolver and cautiously moved forward.

The gusty wind rustled the nearby shrubs, distracting her attention.

"Char? Where are you?"

The breeze shook the shrubs again.

"Char!" Leta called, worried now. She unfastened her walkie-talkie and raised it to her mouth.

Still no sign of Charlene.

"Char!" Leta pressed the SEND button. "903. Trouble here. Do you copy?"

She released the switch and the receiver crackled with static. Was the thing functioning properly?

"Earl! Can you read me? Anyone?"

The static was louder.

"Great! Just great!"

She started up the face of the dune, hurrying, alarmed at Char's absence, wanting to reach the top and yell her lungs out for Earl.

The scraping sound and the growl, coming from behind her, were simultaneous, and she reacted instantly, professionally. She crouched and swept up her revolver, eyes alert, senses sharp, one question burning in her brain—

Was it the thing?

It was.

It dived from the top of the nearest boulder and was on her before she could fire. She tried to dodge and her feet slipped on the shifting sand and she went down, the thing catching her full in the face with a savage, swiping backhand blow as it landed. She tumbled away, rolling to the base of the dune, cocking her revolver as she came to a stop. She made it to her knees and the thing was at her again, snarling, another blow flattening her on her back, the force jarring her spine.

The gun went off.

The thing howled and pounced on her, hairy hands clutching at her throat, its legs pinning her arms.

"No . . ." she managed to croak, sand filtering into her mouth, the fingers tightening on her neck, viselike.

The thing bellowed and applied more pressure.

Leta involuntarily whimpered, more frustrated than frightened. Where the hell was her backup? She couldn't breathe and there was an intense pain in her chest.

The thing pressed against her, and she felt hot breath on her face, hair scraping her skin.

Oh, God! she prayed. I'm dying! Please help me!

"Leta! Where are you?"

The thing stopped choking her and leaped erect, head twisted, listening.

"Leta! Answer me!"

She dimly recognized Earl's voice and knew her fellow officers were closing in. No matter how hard she tried, she couldn't get her vocal cords to respond. She wasn't able to call for help.

"Leta!" Earl was nearer, still not in sight but obviously close.

The thing hissed, furious. It turned one way, then another, and finally bounded into the trees.

"Leta, where are—" Earl ran around the dune, gun drawn, and froze when he spotted her prone form. "Oh, dear God! Here! Here! Over here!"

Leta gasped for air.

Earl was by her side, lifting her head, cradling her gen-

142

tly in his lap. "Dear Lord, please, not again! Not again! Lee! Smitty! Where the fuck are you?"

The five other officers converged on his voice and gathered around him, each of them shocked by the sight of Leta.

"Don't stand there like idiots!" Earl ordered. "Lee, call for an ambulance! Metz, find Charlene! The rest of you, spread out, find the thing that did this! Move!"

Leta attempted to sit up.

"Don't, honey." Earl held her where she was. "Take it easy. Help is on the way. Don't strain yourself. Please."

Leta relaxed, breathing easier now. She wanted to speak, but couldn't do more than shape her lips.

"What is it you're trying to say?" Earl asked. "You shoudn't try to talk. Wait for the ambulance."

One of the officers ran up to them.

"Yeah, Lee?"

"Ambulance is on the way. Ten minutes, they said. How is she?"

"Hanging in there. There's a lot of blood, but it's too dark to determine how bad she is. Shine your light on her."

Lee did as he was told.

"Oh, shit. Turn it off," Earl directed, squeamish at the sight of deep, ragged lacerations on her throat. "Not again!"

"Beg pardon?" Lee said.

"Nothing." Earl could feel a cold sweat covering his body.

Officer Metz rushed over to them.

"What is it?" Earl demanded.

"Officer Winslow."

"Where is she?"

"You better see this for yourself, Sarge."

"I can't . . ." Earl hesitated, torn between duty and emotion. "All right. Lee, watch Leta."

Earl eased Leta's head to the ground, rose, and followed Metz to a nearby boulder. Metz stepped aside and pointed behind it. Earl flicked on his flashlight and aimed the beam at the area Metz indicated. He anticipated the worst.

He found it.

Charlene Winslow was not pretty in death. Her tousled blond hair framed her head with a golden arc.

"Oh, shit." Earl slumped against the boulder.

Charlene's face was contorted, her lips twisted in a gruesome smile, revealing blood-speckled teeth. Her blue eyes were open, blank, and bloodshot. Blood covered the front of her jacket, oozing from gaping tears and slashes in her mangled throat.

"Oh, shit," Earl repeated.

"Should we take her back to Surf Avenue?" Officer Metz asked.

"What?" Earl felt lightheaded and weak.

"What do we do with her?"

"You know the procedure," Earl stated, slowly regaining his control and perspective. "We don't touch a thing. The detectives and the lab boys will remove the body. We've got to lead the ambulance crew here and rush Leta to the hospital. Then we'll have a briefing. We . . ." Earl stopped, fascinated and repulsed by the copious quantity of rich blood still pumping from Charlene's neck.

"It's gonna be a long night, isn't it, Sarge?" Metz nervously questioned him.

144

"It sure as hell is." Earl sighed. "It sure as hell is."

Sunday was his normal day off and he invariably slept in. His mother, usually thoroughly inebriated by late Saturday night, seldom disturbed him. Sparrows chirping and twittering in a tree outside his open window woke him up at two in the afternoon. Harvey rolled over on his back and grinned. The damn headache was gone! See what a good sleep can do for you? he told himself. He sat up and stretched.

Wait a minute!

He stared at the floor, puzzled. How did his werewolf costume get strewn across his rug? Wasn't it on his dresser last night when he went to sleep?

Odd.

Harvey slid out of bed and picked up his mask, hands, and feet. He dropped them on his dresser.

Very odd.

He stretched again, refreshed and eager to enjoy his day. There were several monster magazines he wanted to purchase at the local pharmacy. He opened a drawer and selected a towel and washcloth. Better get his shower before his mother woke up.

Harvey reached for his doorknob and caught a glimpse of his face in his mirror. He stepped into the hall wearing his shorts, knowing his Mom would be irritated if she saw him and not really caring.

What in the world?

He stepped back inside his room and studied his face. What was this? There was a pinkish stain around his mouth, across his chin, and down his neck. It looked like blood. Had he bit his lip while he slept? Weird. He grabbed his robe and hurried to the bathroom, locking the door to guarantee his privacy. The light in the bathroom was brighter than in his bedroom, and he could clearly distinguish the outlines of the pink stain.

Harvey grabbed his toothbrush from the small rack above the sink, squeezed toothpaste on top of the bristles, and began brushing his teeth. He stroked carefully, searching for any tender spots, convinced his lips or gums were cut somewhere. After a minute he glanced down at the sink bowl. No blood. There was spit, toothpaste, and . . . something else. He bent over and examined the area around the drain. There were tiny pieces of a meaty substance clustered along the rim, like scraps of raw beef. Strange. What had he eaten last night? A hamburger and french fries. So where did these specks come from?

"Ladies and gentlemen," Captain Grout announced. "Please bear with us a while longer. We expect the chief to arrive at any minute and then the briefing will begin." He sat down in his chair and muttered to Russ, who was seated beside him at the table at the head of the briefing room. "They'll have a fucking field day with this."

"Don't I know it," Russ agreed.

The two dozen reporters gathered in the large room fidgeted and resumed their conversations, passing the time as they had for the past ninety minutes, waiting for the press conference the chief had called to begin.

"I don't like it," Grout stated.

"What else can the Chief do?" Russ asked. "It's impossible to keep the lid on this any longer. You can never tell. Sometimes these newshounds can dig up information we can't."

"I still don't like it," Grout reiterated. "Police work should be left to police."

Russ elected not to comment, knowing Grout's tirade against the media by heart.

"Nosy bastards," Grout said to press home his point.

Chief Watson, attired in a wrinkled brown suit and puffing on his favorite pipe, entered the briefing room carrying a green notebook tucked under his left arm. The reporters stopped chattering and focused their attention on the front of the room.

"Look at 'em," Grout whispered to Russ, his hawkish features flushed with anger. "They're champing at the bit, all set to fuck up our investigation."

"It's not as bad as all that," Russ answered, restraining his building annoyance.

Chief Watson took his position at the center of the main table and placed his notebook on the table. He methodically tapped his pipe on an ashtray, emptying the contents.

"My lungs thank you, Chief," one of the reporters comented, and many of them laughed.

Chief Watson smiled. "Is that any way for a chain smoker to talk, Tim?" he asked, and again the reporters grinned and giggled. He placed his pipe in his breast pocket, stem down, and faced the group with a stern, somber expression.

"Ladies and gentlemen," he began, "I thank you for coming on such short notice and I apologize for keeping you waiting as long as you have. The delay was unavoidable, as you'll shortly understand. We . . ."

"Someone get a parking ticket?" a stout, balding man joked.

"Thoughtless prick," Captain Grout mumbled.

"We require your assistance," Chief Watson continued, unperturbed. He stopped, his voice faltering. The reporters sensed the magnitude of the coming statements and they hushed, eagerly expectant.

Russ was watching the newshounds, observing their reactions. He scanned the group in the front row of seats and spotted Warren Mckeen.

"Thanks to a premature leak," Chief Watson resumed, pausing to cast a meaningful glare at Mckeen, "you are all aware that late Thursday night, June fifth, a group of bikers was attacked near an area called the Dunes and several of them were injured. Fifteen minutes ago I was notified that one of them, identified as twenty-three-year-old Bert Jackson, had died of complications stemming from the assault."

Chief Watson stopped and the reporters began whispering and gabbling with one another.

They think that's their story, Russ perceived, and sighed. If only it were.

Chief Watson held up his hands, motioning for quiet. They complied. "Unfortunately, Jackson's death is not the reason I've called this press conference. There has been another murder."

The reporters remained silent, their attention riveted.

Chief Watson cleared his throat. "Last night we conducted a stakeout at the Dunes and our officers were fallen upon brutally. One of the stakeout team was killed . . ." He paused, remembering the few times he'd met her, how pretty she'd been. "The slain officer is identified as Charlene Winslow, age twenty-six. You will be issued copies of the official report. Any questions?"

"Anyone else hurt?" a woman inquired.

"Yes," Chief Watson replied. "Officer Leta Ballinger, age twenty-four. She was treated and released. She'll be all right."

"How many officers were involved?" another reporter asked. "What time did all this happen?"

"The reports we're about to release will answer all of your questions," Chief Watson stated.

"Including the identity of their attacker?" someone called out.

"No, not that," Chief Watson said. "We don't know what attacked them. That's where you come in. I want to publicly solicit your help."

"How can we help?" the one called Tim wanted to know.

"I'll lay my cards on the table." Chief Watson glanced at Captain Grout. "My staff is undermanned and our resources are limited. Our force has been putting in ample overtime as it is. Now this. We're nearing the peak of our tourist season, the busiest period of the year. Thousands and thousands of tourists flock to Ocean City at this time of year. We don't have the manpower to put on this case that I'd like in order to insure a speedy arrest. Considering we have a crazed killer on our hands, we naturally want to wrap it up quickly. Mayor Perkins has contacted the governor and been assured of all possible assistance. Let me make one point clear. We want to avoid any widespread public alarm or panic, but by the same token we want it known that there is a murderer haunting the Dunes and we want the public to avoid that area like they would the plague."

"You don't believe the attacks could spread to other

areas?" Tim questioned.

"We have no reason to believe this will be the case. Still, you can never be certain." Chief Watson leaned on the table. "Now we come to the killer himself. The bottom line is simply that we don't have a single, solitary, solid lead to go on. We know the attacker is male. Over six feet tall. Weight, approximately two hundred pounds. We know everyone who's seen him has reported he's a hairy individual. One couple called him a bear. The bikers and one of our own officers liken him to a werewolf. Now, you know and I know there's no such thing as a werewolf. not a real one, anyhow. We could be dealing with someone wearing a werewolf costume. We are checking on that possibility. That's all we know about this guy. We want more. We need more. That's where you news people come in. Previously, we've enjoyed excellent cooperation from the media. I expect this will continue to be the case. If you come across any clues, any information at all, contact us immediately. Many times in the past law enforcement agencies have been aided by the media. I'm asking you, ladies and gentlemen, if you will help us now and, hopefully, enable us to prevent another savage murder. Will you?"

There was a momentary silence, an awkward interval, until Tim and several other reporters rose, followed by the rest. Many of them nodded in agreement, while others yelled an affirmative response.

"You can count on us," Tim remarked loudly.

"Notice how the chief's got 'em eating from his hand," Grout whispered over to Russ.

"Yeah, sure," Russ said. He also noticed that Warren Mckeen didn't nod or say a word. That boy could be trouble, he mused. Real trouble.

"How do you feel?"

"Okay."

"You sure?"

"I'm okay, really."

"Is there anything I can get you?"

"No."

"You sure?"

"I'm fine, Earl, just fine. Tired and sore, but otherwise fine." Leta laid back on her sofa, resting her head on a pillow. Despite her assurances, her throat was throbbing. Superficial, the doctor had said. Nothing to worry about, the doctor had said. Sure hurt like hell, though.

Earl was in the chair across the living room, nervously eyeing her, clearly worried.

"I was never more scared in my life," he said.

"*You* were scared?" She suppressed an urge to laugh, dreading the resultant pain. "How do you think I felt?"

"Thank God you'll be fine. You looked terrible last night. All that blood . . ." He flinched, afraid the memories would upset her.

Leta smiled to soothe him. "Honey, I'm the lucky one. It's poor Char . . . poor Char . . ." She closed her eyes and fought back the tears.

Earl walked over and knelt by her side. "Don't think about it anymore, Leta." He stroked her long brown hair. "Try to get some sleep. You've got five days off and you're going to use every minute of it to rest and recuperate."

"With you watching over me—" she grinned—"I don't think I'll have any choice."

"You bet you won't. Are you sure there isn't something I could get you?"

"For the umpteenth time, no."

Earl returned to his chair and slumped in it, dejected.

"Hey! I thought you were supposed to cheer me up," she goaded him.

"I'm sorry. I just can't help it. I feel so guilty."

"You feel guilty?" She propped herself up on her elbow. "Why should you feel any guilt?"

His forehead creased. "Maybe, just maybe, if I had been closer to you two last night, if I'd been more attentive, Charlene might be alive today."

"What? Don't be silly. What happened, happened. Call it the will of God, or fate, or whatever you want to, but there was no way you could have prevented it. We went by the book and we blew it."

"I wish I could look at it that way. I want to."

"Which reminds me . . ." She paused, tugging at an obscure memory.

"What?"

"Last night you said something about not wanting it to happen again. Not wanting what to happen again?" She saw his face redden and he turned away from her.

"Nothing."

"I thought we had an open relationship."

"We do."

"No secrets?"

"No secrets," Earl agreed.

"I'm waiting."

Earl toyed with the chair arm, running his fingers in circular patterns, delaying, building his courage.

Leta decided to ease off. "Look, honey, if you don't want to talk about it, don't."

"It's okay. I might as well. You'd hear about it sooner or

152

later anyway."

Leta reclined on her pillow, waiting.

"It was about four years ago," he said. "There was a massive drug bust going down. The feds were in on it, the troopers, everybody. You might have heard about it. Simultaneous raids in four cities. Over a million dollars worth confiscated."

"I vaguely recall it," she admitted.

"Well." He clenched his hands into fists. "I was assigned to a routine stakeout, along with a female officer named Jane Clayton, and we were watching this pusher's cottage on the north end of the beach. The feds weren't expecting him to show. They were planning to collar the bum in Atlantic City. What we didn't know was that he was alerted to the impending bust. He split Atlantic City and drove down here the night before. We weren't even aware he was inside the cottage. Dispatch notified us that the feds wanted us to check out the cottage. They didn't mention why. So we walked up to the front door and knocked, not expecting any resistance, and the fucker stuck a shotgun out of a window and blew Jane into three pieces . . . Four years, and I still relive that nightmare over and over again." He sighed and ran his right hand through his blond hair. The corners of his eyes crinkled, the haunting memory agitating him again.

"It wasn't your fault. You can't blame yourself," Leta said.

"Can't I? Then why have I been doing exactly that for four years?"

"That explains it," she stated with dawning understanding.

"Explains what?"

153

"The statement you made last night and the reason you've been extremely protective of me ever since we met. I always suspected there was something you weren't telling me."

"You did?"

"Intuition, you know." She smiled, attempting to lighten the mood. "We females are supposed to be loaded with it."

"You sure are."

"Maybe." She grinned impishly. "But it sure didn't come in handy on my first date."

"How do you mean?"

"You had to be there to appreciate my meaning."

Earl absently nodded agreement.

"Honey, snap out of it." Her heart went out to him, sitting there so grim and filled with remorse. "You're making me feel worse than I already do."

That got to him. He came over to her and clasped her hand.

"I'm sorry. That's the last thing I want to do." He lightly kissed her lips.

"No more Mr. Grump?"

"From here on out I'm Mr. Sunshine all the way."

"Good. I've been neglecting my tan as it is."

"Grout, what the hell is eating you?" Chief Watson angrily demanded. "You've been acting like you've got ants in your pants all damn day. I want to know why."

The three of them were seated in the lounge, sipping coffee and eating hurried sandwiches.

"I said I want to know why," Chief Watson repeated when Grout didn't speak up.

154

"You don't want to hear about it," Grout mumbled.

"Are you hard of hearing as well as on the rag? You'd best tell me, and tell me right this moment, Captain." Chief Watson slammed his cup on the table and spilled some of his coffee.

"All right. I'll tell you. I don't believe you're handling this latest case properly."

"Properly?" Chief Watson glanced at Russ, who shrugged his shoulders. "Translated, that means you think I'm not handling it the way you would handle it. What's your big beef, as if I couldn't guess?"

"You know what it is."

"You bet I do. I haven't worked with you all these years for nothing. I trust you're aware that you can be one royal pain in the ass."

"I can't help the way I think."

"That's the problem. Sometimes I wonder if you *do* think. You'd be far better off if you'd take a second to consider what you're going to say before you open your mouth."

Grout started to rise.

"Sit down. I'm not through with you yet."

Grout slurped his coffee, pouting.

"Damn it, Bob. I know how you feel about reporters. I just wish you'd keep a check on that temper of yours. Your temperament obviously isn't the reason you've risen so high in the ranks."

"You make it sound like my temper is all I've got going for me."

"Bullshit. And since when is a fiery disposition a plus in any career? You've got qualities working for you, all right, like your sharp, analytical mind and your bulldog tenacity. You're not a complete turd."

"Gee, thanks."

"You know what I mean. I want you to . . ." Chief Watson paused, watching a uniformed officer rapidly approach.

"Chief!"

"My call?"

"Yes, sir. Just came in. He's waiting."

"Thank you, Sergeant Bean."

The sergeant departed.

"Call?" Grout asked as Chief Watson rose.

"Yep. Might be a lead. You two go about your business and I'll get in touch with you later." He took several quick steps, then turned, struck by an afterthought. "Russ?"

"Yeah, Chief?"

"Any results on the costume angle?"

"None. We've covered all the local shops dealing in horror costumes with no success. All of them carry werewolf masks during September and October for their Halloween sales, but none of them keep the names and addresses of people who purchase them. Why should they? We're still running down the list of national distributors. It's longer than your arm. Never knew there were so many costume novelty shops in this country."

"I wasn't too hopeful that angle would pan out, anyway. Keep trying, though."

Chief Watson hastened along the corridor to the front desk. Without a word Sergeant Bean handed him a phone.

"Chief Watson here."

"Scott, you old turkey, how the hell are you?" an exuberant voice at the other end exclaimed.

"Well, Nick, I think you've finally attained a grasp of official Bureau jargon."

"Are you kidding? I'm still trying to find the little boys' room without getting lost."

"Glad to talk to you again. What's it been, three years?" Chief Watson asked.

"About that. Sorry I wasn't in the office when you called. I got your message and the courier arrived on time."

"That's good. When can I expect a full report?"

"As soon as possible," Nick answered. "Our lab here in Philadelphia isn't quite as complete and modernized as our one in Washington, but we'll do our best. I can understand the urgency."

"Thanks, Nick. I owe you one."

"What are old buddies for?"

"I still owe you one."

"If you insist. You know, Scott, I never did understand why you didn't enter the Bureau. Seems to me you're stuck in a dead end."

"I don't think so," Chief Watson stated emphatically.

"To each his own."

"The next time you're in town stop on by and we'll shoot the shit."

"Fine by me."

"I'll be waiting for the evaluation."

"I'll personally rush it along. There are two things I can pass on to you now."

"What are they?" Chief Watson perked up.

"Now keep in mind the lab tests are still in progress. We'll know much more when the specimens are processed."

157

"What two things can you give me now?" Chief Watson impatiently prompted.

"There is human saliva in the blood sample and the hair is not human."

"What?"

"Are you getting hard of hearing in your old age? One of the inital tests on the blood sample from her neck contained human saliva. The hair fragments you scraped from under her fingernails are not human. We're running a computer reference link with our primary unit in Washington and expect classification within twelve hours. Anything else I can do for you?"

"You've given me more than I'd expected on such short notice," Chief Watson said, the implications of the information disturbing him.

"Okay, Scott. I'll get back to you once we get anything new."

"Thanks, Nick. Bye."

Chief Watson handed the phone to Sergeant Bean and wandered back to his office, considering his next step. The proportions of this case were expanding by the moment. His boys had determined that Officer Winslow's throat had been torn open by human teeth and now the FBI provided confirmation. The hair development was a stumper. Not human hair? What, then? What the hell were they dealing with?

It was past seven when Warren sealed the envelope on his written report to Fontaine and leaned over to switch on his radio for the next newscast, due on the half hour. He was tuned to WGYN, his main competition, determined to keep abreast of the latest news on his story and concerned that someone else might get a jump on him. He couldn't permit that to happen. It would jeopardize his chances with Fontaine. How could he prevent it? Visiting the Dunes was out of the question. The police had made it clear at the close of the press conference that the Dunes were off limits. Chief Watson had explained that more surveillance teams were staking out the Dunes on a twenty-four hour basis and no one, but no one, was getting in or out of the area without permission. Especially the press. This thing, this "werewolf," for whatever reason, preferred to haunt the Dunes and the police were determined to nab it the next time it appeared.

Where did that leave him?

Fontaine would be expecting results, not excuses. If the werewolf were caught, he'd have to settle for the same statements issued to every media member. There would go his exclusive. Fontaine would not be impressed.

What to do?

Was it possible the attacker was a real werewolf? No, he couldn't accept that superstitious bullshit. A costumed nutcase, then, was the only alternative. Would it be possible to trace this guy through the costume? Doubtful. Too many stores sold monster costumes and if this madman was a tourist the odds against tracing him were astronomical. The police might attempt a trace, they had the resources available, but it could take them weeks, even months, if they found anything at all.

Warren sighed, disgusted.

He had to face facts; there was no way in the world to get to the thing before the police did.

"Shit!" He pounded his desk once in frustration.

No way.

Or was there?

A thought hit him and he grinned. If Mohammed could not get to the mountain, then possibly the mountain would come to Mohammed.

What if the police were wrong in their assumption? They were expecting, or more likely, *hoping* that the thing would confine its murderous activities to the area of the Dunes. But what, he asked himself, if they were wrong? What if it didn't? The thing had to know the Dunes were being patrolled. Surely, even if this werewolf were completely insane, it would recognize the danger and avoid the Dunes. Why would it restrict itself to the Dunes in the first place? Obviously, the remoteness must be a contributing factor. Maybe . . . Warren stood up and began to pace, excited by his line of reasoning . . . maybe the attacks weren't against the persons attacked so much as they were in protection of what it must consider its territory. But would this werewolf continue roaming the Dunes when the area was crawling with cops? Not very likely.

Warren smiled.

It was so obvious! If this guy were deprived of his solitude, his turf, as it were, he'd naturally seek out another area where he could wander without being interrupted. But where?

Warren went to his desk and opened his briefcase, sorted through his papers until he found his map of Ocean City, and spread it open. He placed it on the desk top and studied it. If he could put himself in the place of this guy, think like this werewolf, then he might be able to guess the next move the guy would make.

Okay.

Let's suppose this werewolf doesn't like the fact that the

Dunes are overrun with boys in blue.

Let's suppose it decides to find another secluded area free from intruders.

Where would it go?

There was a small sandy area north of Ocean City, beyond New Castle Road. But it might be too small for the werewolf.

There was another area, though, with definite possibilities. It was west of Ocean City, bordering the Ocean City Municipal Airport. Just north of the airport was the Municipal Golf Course, relatively isolated at night. South of the airport was an even better area, though, with a large expanse of woods and marsh bordered by Pecks Bay on the west.

Warren chuckled, pleased with his deduction.

If he were the werewolf, and if he were denied the Dunes, and if he wanted, for whatever reasons, to remain in the vicinity of Ocean City, then he would choose the area south of the airport as the next best site to enjoy his nocturnal rambling.

Warren sat down and started to hum. If his assessment was correct, and there was no reason to believe otherwise, then all he had to do was keep an eye on this area and wait for the werewolf to show himself.

And what then?

So what if he spotted this guy? The nut was dangerous. He couldn't just walk up to him and ask for an interview. However, he might be able to tail this guy to wherever he holed up during the day. Risky, but it could be done. And if he could accomplish it, then he'd have his exclusive without having to worry about any other reporters butting in.

"I must be a genius," he said aloud, impressed by his deductive insights.

Boy, would Fontaine be eating out of his hand if he could pull it off.

He had to pull it off.

His career was on the line.

June 9

"I WANT TO THANK YOU FOR coming."

"It's my pleasure. This case fascinates me."

"Really, Myrna? I find it morbid."

"You know damn well what I mean," Doctor Myrna Kraft replied. "You've known me long enough, Scott."

"That I have," Chief Watson stated. "And you never cease to amaze me."

"How's that?"

"Well, Myrna, during all these years, all the times I've called you into my office for consultations, you've displayed such little emotion. No matter how grim and gruesome the case, you've analyzed them all clinically and coldly. I've never seen you affected by the cruelty and violence."

"You mean I'm not as squeamish as you'd expected a woman to be?" Myrna asked.

"I didn't say that."

"But I think it's what you meant. Your problem is you're prone to stereotyping."

"Is that a professional judgment, Doctor?"

"I'm a psychiatrist, Scott. I tend to think in psychiatric terms."

"You're also a woman." Chief Watson smiled, openly admiring her proud bearing and stately appearance, her smoldering green eyes and her brunette hair, streaked with touches of gray. "A damn good looker, too."

"That's another problem you have." Myrna grinned. "You can never keep your mind on the matter at hand. You lack singleness of purpose."

Chief Watson laughed. "Okay! I know better than to match wits with you. Why don't you apply some of your expensive psychiatric terms to the case at hand."

"The case of the raving wereling."

"Come again?"

"Never mind. I'll get to that in a moment." Myrna opened a folder she was holding in her lap.

"I'm sorry we don't have more information for you," Chief Watson apologized. "This one is rather sketchy so far."

"I realize the reason," Myrna said. "I can give you some ideas to consider, for what they're worth."

"Some of your ideas have been invaluable in our investigations. Begin." Chief Watson settled into his chair.

"Obviously, we're not dealing with a mentally healthy individual . . ."

"Obviously," Chief Watson concurred, smirking.

"Behave, will you? Exactly what the nature of his psychoses might be, I can't say for certain. I can speculate. I don't think you're after a psychopathic personality."

"He's killed two people, remember?" Chief Watson interrupted.

"True. But we both know people kill for a variety of reasons. What I am simply saying is that I don't believe this one exists purely to kill. I don't think he deliberately

164

plans and executes the murders. I don't think he's a psychopath."

"What, then?" he asked, as usual fascinated by her mind.

"There are a number of disorders which might account for this deviate behavior. He could, conceivably, be a manic depressive, a psychotic depressive, schizophrenic, or suffering from a variety of mental deformities. In this particular case, I'm leaning toward diagnosing a profoundly twisted psyche, possibly even on the order of a split personality."

"You mean, like that Eve woman?" Chief Watson threw in.

"Not exactly the same thing, but along those lines."

"Why?"

"We have several instances here of extremely violent behavior, always at night. Your suspect is wearing some kind of werewolf costume. We could be seeing a rare case of lycanthropy."

"Lycanthropy?"

"A lycanthropic individual suffers from the delusion that they have adopted the characteristics of a wolf or have actually become a wolf."

"Such a thing isn't possible, is it? Turning into a wolf, I mean?" Chief Watson questioned, intrigued.

"Of course not," Myrna answered. "But the history of psychiatry is replete with individuals who have believed they became wolves under certain circumstances. The moon, even night itself, can act as an emotional catalyst on such persons, rendering a perfectly ordinary individual into a demented misfit. I believe lycanthropy could well be the case here."

"You mean . . ." He was trying to absorb her words. ". . . this guy believes he is a wolf?"

"Yes. Or . . . ." She paused, and he could tell she was considering something new. ". . . or he could believe he is a werewolf."

"That would explain the costume," Chief Watson confirmed.

"Exactly. My diagnosis would also explain why you've had no reports of him during the day."

"Werewolves only come out at night!" he said, excited. "But . . ."

"But what?"

"But aren't werewolves associated with a full moon? This guy has been seen on moonless nights as well as nights when the moon was visible."

Myrna smiled. "Who said my theories were flawless?"

"Your batting average is better than most," Chief Watson declared. "Go on."

"As I indicated earlier, this man has an intense mental and emotional disorder. He is not a werewolf, not in the traditional hair-growing and fang-sprouting sense. His personality, I expect, experiences a drastic change at night, a bestial alteration and transformation. The operative word here is change, or, even more appropriate, exchange."

"How do you mean?"

"Your suspect might have two distinct personalities. One, possibly meek, mild, maybe dominated to some degree, is exchanged at night for the wolf nature, for aggression, brute force, and freedom. You've heard the word changeling used before?"

"I think I heard it in connection with a movie," he responded.

"Well, what you have here could be an *ex*changeling."

"An exchangeling?"

"Cute term, isn't it? Should be. I just coined it. Combine the first half of werewolf, the old English *wer*, or man, with the latter half of exchangeling, and you get the term I used before . . ."

"Wereling?" Chief Watson remembered.

"Exactly. Do you like the word?"

"It seems to fit."

"Doesn't it though? I'm pleased with it. It's a Kraft original. I plan to develop a history of this case and present my findings at the next regional symposium. Maybe I'll submit pertinent articles to various publications."

"You enjoy seeing your name is those psychiatric journals, don't you, Myrna?"

"I appreciate peer recognition, Scott. Don't you?" she asked defensively.

"I suppose I do."

"So I officially dub your suspect the wereling. It has a nice ring to it, doesn't it?"

"I guess."

"You're not very enthusiastic."

"Why should I be? It's your word."

"Come on, Scott."

"Myrna, you can throw all the ten-cent words at me you want. But they don't necessarily get me any closer to collaring this maniac. They don't prevent anyone else from being brutally murdered."

"You mean I haven't been of any help?"

"I didn't say that. You might have provided the psychological motive for his actions. But you can't tell me how to catch him."

"I see," Myrna said stiffly.

"Don't get me wrong," Chief Watson elaborated. "I like your new term, Myrna. The wereling. If you say it's appropriate, then it's appropriate. It won't get me the suspect, but it might win you some academic kudos."

"My. Aren't we on a nasty streak?" Myrna sorted her papers and snapped shut her folder.

"Don't take it personally."

"Don't mind if I do." She stood up and walked to his door.

"Myrna, please?"

"I don't know why I bother consulting for you." She took hold of the doorknob.

"Oh, hell!" Chief Watson sighed and threw up his hands in resignation.

"One last thing, Chief Watson." She turned and faced him.

"Anything, you know that."

She ignored his statement.

"I would take it as a personal favor, Chief Watson, if you would keep our conversation to yourself. At least my mentioning my concept of the wereling. I want to be the first to publicly apply the term."

"No problem, Myrna. I'm interested in saving lives, not collecting awards."

"Thanks, Scott." Her eyes blazed for a moment. "That really hurt."

Myrna Kraft spun, yanked open the door, and departed in a huff.

"So long," Chief Watson called after her. "It was nice talking with you," he said to the four gray walls.

"Think it will show?" Doyle asked. He was young, fresh out of the academy, and obviously on edge.

"Who knows?" Earl answered. He was wishing he was curled up alongside Leta instead of squatting behind a cluster of large rocks on the southern tip of the Dunes, freezing his ass at four in the morning.

"Too bad about Charlene, huh?"

"You don't know the half of it," Earl replied. Super! Why did he have to bring that up?

"How's Leta coming along?" Doyle inquired in a whisper. The affection between Earl and Leta was common station gossip.

"Just fine," Earl said testily.

"I didn't mean to pry."

"No offense taken."

Doyle decided to change the subject. "What if this guy never attacks anyone again?"

"Then I guess he won't be caught."

"You don't think so?"

"Slim chance."

"Doesn't it burn you to think he might get away?" Doyle questioned.

"Sure as hell does. I want this one, bad. Real bad. I'll nail this guy if it's the last thing I ever do," Earl angrily declared, allowing his seething inner rage to show.

"Maybe you're taking this thing too personal. Aren't we trained to be objective about things like this?"

Earl shot Doyle a withering glare. "That's sheer bullshit. They try and force feed that objective crap to you at the academy, but don't you believe a single word of it. We're human, Doyle. We have emotions, feelings. We react whether we like it or not. The person who says they aren't affected by all the ugliness we encounter in our line of work is lying through their teeth. None of us are robots or have pointy ears."

"Pointy ears? I don't understand." Doyle was perplexed.

"Forget it, kid."

"Can I ask you one more question?"

Earl sighed. "Sure. Why not. What?"

"Well, we were instructed to catch this guy alive. 'Imperative' was the word Chief Watson used."

"So?" Earl snapped impatiently.

Doyle poked at the sand with his fingers.

"So?" Earl repeated.

"So I get the distinct impression you don't want this guy alive. I have the feeling you plan to blow him away if you're given half the chance. None of my business, I know. But there, I said it."

"If you're right—and remember, I'm not admitting a damn thing—what do you propose to do about it?" Earl watched Doyle carefully, trying to read his features in the murky blackness.

"Technically, I'm required to report you."

"Technically, you're right."

"Personally, I don't see where it's any of my affair. If it were me, if it was my woman this bastard tore up, then I'd probably feel the same way you do."

"Thanks," Earl said sincerely, relaxing.

"So if you get the chance, blow the fucker to kingdom come!"

June 14

THERE WAS A KNOCK ON HIS door. Chief Watson stretched, stirring his circulation. "Who is it?" he yelled.

"Russ, Chief. Can I come in?"

"Oh, sure. It's open." He tossed the Bureau report aside and swiveled his chair to face the door.

Russ walked in carrying a newspaper tucked under his arm. "Have you seen this edition?"

" 'Murderer Still at Large,' " he quoted from memory. " 'Police Still Stymied.' Yeah, I've read that rag. See if I ever help Tim O'Keefe again."

"The same theme is in all the papers and on all the radio stations." Russ sat down in a comfortable chair across from the chief's walnut desk.

"I know. I know."

"The main reason I'm here is to break the bad news to you in person," Russ said, dropping the paper on the floor.

"Bad news? What's that? Never heard of such a thing."

Russ grinned. "I'm afraid I've got to report a dead end on the costume angle. The conclusion I've reached, after an entire week of banging my head on a brick wall, is that there is no way we're going to trace our werewolf through his costume. Very few of the firms dealing in realistic werewolf costumes have provided us with customer lists we could use. They all say they'll check their files for costumes sold in this area, but it could take some of them months. How far back do we look, they want to know. What do I tell them? Did this guy get his costume a week ago, a month, a year or three years? Where do I draw the line? Besides, as you pointed out, what if this guy is from out of town and purchased his outfit in Spokane or Denver or Montreal or Timbuktu? That means we're dealing with a couple hundred masks over the past year alone. The werewolf mask is a very hot item year round, and it goes like the proverbial hot cakes come Halloween . . . Christ, I feel so helpless!"

"Don't chide yourself, Russ," the chief said wearily. "I wasn't too hopeful this tack would pan out. What about the wolf hair?"

"That was a help," Russ brightened. "At least, that's what I thought three days ago when the FBI sent us the information. I checked in the retailers' directory and with a regional distributor in New York City. There are only three firms currently making werewolf costumes using real wolf hair. One in California, two in London. Evidently this type of costume is more than your common novelty. Professionally made and quite expensive, as masks go. The manufacturers in London told me they would mail me lists of all customers on the eastern seaboard, but they indicated they receive few orders from the U.S. The California firm said they've mailed a half dozen werewolf costumes with real wolf hair to our three-state area and for a while I really thought I was on to something. One of the order clerks seemed to recall receiving

172

an order within the past month or so. But when they consulted their files they discovered some dipshit had misplaced orders and screwed up their operational procedure. They blamed it on a part-timer they'd hired to fill in for one of their vacationing clerks. A chronic problem with them, evidently. They're still looking for me, but frankly they're not too optimistic and neither am I."

"Don't be discouraged. You know by now that nine-tenths of all our work is waiting, waiting, and more waiting. Sooner or later we'll get a break."

"It's the later part that worries me, Chief. We've been lucky. A week has gone by without another incident. The men are griping about the long hours spent watching the sand grow at the Dunes. So far, so good. But . . ." Russ let his sentence trail off.

"But," Chief Watson finished the thought, "you think it's just the calm before the storm. I'm inclined to agree."

"So what do we do about it?" Russ demanded.

"We wait."

"I don't see how you can sit there calmly and say that. A civilian and one of our own, dead. The press up in arms. You must be receiving tremendous heat from upstairs."

"Hades couldn't be any hotter."

"Do you think if this guy doesn't put in another appearance that the whole thing will blow over?"

"Two deaths?"

"No, I guess not. Stupid question."

"Say, how is Officer Ballinger doing?" The chief gazed out his window at the setting sun, noting the bright red and orange cast to the horizon, longing for an hour off to go strolling along the beach.

"Fine. Back in uniform and working. The doc has given

her a clean bill of health. Physically, at least."

"Good. So that brings us back to square one, the were-wolf."

"What do we do?"

"Nothing. Absolutely nothing," Chief Watson stated. "The next move is up to him."

"I don't like it out here at night."

"There's nothing to be afraid of. The worst that could happen is you'd trip on a golf ball and sprain your ankle."

"I still don't see why this couldn't wait until tomorrow. We're never going to find it in the dark."

"Daisy, you worry too much."

"I'm a cashier, Curt. I'm not supposed to be wandering around this damn golf course at ten o'clock at night."

Curt laughed and twisted his lanky frame to the side, sweeping his flashlight beam along the perimeter of a stand of maple and oak trees.

"Let me tell you how it is," he said. "Mr. Adams is the manager of the course. Mr. Adams and the mayor were out here this afternoon playing their weekly eighteen holes. The good mayor, that asshole Perkins, lost his wallet. Unfortunately, you and I were the only two on the premises when Mr. Adams called just now and wanted someone to conduct a brief search for the wallet. Why couldn't that blithering idiot Perkins have waited until tomorrow morning to discover his wallet was missing?"

"Is that any way to speak of our beloved mayor?" Daisy sarcastically chided.

"Hey! I'm the pro at this course. I'm the one with the miserable task of giving Mayor Perkins his weekly lesson. I tell you, Daisy, I could be Arnold Palmer or Tom Watson and I still wouldn't be able to teach Perkins a blessed thing. The man has the intellect of a gnat, the ability of a snail, and the density of granite."

"Gee, I didn't realize anyone thought so highly of our honorable mayor," Daisy joked. She swept her beam over a nearby sandtrap.

"Oh, he's okay, in a plodding, political sort of way."

"I still wish I was home. If Mr. Adams had waited five more minutes to call us I would have had my register closed and balanced and been out the door."

"How long have you been working here?" Curt asked, forcing his thoughts away from her luxuriant red hair, her full young breasts, and the fact they were all alone in the middle of the course. "I don't think I've seen you around too often."

"I started in May. I'm just working here for the summer. I go to college in Watertown, New York. I love coming down here for the summer."

"Yeah," he admitted. "The beach can become addicting."

They crossed the green at hole fifteen and slowly walked in the direction of sixteen.

"How about you?"

"What about me?"

"How long have you worked here?"

"Too damn long," he sighed. "I fell into a rut. I was young, about your age, and talented, but I guess I lacked ambition. I lucked across this job and stayed. I regret I never tried to advance in my profession. Take some free advice, Daisy, from a man old enough to be your father. If there's any goal you cherish, any star you've set your sights on, go after it, girl, for all you're worth."

"You do sound like my dad," Daisy giggled.

"I should," he said. "I have a girl your age. I hope you take my counsel more seriously than she does."

"I'm sure she loves you very much," Daisy advised him.

"Sometimes I wonder," he muttered.

"Oh, all parents go through a phase where they can't communicate with their children."

"Oh?" Curt laughed. "Tell me, how did someone of your tender years become so wise?"

"Simple," Daisy chuckled. "I'm majoring in interpersonal communications and interactive societal behavior."

He stopped. "You've got to be putting me on."

"Kind of." Daisy giggled. "I want to be a social worker."

"Ahhhh." Curt noticed his beam was dimming rapidly. "Damn."

"What's wrong?"

"Looks like the batteries in this—"

Curt was cut short by a shrill, eerie howl piercing the night, emanating from a tract of trees ahead.

"What in the world was that?" Daisy asked in a frightened whisper.

"Beats the hell out of me."

"I don't like it."

"Neither do I. Have you heard those news stories about what happened down at the Dunes?" Curt's flashlight was fading faster by the minute.

"Yeah," Daisy acknowledged. "Do you think it's the same thing?"

"I doubt it. But to play it safe, we better head back."

They wheeled and began the trek back to the clubhouse, their pace hurried.

"Should we notify the police?" Daisy glanced over her

shoulder, jittery.

"I don't think so." His beam was barely illuminating the grass ahead.

"Why not?"

"We don't know for certain that the thing we just heard was the killer. It could have just been a dog."

"I never heard a dog howl like that."

"Then we'll call the police. I don't care if I get into trouble."

"Why would you get into trouble?" She could see the lights of the clubhouse a half mile away.

"Haven't you heard about Mr. Adams and that notorious temper of his?"

"You think he'll be upset if we call the police?"

"Not that so much as how pissed off he'll be when he learns I didn't scour the entire course for that damn wallet. Adams and Perkins are good friends. He'll fly off the handle, no doubt about it."

"I don't want to get you in trouble, Curt," Daisy started.

"No problem. I've been taking flak off that old buzzard for years."

"No."

"No, what?" he questioned, hoping.

"No, I won't let you get into trouble with Mr. Adams. You're probably right. It was just a dog. We'll tell Mr. Adams we looked all over the course for the wallet and couldn't find it."

"You sure?"

"Yep. We won't call the cops. I don't want to get you into hot water, Curt."

"Thank you," he said, meaning it.

They fell silent, hurrying. When they were only several hundred yards from the clubhouse Curt laughed and switched off his now useless flashlight.

"Maybe I should talk Adams into installing lights out here for use at night."

"Do you really think he would agree?" Daisy asked.

"Does Mayor Perkins have brains?"

"I'LL CONFESS, WARREN, I'M DISAPPOINTED."

"I'm doing my best."

"Warren, I require results, not excuses," Fontaine arrogantly pontificated.

Warren clenched the receiver, fighting an impulse to inform Fontaine where he could shove his requirements. "It's only a matter of time," he said instead.

"That's all well and good," Fontaine replied. "Only we both know time doesn't sell magazines. Copy does. Exciting, interesting, fascinating copy. All I get from you day after day is the same thing. Nothing to report, but you're on to something and expect new information any day. I expected higher caliber reports from you than those I've been receiving."

"Mr. Fontaine," Warren selected his words carefully. "I know that a man with your vast experience recognizes the obstacles inherent in investigating certain incidents and gleaning further facts to use in follow-up reports."

"You should enter politics, my boy," Fontaine snickered.

"I beg your pardon?" Warren said, realizing full well the meaning Fontaine intended.

"Keep at it, Warren. I should be more patient. Sorry if my call upset you. I just wanted to insure that you weren't becoming discouraged."

Bullshit. "I've meant every word I've written. I'm in a holding stage, awaiting a new development."

"You wouldn't want to elaborate, would you?" Fontaine queried him.

Are you kidding? And relinquish my edge? "I'd like to, but I could be wrong and I don't want to put myself out on a limb and possibly make a fool of myself."

"Very sensible. I can't argue with your reasoning. I'll be waiting for your daily updates."

I bet you will. You just want the story for the next issue of the *Bulletin*. "You'll receive one every day until this madman is apprehended, and I'll cover his trial, too, if you want."

"Warren, you're a good man. I know I can rely on you."

Translation: get your ass in gear. "Thank you for calling, Mr. Fontaine."

"Bye." Warren hung up and heaved a sigh of relief.

June 23

THE FULL MOON HELPED.

How the hell long had he been coming out to this marshy section at night? Two weeks, wasn't it? If Fontaine only knew how hard he was working on this story. No. Maybe it was better if Fontaine did not know how he was spending his time between dusk and dawn. Fontaine would think he was crazy.

Warren shook his head, disgusted with himself.

Maybe he was crazy. Each night he'd drive south on Ocean Drive from Atlantic City to Ocean City. He'd take Princeton over to Bay Avenue and travel north one mile until he reached a gravel road, a seldom used, potholed, weed choked lane leading to nowhere.

Except into the swampy terrain south of the Ocean City Municipal Airport.

His legs were beginning to tingle, going numb, and he shifted his position to restore circulation. He was squatting on an enormous, circular, flat stone on top of a hill overlooking a wide expanse of marsh. The moon illuminated the landscape, the trees, bushes, rotted logs, vines and occasional boulders blending into an uncanny, spectral merging of shadow and form.

Jesus!

If he weren't so eager to update his story for Fontaine, to further his journalistic career, he wouldn't be caught dead out here.

Warren spotted a raccoon foraging along the bank of a small pond, searching for frogs, sniffing the dank air and poking into the weeds and lush grass on the shore. The hunter and the hunted, Warren mused. Just like his situation. He was the hunter and the werewolf was the hunted.

Something suddenly flew by, passing immediately above his head, startling him. He fell back onto his elbows, pain lancing through his arms. There was a momentary flapping of wings, then silence.

Shit!

What the hell was that? An owl? A damn bat? Some kind of bird? He scoured the sky, finding the moon and the sparkling stars and nothing else.

There was a loud splash from the direction of the small pond and he glanced down. The raccoon had pounced on a bullfrog in the shallows and was struggling to retain a firm grip on the slippery amphibian.

Good for you, Warren thought. You've caught your prey, but I think I'm going to pass for tonight. I'm just wasting my time. It must be near four in the morning and my quarry hasn't shown his hairy face.

Warren stretched his legs, picked up his flashlight, and started down the hill. He followed a narrow path he assumed was used by deer and small game as they crossed over the hill to reach the pond. The moonlight clearly revealed the course he was taking and he decided to save his batteries until he reached the dense brush separating the marsh from the gravel road.

The racoon was tearing off chunks of flesh and meat from the hapless frog and chewing with relish. It heard Warren approaching and looked up, the two staring at one another from a distance of thirty feet. Warren stopped, waiting to see what the raccoon would do next, and he was surprised when the raccoon unexpectedly glanced up, over his head, hissed and recoiled and bounded away into the tall grass and weeds surrounding the pond.

What the . . . ?

Warren slowly turned, gazing along the path to the crest of the hill, to the very stone he'd vacated moments before.

"Holy shit!"

The werewolf was crouched on the stone, cocking its hairy head this way and that, studying Warren, evidently amazed to discover an intruder in the marsh.

"Hi, there," Warren said, feeling decidedly foolish, too scared to run, not knowing what else to do. "How are you?" He cautiously inched backward, hoping he could put distance between himself and the werewolf, praying the lunatic wouldn't attack if he weren't provoked.

The werewolf dropped on all fours and growled.

Oh, God, Warren silently petitioned, let me get out of this in one piece!

The werewolf reared erect, poised on the rim of the stone.

God, I'll never make it to the car in time!

The werewolf snarled and took one step.

Fontaine, you can take your werewolf story and shove it up your ass!

Warren broke and ran, panic-striken.

The werewolf howled and leaped from the rock to the path, bounding after its quarry.

Warren raced down the hill, skirting the edge of the pond, wondering if it were at all possible that he could outrun the thing.

He couldn't.

The werewolf howled with fury and pounced, hitting him square in the center of his back, the force of the blow bowling him over and rolling the two of them across the damp ground. The flashlight tumbled from Warren's fingers into the weeds. Warren struggled to his knees, gasping for air, and the werewolf was on him again, claws extended and clamped on Warren's throat.

God, I'm going to be killed!

Warren threw himself backward, pulling the werewolf after him, grasping at the paws, attempting to dislodge the talons. The two toppled to one side, the werewolf bellowing in savage, guttural delight.

Dear God, save me!

Warren renewed his struggles to break loose, almost rising to his feet before the werewolf clamped its claws tighter and surged against him. Their thrashing tossed them to the ground again, carried them over weeds and grass and through thickets.

And into the pond.

The chill, murky water closed over them and the werewolf released its strangling grip and broke to the surface, coughing and sputtering.

Warren gulped fresh air and backed away from the werewolf to the middle of the pond. He barely noticed he was treading water, that his feet were no longer touching bottom.

The werewolf shrieked, racked by pure rage, and came toward its prey. It was six feet from Warren when its footing gave way and it went under. Its arms flailed and it rose to the surface, coughing and spitting.

He's afraid of the deep water, Warren realized, elated. He's afraid of the deep water!

The werewolf made several tentative efforts to draw closer to its victim, and each time, as soon as it reached the sharp incline in the center of the pond where the water was deepest, it would back off, growling.

Warren continued to tread water, resisting the clammy cold, gathering his depleted strength.

The werewolf clambered onto the bank and rested on its haunches amidst a stand of tall reeds. It snarled and glared at its prey.

How long would the werewolf stay there, Warren wondered? All night?

The werewolf stood and slowly circled the pond, searching for an avenue of approach.

Warren kept his eyes locked on the werewolf, expecting another charge at any moment. Surely the thing wouldn't be thwarted so easily?

As if in answer, the werewolf whirled and loped up the slope of the hill.

Warren couldn't believe it!

At the top of the hill the werewolf turned and howled a defiant challenge, then disappeared over the crest.

Warren breathed easier, but he remained where he was. The thing might be circling the hill to come at him from behind. So he waited.

And waited.

Thirty minutes elapsed, during which Warren swam

185

closer to shore and found an area where he could rest his feet on the bottom. He kept alert, waiting for the werewolf to show itself.

An owl somewhere in the swamp voiced its solitary query.

Thirty more minutes passed as Warren shivered and rubbed his limbs to restore circulation, and there was still no sign of the werewolf.

Had it really departed? What incredible luck! And a lesson learned! Warren resolved then and there to abandon this story before it literally killed him. He'd almost been murdered, all for the sake of his career. The goal wasn't worth the possible cost.

More time went by and Warren began to believe the werewolf actually had moved on. Still, he couldn't bring himself to venture from the protective safety of the pond until he . . .

What was that?

He spun at the sound of shuffling steps in the dark brush behind him, fearing the worst, wondering if the water would deter the werewolf this time.

The footsteps came nearer and Warren caught sight of a flash of brown moving towards the pond.

Not again!

Warren stroked backward to the center of the pond and scoured the brush with his eyes, his nerves tingling.

A deer, a small whitetail buck, stepped from the cover of the brush and approached the pond, intent on its nightly watering.

"Jesus!" Warren exclaimed, relieved, and the buck whirled and vanished into the recesses of the marsh.

"Jesus!" he repeated, and cackled, the tension draining

from his tired, aching body. If there were a deer in the vicinity, then the werewolf must be long gone. He was safe! He was safe!

Warren laughed all the way to the reed-covered bank. He sprawled on his stomach and sighed, forgetting his fatigue and stiffness, exhilarated.

Thank God, he was *alive!*

The story could fuck itself, for all he cared. Fontaine could fuck himself. Even the fucking werewolf could go fuck himself! He rolled over and laughed, his mirth impossible to contain. Maybe he could give up broadcasting and raise chickens for a living?

Oh, Jesus!

Warren laughed until his stomach and sides hurt. The breeze on his soaked skin and clothes began to chill his flesh, goosebumps breaking out on his arms and back. Enough was enough. It was time to get his butt in gear. He sat up and glanced around. No sign of the werewolf, the deer, or the raccoon. He was alone.

Not quite.

The owl again wanted to know who was there.

"It's just little old me," Warren answered. "And I'm hauling ass."

He pressed his right arm against the moist ground to provide support as he rose and his hand came into contact with an unusual object. Leathery. Rectangular.

"What's this?"

Curious, he picked it up and examined it. He was holding a black checkbook. The leather cover was clean and neat. Funny, it couldn't have been lying on the ground exposed to all the elements for very long. The checkbook wasn't his. Who did it belong to, then?

A possibility occurred to him and he jumped up, electrified.

The owl hooted one more time.

"That's what I hope to find out," Warren mumbled and broke into a run, forgetting his flashlight, hurrying to his car. The beaming full moon afforded sufficient light for him to make his way. He was twenty yards from the gravel road when his foot became snared in a vine and he tripped and fell, the checkbook flying from his fingers when he struck the ground.

"Shit!"

Warren rose to his knees, his hands probing the weeds and vines for the checkbook.

"Where the hell is the damn thing?"

If his assumption were correct, if the checkbook belonged to the werewolf, and if he lost it now . . .

"Where can . . ."

His hand closed on the checkbook and he stood up. There was no one else it could belong to. The guy in the werewolf mask must have lost it while they were fighting.

Warren jogged the remaining distance to his car, more careful of his footing. He opened the door and sat down behind the steering wheel, leaving the door ajar so the overhead lamp would stay on.

Please, he mentally prayed, please let it be his!

Warren flipped the checkbook over and rested his eyes on the handwritten name and address.

"Harvey Painter," he read aloud. "Four thirty-two West Avalon."

Warren placed his head on the top of the seat, closed his eyes, and grinned.

"I've got him," he said, delighted. "I've got him!"

188

Maybe, he thought, he should stick with this story after all. Why give up when he had an ace in the hole? Besides, chicken farming never had appealed to him.

"THIS IS CHIEF WATSON. MAY I help you?"

"Hello, Scott."

"Well, well, well. Myrna. I thought you weren't talking to me anymore."

"Listen, Scott, I'm terribly sorry about the other day. I had no justification for taking your head off."

"Apology accepted." Chief Watson leaned back in his cushioned chair and propped his shoes on his desk. "What can I do for you?"

"I'm polishing my symposium paper on my operational definition of the subject of our recent consultation."

"Do you read dictionaries as a hobby?"

"What?"

"Nothing. What's an operational definition?"

"Specifically, defining any variable—in this case your suspect—in terms of psychological phenomenon."

"I'm sorry I asked."

"Scott, have you any new developments to report?"

"No, Myrna. Unfortunately."

"You sound depressed."

"I don't like knowing there's a killer loose somewhere in my town and there's nothing I can do about him until he makes another move." He switched the phone from his right hand to his left. The arthritis in his right hand was particularly bothersome today.

"The wereling will put in another appearance sooner or later."

Chief Watson snickered. "You think so, huh?"

"What's so funny?"

"I'd forgotten all about that fancy word of yours."

"Scott, has anyone ever informed you that you're behind the times?"

"The little woman, every time I refuse to help her with the dishes or the laundry."

Myrna giggled.

"I wish I did have more information for you," Chief Watson sighed. "We're running down dead end after dead end."

"Be optimistic. As I said before, the wereling will show himself again."

"That's what worries me, Myrna."

"Why? I thought you wanted to apprehend him?"

"I do. But every time he shows his hairy face someone gets hurt. He's killed two people, one of them one of my officers. I want this guy, Myrna. Bad."

"You'll get him. I hope he doesn't kill again. I can only begin to imagine the responsibility weighing on your shoulders. Scott, believe me, you have my sympathy."

I appreciate that, Myrna, but his next victim will need it more."

What to do? What to do? Here he was, virtually handed his future on a silver platter, and he couldn't decide how to proceed. Indecision. Indecision. To act, or not to act, that was the question. Bullshit. How to act, that was the damn question!

Warren sighed and rolled over onto his back, the springs under his mattress squeaking as they bounced.

Two days! Two fucking days! His course of action wasn't clearcut and he was pissed with himself because he couldn't select the wisest step. For two days he had held onto the checkbook, actually twirled it in his fingers and stared at the blasted thing, speculating on the path to pursue. Should he notify the police of the attack and tell them about the checkbook? They'd undoubtedly confiscate the checkbook as evidence, arrest this Harvey Painter, and that would be that. End of his scoop. He could kiss his job with the *Bulletin* goodbye. No way! That choice was definitely out of the question. What else? He could recount the assault to Fontaine and show him the checkbook. Then what? Would Fontaine hire him on the basis of his performance to date? Not very likely. That crafty fox would find some way to exploit the checkbook to his own advantage, maybe even to the point of excluding his prospective employee from the picture entirely. So what else was left him?

"What do I do?" he asked his darkened ceiling. "What do I do?"

The phone rang.

Warren glanced at his clock radio. The glowing hands indicated one in the morning. Who the hell . . . ?

He groped for the phone on the nightstand beside the bed, found the receiver, and picked it up.

"Hello."

"Hello, Warren. How are you?"

Shit! Fontaine.

"I'm fine, Mr. Fontaine. What a surprise." Warren sat up and rested his back against the headboard.

"Did I wake you up?" Fontaine inquired.

"No, as a matter of fact, you didn't."

"Good. I just got in from a rather boring social function and remembered I had wanted to talk to you today."

"What about?" Warren knew why he was calling. Think fast, he told himself.

"Well, as you know, it's been a week since we last talked. I was wondering how your investigation of the werewolf story is coming along?"

You asshole. You're receiving my daily reports!

"Haven't you received my reports?" Warren asked.

"Yes, I have," Fontaine hesitantly answered. "That's one of the reasons I'm calling."

"Mr. Fontaine, my dailies are as up to date as I can get them."

"I believe you Warren. But you're not uncovering any new information. I could get the same intelligence from any other reporter covering the story."

"I'm performing the best I'm able," Warren interjected before Fontaine could continue.

"I know, Warren. I know. Quite frankly, that's what worries me."

"Oh?" Crap! I need this at one A.M.!

"Yes. The caliber of ability you're displaying is not commensurate with the professionalism the *Bulletin* requires."

Translation: I ain't cutting it. "I don't see how anyone could perform any better, given the circumstances," he commented.

"Warren," Faintaine began, "I understand and appreciate the difficulties inherent in this story. You're correct in

193

one respect. An average reporter wouldn't do any better than you are doing. But I'm not inclined to hire an average reporter. I want initiative. I want style. I want a certain flair I believed you possessed. Evidently I was wrong."

"But Mr. Fontaine . . ."

"Warren, hear me out. I need to fill the open position soon. Very soon. I promised you serious consideration if you could produce. You are not producing. You don't allow me any recourse."

"How do you mean?"

"I'm afraid I'll have to give you a deadline."

"A deadline?"

"Yes."

"What kind of deadline?" Warren punched his bed in frustration. Shit!

"Four days, son. I'll give you four days to dig up something new, an angle no one else currently has. I—"

"Four days?" Warren couldn't contain his resentment. "Isn't this being a bit unfair, Mr. Fontaine?"

Fontaine was silent for a minute.

"Possibly, Warren," he finally admitted. "But I've got to do what is best for the sake of the *Bulletin*. I'll extend you four days to prove yourself to my satisfaction, and then . . ." Fontaine paused and cleared his throat.

"And then?" Warren demanded impatiently.

"And then I shall give other applicants precedence."

"But, Mr. Fontaine, you can't . . ."

"I can because I must." Fontaine sighed. "Warren, I hope you won't harbor any ill feelings. Can you see my point?"

"Sure, Mr. Fontaine," Warren muttered without conviction.

"Well, then," Fontaine stated wearily, "I'll expect to hear from you within four days."

"Certainly."

"Bye."

"Goodbye."

Warren hung up his phone and slumped into his pillow. Blast! That fucking Fontaine! How could he do this? What the hell was he trying to prove? Maybe there was another reason for the deadline. The *Brotherly Bulletin* was a monthly publication, right? And if he remembered correctly, their publication date was one week away. That fucking prick! That was the reason for the damn deadline! Fontaine needed the story for the next issue of the *Bulletin*.

But if he didn't come up with what Fontaine wanted before the deadline, even if he did recognize the real reason behind it, he'd still be out of a job with the *Bulletin*. So long, career.

"Damn!"

Well, he couldn't sit in bed all night and sulk. Now he had no option. He had to decide his next move. Going to the police was out of the question. So was approaching Fontaine with what he knew. There was no way he could capture this Painter by himself. The guy was too immensely strong for that. Not to mention being off his rocker. What, then? What course of action would he take that would combine practical with spectacular, desired results with necessary safety? Walk up to the werewolf and ask for an interview?

Warren started laughing.

Oh, sure! He could see it now: *"Hello, Mr. Painter. I'm a reporter and I know you're the werewolf everyone has been looking for and I wonder if you might take the time to ex-*

plain your motivation. Do you enjoy mauling and killing people? What type of childhood did you have? Do you have a hair fetish?"

An interview! Warren snickered.

Wait a minute.

Why the hell not?

Warren sat up, his mind whirling with possibilities. Sure. Why not? I could work. Approach this guy during the day, in a public place. Do it carefully so as not to spook him. Get an interview on tape, then turn him in to the Ocean City police. Call Fontaine and offer an exclusive, tactfully implying the interview in exchange for the position with the *Bulletin.*

Warren stood up and began to pace.

If he were cautious, planned the interview wisely, and didn't intimidate Painter, he could pull it off and salvage his future!

"What an inspiration," he said, grinning. "I'm a genius!"

"THANK YOU, SIR, AND COME AGAIN." The pretty young cashier beamed a mechanical smile and turned to the next customer.

Harvey picked up the bag containing his magazines and walked out the pharmacy door. The morning sunshine struck him full in the face and he squinted to reduce the glare. Another hot, sultry day was in the works. He turned right and headed home, longing for the coolness, quiet, and solitude of his room. Mr. Salisbury had scheduled him for the afternoon shift. He wanted to relax for a few hours reading his monster magazines before going to work.

Harvey came to a curb, stopped, glanced both ways, and crossed Palmer to Avalon. He was two blocks from his house.

A small dog, a white poodle, suddenly broke through a hedge surrounding a yard he was passing and stood in his path, yapping furiously.

"Beat it, mutt," Harvey ordered.

At the sound of his voice the poodle growled and increased the volume of its barking, prancing back and forth.

"Get lost!"

Harvey swung his foot at the dog and the poodle easily jumped to one side, avoiding the blow.

"Beat it!"

Harvey was angry and a bit worried. The damn dog might attract attention to him and that was the last thing he wanted.

The poodle dashed in close and snapped at Harvey's pants, catching the hem of his jeans in its mouth and tugging.

Damn!

The dog frantically pulled on his pant leg, bouncing up and down, twisting and tugging, snarling the entire time.

"This is your last warning, dog," Harvey said quietly, his teeth grating, his anger increasing. He studied the street and noticed the only other person in the vicinity was a small child riding his tricycle a block away. Avalon was a residential street and normally pedestrian traffic was at a minimum.

The poodle savagely wrenched at his pants, and the seam on the side of his jeans split with a loud ripping noise.

Before the dog could react, with a speed quicker than its sharp reflexes Harvey leaned over and fiercely grabbed the poodle by the scruff of its neck. He squeezed and the dog released his jeans and yelped in pain, struggling to break free of his constricting grasp. Harvey raised the whimpering animal on a level with his eyes and glared his hatred. The poodle cowered and whined. Harvey snarled, rumbling deep in his massive chest, and contemptuously tossed the dog aside into the hedge.

The boy on the tricycle rode by slowly, gaping,

astonished.

Harvey grinned at the child and continued his walk home. The incident left him tingling with excitement. He was pleased with himself. He reached his walk and glanced back. Neither the boy or the dog was in sight. Good. He strolled to the front door, checked once more to insure he wasn't being watched, and went inside.

What a great way to start a day!

"Harvey, is that you?" his mother's rasping voice called out.

Harvey stopped at the foot of the stairs. Maybe he could sneak back outside?

"Harvey, I know you're there!" She was somwhere upstairs. "Come up here this very instant."

Damn!

"What is it now, Mother?" He didn't want her invariably bitchy mood to spoil his day.

"I want you up here, now!"

What was she ticked off about this time? Harvey bounded up the steps and walked into her room. She wasn't there. Where was . . .

"Harvey!"

A realization hit him then, and he whirled, instantly enraged, and ran along the hall to his room.

She was standing next to his bed.

And she was holding the werewolf mask in her hands.

"Mother!" Harvey stopped in the doorway and glowered, his fists clenched, his knuckles white. "What are you doing in my room?"

"I want to know what this is?" she demanded, ignoring his question.

"What are you doing in *my* room?" he asked again, his

voice rising. "How did you get in my room?"

"You left your door open," she answered. "Now, what is this thing?"

"I never leave my door open," he stated, but not with conviction. Was it possible? Could he have done it? He'd been doing quite a number of stupid things recently. But this?

"And I tell you that you did!" she retorted angrily.

"Impossible," Harvey muttered.

Gretchen shook the werewolf mask in his face. "Are you going to tell me what the hell this is or not?"

Her stale, putrid breath caused him to turn his face aside and she misinterpreted his action.

"Don't you ignore me, Harvey Painter. I demand an answer and I demand it this minute! What is this thing?"

Harvey sullenly, silently, stared at the floor.

"Answer me, damn your hide!"

Harvey closed his eyes and frowned as his temples began throbbing.

"Is this some kind of costume? It is, isn't it?" Gretchen rattled on. "It's a monster mask, right? What kind is it?"

Harvey dropped his bag onto the floor and pressed his palms against his forehead.

"What are you doing with this?" Gretchen was examining the mask closely. "Are you crazy? A boy your age having a thing like this?"

Harvey bit his lower lip. The pain was intensifying.

"I didn't know you had this mask. When did you get it?"

Harvey opened his eyes and scowled at her.

"What's the matter with you? Are you sick or something? Are you paying attention to me?" Gretchen threw the mask at him and, without thinking, he caught it. "It's a *werewolf* mask, isn't it? I've seen enough werewolf movies to know a werewolf mask when I see one. Question is, what are you doing with it?"

Harvey held the mask limply in his hands, still refusing to respond.

"Are you all right, boy?" Gretchen placed her hand on his forehead. "You're burning up. You better see the doctor."

"I don't need a doctor," he mumbled feebly.

"Ahhh. At last. You *are* alive, after all!" she sarcastically cracked. "I was beginning to wonder."

"I'm okay."

"I don't think so."

"Leave me alone."

"What?" She placed her hands on her hips and defiantly confronted him. "Is that any way to talk to your mother?"

"It's the only way."

"*What?*" Gretchen recoiled, shocked.

"You heard me."

"I don't believe my ears are hearing this!" She shook her head in disbelief, her tousled hair swaying."

"You should have heard it a long, long time ago."

"Harvey Painter, you shut your mouth!" she ordered, her cheeks reddening.

Harvey straightened up to his full height and glared down at her. "No, Mother. I will not shut my mouth. For once *I'm* going to do the talking and you're going to do the listening."

"I most definitely will not!" she asserted and started to brush past him on her way out the door.

"*No!*" Harvey exploded. He took hold of her arm near

her elbow and pushed her back into the room. "You are going to hear me out."

"What do you think you're doing?" Gretchen, mad, flustered, would not give ground.

"I should think it was perfectly clear."

"Harvey, you let me out of this room!"

"No, Mother."

"Are you crazy?"

Harvey laughed. "Possibly. And I know who to thank for my problem."

"What are you babbling about?" Gretchen waved her fist at him. "For the last time, let me by you."

"For the final time—" Harvey grinned, taunting her— "no."

"I'm calling your Uncle Russ and telling him how you're behaving," she threatened him.

"No, I think not." Harvey crossed his arms. "Uncle Russ has enough of his own problems. He doesn't want to hear about yours."

"Oh? How do you know, smart guy?"

"I just know."

"You don't know shit!"

"You think so, don't you? But then, you always have." Harvey pointed at the werewolf hands lying on his bed. "Hand them to me."

"What?" Gretchen glanced at the gloves. "Why?"

"Be a good girl," Harvey mocked her, "and give me them."

Gretchen hesitantly picked up the hands and gave them to Harvey.

"What are you planning to do with them?" Gretchen asked.

Harvey grinned, hiding his headache, focusing his thoughts with extreme difficulty. "You wanted to know why I bought this costume, right?"

"Yes." She was studying his face, trying to read his feelings.

"Well, you're about to find out. You were right, you know. This is a werewolf costume." Harvey stared at the mask and hands for a minute, silent, reflective.

"It's stupid!" Gretchen said maliciously. "A boy your age with a Halloween costume."

"Ahhh, but dear Mother, this is far more than a Halloween costume."

"You'd never know it by looking at it," she retorted, smiling broadly.

"Ever the brilliant wit, huh, Mother?" Harvey was pleased when her face reddened. "But, for this unique moment in time, let's cut the crap and stick to basics."

"Honestly, I don't for the life of me understand a word you're saying." Gretchen shook her head in disapproval.

"You just hit the nail on the head."

"What?" Gretchen was completely perplexed.

"First things first." Harvey closed his eyes for several seconds, suppressing a sharp pang. When his eyes opened Gretchen noted that his pupils were dilating. "Mother, do you have any idea how damn difficult living with you over the years has been?"

"What?" She was instantly defensive. "The hell you say!"

"Yep. That's it. Sheer hell."

"Are you on drugs?" Gretchen inquired gravely.

Harvey laughed. "Leave it to you to make such a ridiculous supposition!"

"Will you let me go now?"

"Nope."

"Why the hell not?" she demanded.

"We're not finished yet."

"What's to finish?"

"Our relationship," Harvey replied, smirking.

"Oh? Are you leaving?"

"When I'm ready. You see . . ."

"No, I don't see," she interrupted. "And I'm warning you, Harvey, you're getting me mad!"

"Should I panic now or later?"

"You bastard!"

"You should know." Harvey chuckled.

"Well, can we get this over with, then? I'm missing my morning shows."

Harvey grinned, exposing his gleaming teeth.

"What the hell is so funny?"

"Never mind. The irony would escape you. You want to get this over with, we'll get this over with. Too bad. I wanted to draw this out and savor it."

"Draw this out? Harvey, you're making no sense at all." Gretchen, exasperated, crossed her arms and stamped her foot.

"Then it's time for the final curtain." Harvey turned the werewolf mask so the back of it was facing him.

"Harvey, this is the last straw!" Gretchen stepped up to him and glared into his eyes. "I'm going to have you examined by a psychiatrist and—"

"You're too late."

". . . you need help, son. Professional help. I tried to tell Uncle Russ—"

"He's going to get his, someday soon."

Gretchen again ignored him. "But he wouldn't listen.

There is something drastically wrong with you. There—"

"Would you like to know what?"

His question threw her off stride. "What?"

"Would you like to know what is wrong with me?"

"You know?" she asked incredulously.

"Of course."

"What?"

"You. You, Mother, are what is wrong with me."

"Talking with you is like talking to a brick wall," she said, peeved.

"I can see you don't believe me. Would a demonstration help you see the light?"

"Demonstration?" Gretchen was thoroughly confused and it showed. "Sure. Show me what's the matter with you."

"I thought you'd never ask." Harvey smiled and raised the mask over his head. He slowly pulled it over his face and tucked the neck under his shirt.

"What the hell are you doing now?" Gretchen demanded.

Harvey stood for a minute, his eyes blinking rapidly, his breathing labored.

"Is this some kind of strange game?"

Harvey pulled the left werewolf glove over his hand.

"I don't like this, Harvey?" Gretchen poked him in the chest with her finger. "Cut it out."

Harvey placed his right hand in the corresponding werewolf glove.

"Harvey! Take the damn thing off, now!" Gretchen poked him again, harder.

Harvey leaned against the bedroom wall. Through the slits in the mask she saw his eyes beginning to focus. His breathing became normal.

"Harvey! Damn you!"

Gretchen forcefully poked his chest a third time.

Harvey growled, a rumbling, feral warning, chilling her blood, stopping another poke halfway to his breast.

"What in the world . . ." She paused, at a loss for words.

Harvey crouched and hissed.

"Harvey," she mumbled, surprised and frightened. "This isn't funny!"

Harvey stepped up to her, sniffing loudly.

"Stop it!"

Gretchen shoved him with all her strength and he stumbled back and struck his dresser.

"You're scaring me!"

Harvey hissed and took a slow, menacing step towards her.

"Harvey!"

Gretchen ran to the doorway.

Harvey was at her side in a single bound. His hand lashed out, striking her on the shoulder, and she spun around and crashed into the wall on the opposite side of the hallway.

Gretchen screamed. She recovered her balance and fled to the top of the stairs, adrenalin lending speed to her legs. She gripped the railing for support and glanced over her shoulder.

Quick as she'd been, she was no match for Harvey.

He was on her, snarling, his arm sweeping in a full arc, catching her on the side of her head. Something cracked and she twisted, the brutal blow propelling her through the air to the very base of the stairs. She struck the hard wooden floor and crumbled into a distorted, jumbled heap.

The werewolf, gloating, threw his head back and howled his victory cry.

June 28

WHAT A WASTE OF HIS TIME!

Warren stared at the half-eaten mustard-and-onion covered hamburger on the car seat beside him and frowned.

Christ! He was tired of buying his meals at fast food joints. Combine that with all the sitting he was doing and it was no wonder he felt constipated. When was this wacko going to show his ugly puss outside of his house?

For two days he'd used every spare hour he had to drive down to Ocean City and park his car on Palmer Street. Parking on Avalon, he thought, would be too obvious. Besides, just around the corner, at the junction of Avalon and Palmer, was a vacant duplex for sale. He could park in front of the duplex, keep his eyes on 432 West Avalon, and none of the neighboring residents would be likely to complain. Once yesterday afternoon he'd spotted a police cruiser approaching in the rear view mirror. He'd ducked down below the dash, waited an adequate length of time, and sat up. The cops were four blocks away and continuing their patrol. They hadn't seen him.

Warren studied the Painter house for the umpteenth time; it was one of those white, two-story jobs prevalent in a resort city. Atlantic City, Ocean City, all the resort towns had them in abundance. A wooden frame, slatted wood sides, and shingles on the roof. This one was in pronounced disrepair. The paint was peeling, dozens of the wooden slats were split or cracked, one of the ground-floor windows was broken, and the weed-choked yard looked like it hadn't been mowed all summer.

Where the hell were the occupants? For two days there'd been no sign of anyone coming or going, not even at night. Yesterday, shortly past noon, the mailman had deposited a letter in the small black box to the front door, but to Warren's knowledge no one had claimed it yet.

How many lived there, he wondered? He wasn't about to ask the police for information, nor any other governmental bureau. They'd demand to know his reason for asking and he couldn't afford to arouse their curiosity. Asking the bank Painter had his checking account with was definitely out of the question. They would regard such information as confidential, and rightly so.

Was anyone living there? Was he wasting his time?

The front door opened and a tall, strapping, muscular young man came out on the porch and opened the mailbox.

"At last!" Warren stated to himself. Was it Harvey Painter? Had to be. Right size. And dear God, look at those biceps!

Painter examined the solitary letter, glanced up at the sky once, and went inside.

Shit! Was that it? Didn't the guy ever go to the supermarket? How was he going to catch this weirdo in a public place to conduct an exclusive interview if the son-of-a-bitch stayed indoors all the time?

Was it smart, Warren wondered, to attempt an interview? Initially he'd thought so. But with subsequent reflection the idea appealed to him less and less. What if Painter didn't care if there were witnesses? What if he spooked and went berserk? What then?

There was movement in the doorway of the Painter house and Warren bent over until only his eyes were above the dash.

Hercules was outside again. He shut the front door and sauntered down their walk to the sidewalk.

Eureka! The bastard was going somewhere.

Painter turned left, away from Warren's position, and strolled off.

Warren sat up. Here was the moment of truth. What should he do? Confronting Painter was absolutely a no-no, especially now that he'd seen how big he was, how strong he looked.

Painter was almost out of sight.

An alternative course of action occurred to Warren. Maybe he could get inside the house and discover some incriminating evidence. Why not? Painter obviously lived there alone. there must be something inside that house implicating Painter as the werewolf. The risk should be minimal. Painter couldn't return for at least five minutes, and in all likelihood he would be gone longer. That gave Warren ample time to get in, conduct a quick search, and get the hell out before musclebound returned. If Painter found him inside the house . . .

If he was going to do it, he had to do it now!

Warren opened his door and stepped onto the curb.

Painter was gone, blocks distant, en route to his unknown destination.

Warren closed his car door and hurried to the corner of Palmer and Avalon. He crossed Avalon and hastily walked the distance to the Painter house. Sweat formed on his forehead, and he knew it was caused by more than the hot afternoon sun. He prayed none of the neighbors were paying attention to him.

Then he was there, facing the chipped, flaking paint on the Painter front door, and he froze. This was insane! What if Harvey Painter caught him? What if there were somebody else living here? He started to turn, to leave, and he remembered Fontaine, recalled the ultimatum, and realized he couldn't afford to stop now.

Damn it! He had no choice!

Warren knocked several times, pounding on the door, hoping he'd hear a commotion on the other side so he could haul ass and forget the entire idea.

No one came to the door.

Just his luck!

He rapped his knuckles on the door again. Just to be sure, he told himself.

Again, his knock went unanswered. He glanced over his shoulder, searching for Painter. The street was deserted.

Warren sighed and grabbed the doorknob. To his utter amazement, the knob twisted and the door swung open.

Uh-oh. I don't like this, he warned himself, abruptly very alert and extremely suspicious. This shouldn't be. Too easy.

"Anyone home?" he called, hoping someone would respond in the affirmative. He still had time to split.

"Is there anybody here?" he asked.

Warren cautiously stepped inside. The lights were on. A

hallway straight ahead, stairs to his right. He opted for the stairs. The bedrooms, most likely, would be on the second floor. And he wanted to see Harvey Painter's bedroom.

At the top of the stairs he stopped. There was a dark hall, one closed door on his left, an open door several feet farther on his right. He chose the open room.

Warren nervously edged along the wall to the doorway. The tomblike silence was unsettling.

Was that a noise?

He froze, listening intently. Had he heard a scraping sound? From downstairs? He waited a minute, pressed against the wall, but the noise wasn't repeated.

Just nerves.

Warren reached the doorway and peeked around the corner, expected the worst.

Son-of-a-bitch!

He gawked at the posters littering all four walls. One of the walls was covered with various monsters, another with vampires, and another with . . . with . . . *Jesus!* Werewolves, werewolves, everywhere. There was no doubt about it now. Painter was the guy they were after.

Warren backed away from the room. How much time had elapsed since he came inside? Two minutes? Three? He couldn't remain much longer.

There was still the second room to check.

Warren wasn't surprised when the door easily opened with a flick of the knob. Unlocked doors seemed to be his speciality today. The room was pitch black, the lights off and the shades drawn. He stepped inside, closed the door behind him, fumbled for the light switch, located it and turned on the overhead light.

"Holy shit!"

She was lying in the center of the bed, on top of the bed-spread, positioned with her legs primly crossed and her hands neatly folded on her lap. Her thin features were pale and stark. She was attired in a blue evening dress.

Warren moved to the foot of the bed.

The woman must have been dead several days. There was a distinct odor filling the musty room. He saw that her right elbow had been shattered, the gleaming bone exposed through her torn skin, and his stomach went queasy. He gripped the metal bedrail for support.

Who was she?

"Say hello to my mother."

Warren spun, his heart pounding, his legs suddenly weak.

"I'm Harvey Painter," the giant figure in the doorway said. "I think you already know that, though."

Warren felt numb from his hair to his toes. He attempted to speak, but couldn't.

"Are you scared?" Harvey Painter asked. "Understandable. I guess I would be, too, if I were in your shoes."

"Don't . . . don't . . ." Warren stammered, forming his syllables with extreme difficulty. "Don't hurt me!" he finally blurted. ·

Harvey Painter laughed. "It isn't me you have to worry about, mister. It's him you need to be afraid of."

"Him? Him, who?" Warren tried to stand erect without the aid of the bedrail. His knees began shaking.

"Calm down," Harvey Painter suggested. "You have plenty of time left."

"Time?" Stall, Warren told himself. Delay this bastard until you regained your composure, then run like hell.

"Who are you?" Harvey Painter demanded. He walked

into the room and stared at his dead mother.

"Warren Mckeen."

"What do you do for a living, Warren?"

"I'm a reporter with radio station WREN in Atlantic City."

"Really? I'd assumed you were a policeman. I'm glad you're not." Harvey pointed at an oak chair next to a vanity table. "Have a seat, Warren."

"Okay, Mr. Painter." Did he have any choice?

"Call me Harvey," Painter directed as Warren sat down.

"Okay, Harvey." Warren was thankful he was sitting. At least his legs weren't trembling anymore.

Harvey stood by the bed and gazed at the woman on the bedspread. For several minutes he remained silent, his forehead furrowed.

"You said she's your mother?" Warren asked gently. Maybe he could talk Harvey into giving himself up to the police.

"Yes," Harvey replied, his deep voice husky and strained. "Gretchen Painter was her name."

"I'm sorry she died."

Harvey glanced at Warren. "Why? You didn't know her or you wouldn't be saying that. Don't feel sorry for her. She was the supreme bitch of the western hemisphere. No one liked her. I didn't. He didn't."

"Who is this 'him' you keep referring to?"

Harvey shot Warren a meaningful look. "You know."

Warren elected to change the subject. "Harvey, did you know I was in here when you returned from wherever you went a while ago?"

Harvey gestured at the woman on the bed. "Did you hear that, Mother?" He chuckled.

Warren flinched. God, he was a lunatic!

"I knew you would be here before I left. In fact," Harvey said with a laugh, "that's *why* I left. To give you time to make your move."

"What?"

"Sure. I'd been expecting someone ever since I discovered my checkbook was missing. I suspected he lost it, but I couldn't be certain. For two days I've watched you from a downstairs window. You probably thought you were being clever, but really, Warren, you stood out like a sore thumb. I waited and waited for you to do something until I couldn't wait any longer. You evidently required encouragement. So I walked six blocks from the house, returned by the back alley, came in the back door, crept up the stairs, quietly opened the bedroom door, and here you were. Not bad, huh?"

"Not bad," Warren agreed, impressed. A lunatic, yes, but a clever lunatic. "What do you plan to do with me?" he bluntly demanded, hoping to catch Harvey off guard.

"You should know better," Harvey smiled. "Your fate isn't in my hands. It's up to him."

What should I do? Warren speculated. Humor him? Or goad him a bit, agitate him, force him to drop his guard for the seconds it would take to dash down the stairs and run outside?

"What are you thinking about?" Harvey inquired, his gaze still on his mother.

"I'm wondering why you keep playing games with me."

"Games?" Harvey turned his attention to Warren. "What do you mean by games?"

"What do you mean by referring to the werewolf as 'him' and 'he'? We both know who you're talking about.

215

We both know the werewolf and you are one and the same." Warren wiped his sweaty palms on his gray pants.

"You still don't understand, do you?" Harvey sighed and shrugged his broad shoulders. "I can see I'll need to explain it to you. Yes, that would be fitting."

"Explain what?" Warren glanced at the doorway. Could he make it?

"Are you stupid?" Harvey asked.

"What?" Warren temporarily forgot his escape consideration, surprised by the question.

"I asked you if you're stupid."

"Who am I to say?" Warren replied, uncertain of Harvey's point.

"I didn't think he was, Mother," Harvey addressed the deceased. "After all, he was able to trace me this far. But now I'm not so sure. He hasn't perceived the truth."

"Truth? What truth?"

"You honestly don't comprehend, do you?"

"I'm sorry." What the hell was he babbling about? "I'm afraid I don't."

"I see." Harvey walked around the foot of the bed and sat next to his mother. He crossed his legs and rested his hands on his knees.

Warren noted Harvey's jeans were frayed along the hem.

"I'll try my best to enlighten you, but it'll be hard. I didn't see the light myself until after he killed my mother."

"Are you trying to tell me you're not the werewolf?" Warren interrupted.

"Precisely."

"Well, if that's the case"—Warren began to rise—"I see no reason to stay here and bother—"

"Sit down," Harvey ordered, and Warren did. "You didn't let me finish. I am not the werewolf, but the werewolf is me."

"Come again?" Warren was captivated by their conversation, disregarding his obvious peril.

"When he killed my mother," Harvey began, "I went into shock for a day. Couldn't eat. Couldn't sleep. I sat at the top of the stairs and stared at her lifeless body. I couldn't believe what had happened. I wanted to be free of her, but not this way. I was going to leave, travel, see the world. He doesn't want to leave Ocean City, though. He prefers this area. It's his."

"Are you referring to the werewolf?"

Harvey shot Warren a disgusted look. "Who else, dummy? Who else murdered that biker and the policewoman and now my mother? Who else?"

Warren shrugged his shoulders.

"You think it was me, don't you?" Harvey angrily demanded.

"No. No. Of course not." Warren didn't like the emotional upheaval this talk was generating in Harvey.

"Liar. You do too. I can sense it. Rather, *he* can sense it."

"Tell me, Harvey"—Warren glanced about the room for something he could utilize as a weapon: zilch—"where is the werewolf at this very moment?"

"Staring right at you."

"What?" Warren checked the doorway and the windows. "I don't see him. If you aren't the—"

"You're an idiot," Harvey flatly stated.

Warren smiled weakly. Who was he to argue?

"The werewolf is right here." Harvey reached his right hand up and pointed at his own face.

217

"So you are the werewolf!" Warren gloated.

"No! No! No!" Harvey rose to his feet and glared at Warren. "Don't you see him? Here! Here!" Harvey tapped his index finger on his nose. "He's in here, looking out at you this very second."

"Oh," Warren simply said, flabbergasted.

Harvey straightened. "You know, I didn't see it at first, either. I thought it was me. I didn't realize the significance of the headaches. I—"

"Headaches?" Warren interjected quickly. "What headaches?"

"Didn't I tell you? I finally figured it out. Lately I've been getting these awful headaches. I come down with one when he's on the verge of busting loose. It doesn't do me any good to resist. Only makes the pain worse. He's just too strong. He stores me away until he's ready, then he releases me. Now do you understand?"

"I think I'm beginning to."

"Good. Good." Harvey walked to the door. "Are you thirsty?"

"Uh, sure. Sure am."

"I'll get you a glass of water. Would you like that?"

Why did he feel like he was being treated as an adolescent? "Water would be nice."

"Okay. I'll return in a jiffy. Stay where you are."

Why should I? Warren asked himself.

"You might run into him if you leave this room," Harvey said, and left. The door stood open.

That's a damn good reason. What the hell do I do now, Warren reflected. Leave? He might be waiting downstairs for just such a move. The guy was thoroughly bananas. Killed his own mom, for Christ's sake! Was there a chance he could be enticed into giving up? Doubtful. He was too far gone. Overpowering him was definitely an absurd idea. Even his muscles had muscles! That only left making a break for it. When? Now? Maybe he wasn't waiting in the hallway, ready to pounce. Wasn't there any way out . . .

The windows!

Warren jumped up and ran to the nearest window. So what if he was on the second floor? The fall wouldn't kill him. He raised the green shade, pushed a blue gingham curtain aside, and tugged on the window sash.

Damn it!

The thing wouldn't budge!

Warren threw his back into his effort, straining, his fingers aching. Come on, baby, he silently coaxed. Come on!

Shit!

His attempt was useless. The window refused to budge an inch. He studied the windowsill and discovered the reason. The windows were nailed shut.

"You're really working up a thirst."

Warren resisted a tempting urge to faint. Instead, assuming a cool, collected exterior, he turned. "Can't blame a guy for trying, can you?"

"Guess not. Anyway, what I think doesn't count. Here's your water." Harvey brought a large glass over and gave it to Warren. "It's cold."

"Thanks." Warren gulped several mouthfuls. It refreshed his parched throat.

Harvey pointed at the chair.

Warren nodded and took his seat, holding the glass in his hand. What next?

Harvey stood over his mother and straightened several

wrinkles in her dress. "We must be neat at all times, Mother," he said. "Isn't that what you always told me?"

Warren finished the water. What was this wacko planning? Why was he being so polite?"

"Do you have a mother?" Harvey asked.

"Well . . . uh . . . sure." Warren placed the glass on the vanity table. "I do."

"You don't mind if we talk a bit, do you?" Harvey began smoothing his mother's hair.

"No."

"Good. I don't get many chances to talk with others. You're sure you don't mind?"

"No."

"We've got some time to kill before he arrives."

Warren nervously bit his lower lip. What would happen if he just bolted? Would Harvey kill him without provocation? Who could tell? Harvey was over the deep end, too far gone to be predictable. Maybe his best bet was simply to wait until Harvey gave him an opening. But would he?

Harvey sat down on the bed, careful not to disturb his mother. "Do you love your mother?"

This isn't happening to me! "Yes." What do you say?

"I don't think I ever loved mine. Oh, possibly when I was real small, until . . . until . . ." Harvey stopped, his voice faltering.

"If you'd rather not talk about it . . ." Warren suggested, feeling uncomfortable. What did Harvey think he was, a psychiatrist?

"It doesn't matter. Still, no matter how much I disliked her, I wouldn't have killed her. I wonder why he did it?" Harvey frowned, considering his question. "I certainly

220

don't know. But then, I can't understand some of the things he does. Do you have a brother?"

"No."

"Neither did I, until now."

"You mean the werewolf is your brother?" Warren's interest increased.

"In a sense."

"Harvey," Warren confessed, "I don't understand you."

"You don't?" Harvey appeared genuinely surprised. "After all I've told you?"

"I'm sorry."

"Amazing." Harvey shook his head. "Maybe no one would understand. I'll try to explain it to you again. For years I've felt something inside me, trying to get out, to express itself. I assumed I possessed a rare quality, a certain appreication of nature most of my peers lacked. Little did I know!" Harvey grinned. "Little did I know! All these years he was trying to bust loose. How was I so fortunate?"

How could he be so lucid and articulate, and insane at the same time? "How do you mean?" Warren wanted an elaboration.

"How many people get to know him during their lifetime?"

I can think of three, and none of them would give him rave reviews. "Harvey, you make it sound like the werewolf has a mind of its own."

Harvey slapped his leg in annoyance. "I'm rapidly losing patience with you, Warren. I'm convinced you'll never understand. Besides"—he gazed out the window at the darkening sky.—"I think we've run out of time."

Shit! Think fast, Warren, think fast!

Harvey stood and stretched. "Thanks for listening, Warren, although I don't think the conversation helped you very much."

You can say that again! "Is it time for you to go somewhere?"

Harvey grinned at Warren. "Don't be naive. You know why I've got to leave." He took a step toward the doorway.

"You'll never get away with it!"

Harvey laughed. "I won't need to. He'll take care of everything."

"The police will catch you." Warren racked his mind for more objections.

"You know, when I first realized what had happened to me, I expected them to show up at any time. Now I know better. The last smart cop was my dad. The rest are all dummies. No, they won't catch him."

"Others know I'm here!"

Harvey paused in midstride. "That occurred to me, Warren. Do you know what I decided?"

"No." Warren's palms were sweating profusely.

"Why did the reporter come alone, I asked myself? Strange, considering what he expected to find here. You'd think anyone with any brains would bring friends to help in case danger presented itself."

Warren squirmed and wrung his hands together. Damn this madman!

"From what I can tell, you're not even armed. Are you?"

Warren bleakly shook his head.

"Are all reporters so absent-minded?"

Warren didn't bother to reply.

"If they are, your profession is in big trouble." Harvey laughed. "Well, Warren, it's been a lot of fun."

"Don't go!" Warren jumped up. "Please!"

Harvey pointed at the chair. Warren reluctantly seated himself on the edge of the chair.

"Man can not evade the inevitable," Harvey sermonized. He smiled broadly, waved his right hand in parting, and left.

Oh, shit! What the fuck should he do now? Warren started to rise, but just as quickly sat down again. Harvey would be waiting for him out there. No, not Harvey. The werewolf. And there was no doubt what the werewolf would do to him. Why? Why the hell had he waltzed into this place without an escape plan of some kind? No one knew where he was. If the werewolf killed—Warren changed his flow of thought, too upset by the implications to continue. He had to think positively. There had to be a way out of this house. Had to. The windows in this room were nailed shut, but what about the windows in the other room on this floor, in Harvey's room? Harvey's room! No way would he go in there! There was only one option remaining. The front door. The fastest route between two points was the straightest. The front door was all that stood between him and freedom, between him and his car.

The front door it would be.

Warren stood, fighting the trembling in his extremities, and haltingly moved to the doorway. He leaned against the wall for support, catching his breath, gathering his courage. There would only be one chance. He had to do it right the first time.

Now or never!

Warren crouched and peered around the corner. The

223

hallway was empty. Harvey's door was open and light was streaming into the hall. The head of the stairs was in view and Harvey was nowhere near it.

Go!

Warren ran the ten feet to the stairs and stopped behind the bannister. The stairs were clear. He had a limited view of the downstairs hall.

Still no sign of Harvey.

Warren fixed his gaze on the front door, gripped the railing, and rose slowly. His mind flashed back to his track days in high school. A mediocre record, to be sure, but it reminded him he could move when he had to.

So move!

Warren sprinted down the stairs, three steps at a time.

He gained too much speed, wasn't able to stop when he reached the bottom, and he crashed into the wall. A sharp pain stabbed up his arm. He clutched his wrist, staggered to the front door, and yanked it open.

Can't give up now, he told himself. Can't give up now!

Warren reached the front porch and glanced over his shoulder. Harvey was not behind him; the stairs and downstairs hall were clear.

Where the hell was he?

The sun was touching the horizon and the shadows of evening were descending. Warren forced his legs to function, to pump, and he ran to the curb, cut across the street, and sprawled on the hood of his car.

A young girl, in the midst of jumping rope, stopped and gawked at him.

Warren found his keys in his pants pocket, remembered the doors were unlocked, tore open his door, and collapsed behind the wheel. He groaned and rested his forehead on top of the steering wheel.

God, his left wrist hurt! Was it broken?

"Hey!" The girl was perched on the curb, peering into his car. "Is anything wrong?"

Warren shook his head. "No. I'm okay. Really. Thanks." He gritted his teeth, grappling with waves of agony, and started the engine.

The girl backed away and smiled.

Warren grinned in response, admiring her dimples and blond pigtails, not wanting to alarm her. He shifted the car into drive and drove off.

He'd done it! Actually done it! What the hell had happened to Harvey?

Despite his agony, he laughed, delighted and relieved.

Who the hell cared what had happened to that damn wacko? Harvey and that spooky house were behind him now, and there was no way he was going back! Under any circumstances!

Warren was suddenly racked by intense spasms in his left wrist. He eased his foot off the accelerator and involuntarily pressed his arm against his stomach, doubling over. Jesus! Why was his wrist hurting so much? Had he busted it when he slammed into that wall? Terrific!

An intersection came up, the junction of Palmer and Newton. He turned left on Newton, searching for a spot to pull over so he could examine his arm. If it was broken he'd head for the nearest doctor and get it tended to. Then a quick call to the police. Screw Fontaine and the *Brotherly Bulletin* and, yes, even his literary career! Twice he'd almost lost his life because he didn't possess enough common sense to know when it was time to come in out of the rain. Never again! He'd learned his lesson.

A church appeared ahead, on the right-hand side of the street. Across from the church was a large empty parking lot. Perfect. Just what he needed.

Warren wheeled into the lot and parked his car in one of the rear rows. He switched off the ignition and settled his head on the back of the seat. God, he felt tired! He couldn't afford to fall asleep yet, though. Not until that bastard was safely behind bars.

Got to get that prick!

Warren gingerly raised his left arm. The pain was diminishing. Maybe it wasn't broken after all. He concentrated and attempted to move his fingers, to make a fist. Slowly, reluctantly, his fingers reponsed and bent slightly. Good. He could forget the doctor and drive directly to the police station and report Harvey Painter.

Going to nail that son-of-a-bitch to the wall!

Warren reached for the key. He gazed over the parking lot, surprised at how dark it had become, and automatically glanced into the rear view mirror.

Strange. The mirror was a black blur. He couldn't see anything in it, not even the back seat. What . . .

The snarl froze his bones to the marrow.

Warren clutched the steering wheel with his good hand, his eyes widening. He could detect a huge, looming figure reflected in the mirror.

"Oh, dear God!" he exclaimed, grabbing the ignition key, beginning to twist it.

Hairy, enormous, immensely powerful hands clamped around his constricting throat.

Father Mulvane closed and locked the outer doors to

Christ the King Catholic Church. He checked his watch and noted the time was ten minutes past ten. Brilliant stars were twinkling in the night sky. He turned his steps toward the nearby rectory. The propect of a late snack and an hour or two of studying the latest issue of the diocese newspaper, *The Register*, appealed to him. The hours of the day had passed slowly and had been filled with several unexpected surprises. Mrs. Diamond's confession had perturbed him greatly. Imagine! With her own brother! All these years! The poor, pathetic woman. Of all the possible personal spiritual problems, unnatural lust was exceptionally devastating to Father Mulvane.

The priest reached the steps to the small brick rectory and absently glanced around at the serene nighttime setting. He spied a car parked way at the back of the church parking lot and he sighed.

When would these kids learn? How many times in the past year had he been compelled to chase young neckers off the premises? In his day and age such blatant sexual acts had been frowned upon and actively discouraged. Nowadays the exact opposite was the prevailing case. Society encouraged materialism and premarital promiscuousness.

Father Mulvane approached the parked vehicle warily. A marauding gang of ruffians were pestering the neighborhood recently, spraying graffiti and harassing the elderly. What had happened to the traditional moral fiber of this country, he wondered. Was America to follow in the footsteps of Rome? He stopped ten feet from the car.

"You in the car!" Father Mulvane called out. "What are you doing?"

Nothing happened.

"Did you hear me?"

There was no indication of movement.

Father Mulvane moved forward five paces.

"Do you hear me? You're parked on private property and you must move."

Still no response.

Surely if the car were occupied someone would have responded by now. He walked up to the door and peered inside. The interior was inky black, and he couldn't be certain, but he thought he could discern someone slumped over the steering whee. So. Not two neckers. A drunk.

Father Mulvane pulled open the door. "Listen fellow, what do you think . . ."

Stunned silence struck him as the occupant fell from the car to sprawl on the tarmac.

"I say!" Father Mulvane regained his speech. "Snap out of it!" He bent over, placed his hands under the man's shoulders, and lifted so he could get a closer look at the face. Passed out from excess alcohol, the priest assumed.

"Wake up!" Father Mulvane shook the man and peered into his face. "What's the matter with—" He stopped abruptly, for the first time seeing the contorted face, the protruding tongue, the ruptured neck, and the wide, lifeless eyes.

"Heavenly Father!" Father Mulvane exclaimed, dropping the body.

The head struck the blacktop with a ponderous thud.

June 29

RUSS RAPPED ON CHIEF WATSON'S DOOR.

"Come in." Chief Watson beckoned.

Russ entered the office and nodded at each of those present; Chief Watson, Captain Grout, Mayor Perkins, and a representative from the governor's office, a Mr. Randall.

"Is it confirmed?" Chief Watson inquired as Russ seated himself.

"His parents just provided positive identification." Russ frowned. "As if any were required. We knew who it was last night."

"That we did," Chief Watson agreed. "But regulations are regulations. At least now, with the next of kin duly notified, we can release the information to the media."

"Bloodthirsty bastards," Grout commented.

"Must we release it?" Mayor Perkins wanted to know. He was nervously wringing his sweaty hands together.

"We've got no other option." Chief Watson tapped the top of his desk with his pen. "Do you realize the magnitude of this situation?"

"Couldn't we just sit on it awhile?" Mayor Perkins whined.

"For what purpose?" Chief Watson snapped impatiently. "This is the third known victim of this killer. The sooner we nab this guy, the better it will be for all of us."

"I agree," Mr. Randall stated. He was a personal assistant to the governor, a professional politician. His balding pate and bulging paunch did little to detract from his immaculate appearance. "The gravity of the situation is bordering on the extreme. Are you aware of the latest retail figures for this month?" He directed his query at Perkins.

"No. Can't say that I am." Mayor Perkins eyed Randall defensively.

"You're having a lousy month, both on the boardwalk and in the city. The proper time to sit on this was at the very beginning, when the first murder occurred." Chief Watson glared at Randall and he noticed. "But the governor recognizes that such a course of action was unwise and impossible. We can't waste time bemoaning the past. We must concentrate on the present, on a feasible means of stopping this son-of-a-bitch before Ocean City loses an entire summer of tourist income."

"What other type of income do we have?" Grout quipped.

"You all know how shaky the economy of a resort is," Randall continued, ignoring Grout. "Any number of calamities can throw the balance off-kilter. Adverse weather. Disease. A murdering psycho. The other coast resorts won't mind your run of bad luck. Atlantic City and the rest will benefit from the rechanneled tourist flow. How long, gentlemen, do you think your merchants can stay afloat if your tourism dwindles to a trickle? The loss of life is reprehensible, certainly, but the bottom line here is the bucks, the dollars and cents. The governor must perceive the many facets of any issue or incident. He recognizes the harmful repercussions to the state economy if Ocean City experiences a rotten year. The state budget is critically balanced as it is. Any strain would be particularly deleterious in many respects. Any questions?"

Is this what is meant by political expedience?" Grout asked, and Randall blushed.

"Let's keep our attention on the matter at hand." Chief Watson changed their topic of discussion. "So what do we have?" He looked at Russ.

Russ cleared his throat, opened a manila folder he'd carried into the room, and studied the contents, speaking as he read. "There is no doubt the werewolf has struck again. Same M.O. as in previous attacks, with one notable exception."

"What's that?" Grout demanded.

"This time our werewolf took the time to empty the pockets of the victim."

"But why?" Chief Watson leaned back in his chair, puzzled. "What was his motive?"

"Robbery?" Randall suggested.

"No. He didn't rob his previous victims. Why should he start now?" Chief Watson knit his brow in deep thought.

"This one raises a host of questions," Russ resumed. "What was Mckeen doing in the church parking lot? Why was he in Ocean City in the first place? Was he following a lead, one we don't have? Or was it just coincidence that the werewolf attacked him? Why did the killer take the time to empty his pockets? Was he looking for something? Or did Mckeen deliberately leave his pockets empty? I can't see him driving around without his license and press pass. They weren't on him and they weren't in the vehicle." Russ closed the folder and shook his head. "I couldn't believe it last night when I arrived at the scene and recognized his body. He had to be onto something."

"I agree," Chief Watson concurred. "But what? I can't accept his murder as a coincidence. For some reason McKeen was dogging this story. Maybe he discovered something, the killer found out, and he was murdered. But even that idea raises more questions. What did he find out? How? With all our resources we haven't unearthed a single clue. Did Mckeen meet the killer deliberately? Damn stupid if he did. If he didn't, how did the murderer know about him? How did the killer get into the car? And why on Newton Street this time? Not the Dunes. Right smack in the middle of the city. You have something?" He noticed a peculiar expression on Russ's face.

"Nothing definite. There's something about Newton Street, though," Russ answered. "Something in the back of my mind, but I can't place my finger on it."

"Keep trying," Chief Watson directed. "Any other comments?"

"I just wish this whole mess was over," Mayor Perkins sniveled.

"Don't we all," Randall did not bother to hide his disgust. "Where do you go from here?"

"Well, the car is still being dusted and torn apart. Doubt we'll get any results except the discovery of more wolf hair and human saliva in the neck wound." Chief Watson grimaced. "Mr. Randall, you have no idea how bad we want this guy."

"I think I do."

"Anyway, we're still questioning the area residents, hoping someone saw something unusual. But our hopes aren't very high." Chief Watson dropped his pen on the desk. "It looks like we do some more waiting."

"How long can we afford to?" Randall inquired.

They stared at one another, not bothering to answer the question, each of them recognizing the truth of the matter; they couldn't afford to wait at all.

"Time had already run out for three lives," Russ eventually said. "How many more before this guy makes a mistake? How much longer can he keep making assholes of us?"

"That was a wonderful meal."

"I'm glad you had a good time." Earl unlocked the door to Leta's apartment, stood aside to allow her to enter first, then followed her inside.

"Would you like a drink?" Leta asked. She switched on the lights and draped her fur wrap over an easy chair.

"No, thanks," Earl secured the door.

"You sure?"

"Yeah. You know, you look positively gorgeous in that gown."

Leta spun in a complete circle and batted her eyelashes at him. "Well, thank you, kind sir."

Earl sat down on her sofa and loosened his tie. He was wearing a leisure suit. "I mean it, Leta."

"You're so serious tonight." She smiled and reclined beside him.

"Maybe it's time we got serious."

"What?"

He adjusted his position so he could clasp her hands in his own. "How long have we known one another?"

Leta reflected for several seconds. "Oh, about a year,

I think. Why?"

Earl gently squeezed her hands. "And how long have we been going together?"

"Nine months or so. Say!" She glanced down at her tummy. "Do you think I'm pregnant? You mean to tell me the pill isn't foolproof?" She laughed and stuck her tongue out at him.

"I'm serious, Leta." He didn't even smile.

"So you keep telling me." Leta used her right hand to stroke his brow. "And there's no need to be. It's been three weeks since Charlene died. I'm recovering, slowly but surely."

"For which I'm thankful. But it isn't Char I want to talk about. It's us."

"Earl don't. Not now." Leta crossed her arms and gazed out her window at the neon lights of the city.

"Then when? We can't put it off any longer."

"Why not?"

"Because."

"Terrific reason."

Earl shifted uncomfortably. "Because I love you and I want to marry you. There. I've said it."

"Damn!" Leta stood and walked to the window. The night sky was obscured by dense clouds. Rain was predicted for the next morning.

"What's the matter?" Earl asked.

"Why did you have to ruin a good thing?"

"What do you mean?"

She smiled at him to reassure him. "Honey, I'm happy with the way things are. I don't want to change them."

"You can't mean that."

"But I do!" she protested. "I like being able to see you

when our shifts don't conflict. I enjoy dating you. I love you, Earl. You know that. But I'm not ready for a serious commitment. Not yet."

Earl came up behind her and placed his arms around her slender waist. "Why not? You love me and I love you. What more do we need?" He kissed her on her neck.

"Stop distracting me! No fair!" She giggled and turned, grinning. "The timing isn't right."

"Oh." He frowned. "Too close to Char's death?"

"More than that." Leta pecked him on his chin. "I'd like to say yes. I really would. But I'm not quite ready for marriage. Soon, maybe. Very soon. Can you understand?"

"No," he admitted. "I'll try to, though."

Leta pressed against him and their lips met in a lingering kiss.

"Thank you," she said after a minute. "I appreciate it."

"Just don't take too long to decide you're ready."

"Why? Do you turn into a pumpkin?" she teased.

"No. But . . ." his eyes reflected an inner sadness . . . "if you let opportunity slip away when it knocks on your door, it may never knock again."

"Are you implying you'd change your mind?" She pinched his ribs.

"You know better than that." Earl embraced her passionately, the pliant feel of her voluptuous contours arousing him.

Leta relaxed and enjoyed the feel of her surging sensual sensations. Several minutes elapsed.

"Leta, I love you so very, very much," Earl affirmed at last.

"Don't I know it, tiger!"

235

July 4

"I JUST DON'T LIKE IT, SIMON. We should have went to Atlantic City or Cape May."

Simon Reid faced his plump, irritated wife. "Can it, Jackie!" he ordered, frowning, irate himself. "Can't you just let yourself go for one night? We're here to have a good time."

Jackie adamantly refused to knuckle under. "Oh, sure! Have a good time with a killer running around loose? Are you crazy?"

Simon glanced down at their two children. Shawn, age six, was patiently waiting for them to continue their boardwalk stroll. This was his first visit to the shore and he was fascinated by the activity and the lights. Beth, eleven, was leaning against a green bench, sheer boredom conveyed by the set of her lean features.

"For the sake of the children," Simon urged, "I will agree to avoid an argument if you will."

"Maybe I don't want to avoid an argument!" Jackie fumed. "Was I consulted about the place where we would take our four-day vacation? I was not. Was I given any say at all? I should say not! And now here we are, with the children, in mortal danger!"

"Bullshit."

"What did you say?"

"I said bullshit! Look around you." Simon waved his arm in a circular, expansive gesture. They were standing at the top of the steps leading to the northern entrance to the boardwalk. Groups of people were passing constantly. Thirty yards farther south row after row of amusements and eateries began, and despite the bad publicity generated by the murders the press had dubbed the "werewolf" killings, several thousand people were crammed onto the boardwalk, delighting in the holiday festivities. "Do you see all those people? What the hell do we have to be afraid about? You think you'll be attacked in public, right on the boardwalk? You're crazy."

Jackie watched the throngs for a while. "Well, maybe you're right," she finally admitted.

"I know I'm right. Now let's get started, shall we? There's a lot to see and do."

"Okay."

Leta, in uniform and on duty, lounged against the protective railing on the ocean side of the boardwalk and studied the passersby. There was the usual assorted mixture of vacationers, interspersed with a few locals and those employed for the summer by the resort retailers. She always could readily identify the latter: their bodies were bronzed by the protracted exposure to the sun.

"10-8, unit 970," her walkie-talkie crackled. "Unit 942, do you copy?"

"10-4," she acknowledged. Earl was back in service after a nature break. He was stationed only a block north of her location, which was at midpoint on the boardwalk.

She stood on her toes and craned her neck, but the packed crowds prevented her from spotting him.

"Cutie," she heard him faintly whisper over the air, and he clicked off.

That idiot! She grinned. He could get in trouble fooling around like that!

Jimmy Watton ran his eager fingers over his girlfriend, caressing her firm breasts through her scanty bikini.

"Anita, I love you." He sighed, altering his position so he could wedge his knee between her trim legs.

Anita Seers ran her hands through his red hair, pressing him close, wanting him, yet disturbed by nagging thoughts of her mother and father. What would they say, she wondered. Their daughter, necking under the boardwalk with a boy she'd only known two days! She could hear her mom now. Shameless! Hussy! She was raised better! A senior in high school, no less! But Jimmy was so . . . *perfect*. Her ideal of a hunk. And a college freshman!

Jimmy slipped the top of her red bikini aside and traced her nipple with his tongue.

"Oh, Jimmy!" she moaned as her feelings overwhelmed her.

"Anita!"

His right hand stroked the damp area between her thighs. She arched her back and dug her long red nails into his back.

Jimmy suddenly stopped, his lips poised over her navel, his muscular body tensed.

"What is it, honey?" she asked huskily, surprised.

Jimmy was staring across her naked chest, gazing up at something. His eyes were wide, scared.

238

"What's wrong?" Anita rose on her elbows, alarmed, following the direction he was looking, thinking a cop had found them. Blast! Jimmy had told her the police rarely patrolled this far north. "What do you—" she froze, seeing what he saw, recognizing what it was despite the gloom.

The werewolf was on them.

Jimmy tried to rise, but too late. The hairy fist smashed into his jugular and he collapsed, gagging, spitting blood.

Anita screamed, hoping someone would hear her over the hubbub on the boardwalk above. She crawled backward, kicking sand at the werewolf, attempting to slow it down long enough for her to get on her feet.

She didn't.

The werewolf snarled and pounced, its knees slamming into her stomach. Its huge hands encircled her neck.

"Did you hear something, Daddy?" Beth Reid asked, her head twisted to one side, listening. The family was standing alongside the green bench, waiting while Jackie buttoned Shawn's jacket to protect him from the stiff sea breeze.

"No, honey. Why?" Simon noticed his wife had missed a button. "Like what?"

"Like a scream."

"Scream?" Jackie stood. "Did you say *scream?*"

"Don't go flying off the handle," Simon cautioned his wife. "Look over there." He pointed at the nearest amusements. One of them was a roller coaster. "Beth probably heard someone on that ride."

"No, Daddy," Beth hastily disagreed.

"No?"

"No. I think it came from down there." Beth indicated the boardwalk.

"Under the boardwalk?" Jackie asked, aghast.

"Don't get excited." Simon gripped his wife's arm. "It's just some kids clowning around, more than likely."

"How do you know?"

"Bet you anything."

"I don't gamble with my children's lives!" Jackie took Shawn and Beth by the hand. "Come, children, we're leaving."

Simon mentally maligned her for being such a hyper bitch. Smiling, he blocked them from leaving, standing in their path. "Will you wait a minute, Jackie? I'll prove to you that you're worried over nothing."

"How?" Jackie demanded.

"Easy." Simon spun and walked to the nearest steps leading down to the beach.

"What the hell do you think you're doing?" Jackie inquired angrily.

"What does it look like?" Simon started down the steps.

"Don't be an idiot!" Jackie walked a step towards him.

"Daddy, don't!" Beth called out.

Simon grinned and reached the bottom of the steps. He'd show Jackie who wore the pants in this family! He might be in retailing, but that didn't mean he was a wimp! Couldn't they do anything without her griping about every little thing? Sometimes he wondered why the hell he'd even married her.

"Get back up here!" Jackie ordered.

Simon turned and waved at them. "See. There's nothing to worry about."

The werewolf hit him between the shoulder blades,

charging from under the boardwalk, striking swiftly, savagely, before he could begin to react.

"Simon!" Jackie managed to scream before she fainted, the sight of her husband being brutally slammed into the sand too much for her frail nervous system.

The werewolf, growling, bounded up the steps and leaped onto the boardwalk. It ignored the two bawling children and faced the teeming crowd, many of whom had observed the assault and were gaping in astonishment.

A woman shrieked in terror.

The werewolf reared erect, howled, and rushed into the throng, tearing and rending at will, the frightened vacationers stumbling over themselves in their eagerness to avoid his primal fury.

One large man, braver than the rest, jumped on the werewolf from behind and locked his brawny arm around the werewolf's neck.

The werewolf stopped, reached over its shoulder, grabbed the man by his hair, and swept him to one side, crashing him head first into the sturdy boards underfoot. His cranium split, blood spurting through the air.

Another person fainted.

Pandemonium exploded on the boardwalk as men, women, and children frantically sought to flee. A number of them fell and were trod on by others.

The werewolf reveled in their fear, chasing them, maiming the slower ones, baying all the while.

Leta suppressed a yawn. This was certainly one of the more boring shifts she'd worked in some time and, for once, she didn't mind. Ever since Char's death she looked forward to quiet shifts. She'd had enough so-called excitement to last her a lifetime.

"All units," her walkie-talkie abruptly blared, "10–98 in progress. Repeat. 10–98 in progress."

Leta unclipped the walkie-talkie from her belt. A 10–98? A riot or mass disturbance? It couldn't be.

"What's the 10–20 on this 10–98?" she heard Earl question the sender.

"North end of the boardwalk. Hurry! Hurry!" The officer sounded panicky.

"Calm down, Fritz!" She overheard Earl order the officer.

"Sergeant!" Fritz was not adhering to the code signals. "Sergeant!"

"Damn it, Fritz! Calm down! What is it?" Earl sounded mad.

"It's the werewolf! The werewolf!"

"What? Where?"

"Right here on the boardwalk! He's . . . he's . . ." Fritz paused and Leta could detect his rapid breathing. "I'm looking right at him and he's hurting people and it's terrible . . ."

"Get a hold of yourself!" Earl commanded, breaking in. "We're on our way! All units, 10–34. North of the boardwalk."

Leta pressed the walkie-talkie against her right ear and merged with the crowd, moving toward the north end, hurrying as fast as she could, hindered by the number of people and the volume of noise.

"Move aside! Police officer!" she yelled, but it was no use. Only those within immediate proximity could hear her, and they were too sluggish in responding and getting out of her path.

"Sergeant!" There was no denying the inflection and tone to his voice: Fritz was petrified.

"We're coming," Earl assured him.

"Sergeant! He's seen me! He's coming my way! What do I do?"

"Shoot the son-of-a-bitch!"

"Yes, sir."

Leta was still several yards away from the north end of the boardwalk, but she distinctly heard the *crack-crack-crack* of a service Magnum and knew Fritz was obeying Earl. Good boy! She felt a momentary regret that she wasn't the one turning the werewolf into Swiss cheese.

"Sergeant!"

"I'm almost there," Earl answered.

"But I hit him. I know I hit him."

"What? Give me thirty seconds. Will you get out of my way, lady?"

"Sergeant, I shot him three times. He's still coming . . ."

"Fifteen seconds, Fritz!"

Leta heard a siren wailing, and glancing to her left and down one of the side streets, spotted a patrol car racing north on Meridian.

"Fritz?" she heard Earl shout over the walkie-talkie. "Fritz? These people are going crazy. Where are you?"

Leta saw a large cluster of men, women, and children on the opposite side of the boardwalk, running and shoving and yelling as they hastened south, away from the end of the boardwalk, away from the werewolf. Other families and strollers, those not aware of the situation, were standing and staring, puzzled and alarmed by the confusion and fear. She was confronted with increasing difficulty in maneuvering through the press of vacationers. A narrow gap opened up along the center of the boardwalk and she took advantage of it, running now, making headway.

Suddenly there were two more shots, followed by screams, and everyone in front of her was turning and striving to get past her, pushing her and bouncing her from one person to the next.

"I'm a police officer!" Leta screamed, resisting the flow of the mob, trying to keep her footing.

Someone gouged her in the ribs and the pain doubled her over. Before she could straighten, a crush of scared people swept by her and one of them bumped into her and she tripped and sprawled onto the boardwalk, a large splinter slicing into her hand. She curled herself into a ball and placed her hands over her head, afraid she would be squashed by the hundreds of feet sweeping along the boardwalk. A minute elapsed and she was surprised because very few of the crowd stepped on her. Finally the mob was past her and streaming south, and the noise began to subside. She was, it seemed, alone.

Leta sat up and examined her hand. The wooden splinter was over an inch long and was protruding from the fleshy area near her thumb. Damn, but the thing hurt!

Something snarled, and the sound was so close to her that, startled, she jumped.

Leta looked up.

The werewolf, blood-splattered and grim, was only ten feet away, crouching on all fours and eyeing her quizzically.

Leta froze, the memory of his hairy hands on her throat overcoming her, paralyzing her. She remembered the

244

claws digging into her skin and the pain she had felt.

The werewolf stood and hissed.

Leta moved, the spell broken, rising to her knees and drawing her revolver, the standard issue .357 pointed and aimed, and the werewolf leaped as she fired, the gun bucking in her hand.

The werewolf, as if slammed by an invisible hammer, crashed to the boardwalk and lay still.

Leta rose to her feet, her revolver trained on the prone werewolf, waiting for it to charge again.

The werewolf remained immobile.

Leta stopped a foot from the thing, unable to believe that it was dead, unwilling to accept that it was finished.

It wasn't.

The werewolf was up and on her in the time it took her to pull the trigger, growling and reaching for her neck.

Leta missed. The bullet tore into the boardwalk, slivers flying.

The werewolf grabbed her throat with his left hand, lifted her off her feet, and struck her once across the face with his right. She groaned and went limp and he drew back his fist to hit her again.

Two officers burst into view, coming up one of the entrance ramps to the boardwalk, and bore down on him, drawing their revolvers.

"Hey you!" one of them shouted.

The werewolf contemptuously flung the woman aside and faced his new threat, growling.

The officers closed the distance between them and their suspect, concerned for the officer lying on the boardwalk, glimpsing six or seven other bodies scattered behind the werewolf.

Snarling, the werewolf suddenly whirled and ran toward a clothing store.

"Shit!" the other officer exclaimed as the werewolf leaped, smashing through a plate glass window into the vacant store. The occupants had fled during his earlier rampage, but the lights were still on and the interior was clearly visible. The officers stopped outside the shattered window and searched the aisles of garments.

"See him, Petey?" the shorter officer asked.

"Nope," the other answered. "Not on this side."

"Where the hell is he?"

There was movement at the back of the store, and the werewolf came into view from under a dress rack.

"There he is!" Petey yelled, aiming his Magnum.

The werewolf sprinted a few paces and vaulted a table, striking a rear window, demolishing the glass, and tumbling through to the other side.

"After him!" Petey directed, and the two of them raced around the store. The night was being rent by over a dozen caterwauling sirens as every available unit converged on the boardwalk. They reached the window the werewolf had used for an exit, broken glass littered the ground. The side street behind the clothing store was deserted except for three parked automobiles and a row of garbage cans.

"I don't see him." Petey knelt to peer under the cars. "Do you, Monty?"

"Nope. He's got to be here, though."

"Oh?"

"A person can't just vanish."

"Who says this thing is human?"

"Come off it, Petey."

"I'm serious."

Monty shook his head. "You're crazy. But that's beside the point. What do we do now? Look for your monster or help those poor victims on the boardwalk?"

"The victims need us more. Let's go." Petey glanced over his shoulder at the empty street and led the way to the front of the store.

"Holy shit!" Monty declared, surveying the carnage. "I hope none of them are dead."

Petey holstered his revolver. "I'll tend to them while you call for an ambulance."

"Right." Monty lifted his walkie-talkie.

"Hey!"

"Yeah?" Monty looked up.

"Make that as many ambulances as they can send."

"Got it."

Petey hurried over to the injured officer and gently turned her over. "Damn! Leta!" He gazed at the ragged line of bodies extending northward on the boardwalk. He wiped the back of his right hand across his perspiring brow.

"Dear God!"

July 5

CHIEF WATSON PRESSED HIS KNUCKLES AGAINST his tired eyes and rubbed them. "I haven't been this tired," he said to Grout, who was seated in a chair near his desk, "since that night seven years ago when we had that triple homocide. I had to stay up all night then, too. Every pore aches."

"You aren't the only one," Grout stated.

There was a knock on the office door and Russ entered.

"Well, what's the final tally?" Chief Watson asked, dreading the expected answer.

Russ sat in a chair and sighed. "I just phoned all three hospitals the injured were taken to, as you requested, and spoke with the heads of each one. They've released brief official statements, but not the identities of the deceased or the injured."

"And the total count?"

"Thirty-one injured, seven seriously, and four dead."

"What?" Grout was on his feet. "I don't believe it!"

"Sit down," Chief Watson instructed, and Grout complied. He glanced at his clock and noted the hands indicated ten past four.

"Most of the injuries are minor," Russ resumed. "From

what I was told, five of the seven on the critical list could go at any time."

"How could the damn thing get so many?" Grout queried, incredulous.

"Most of the injuries were caused by the crowd on the boardwalk when they panicked and ran over one another," Russ replied. "As near as we can make out, the werewolf attacked only a dozen or so. Four of them are dead."

"How are the officers the thing assaulted?" Chief Watson questioned.

"Officer Ballinger is resting at home. She suffered a bruised jaw and some lacerations. Nothing serious, though."

"Poor girl," Chief Watson commented, crossing his arms. "That's twice the thing has nearly killed her. She lives a charmed life."

"Sergeant Patterson wasn't so fortunate. He's in a coma and the doctor rates his chances at fifty-fifty."

"Damn!" Chief Watson felt his anger boil and he restrained an urge to pound his desk top. "What about the third one, the rookie? Fritz, wasn't it?"

Russ nodded. "He's doing fine. His collarbone is busted, but he's conscious and recuperating."

"Did you talk to him?"

"Yes, sir."

"And?"

"He still claims, and a dozen witnesses confirm him, that he shot the werewolf three times at point-blank range."

"Bullshit!" Grout interjected. "The kid pissed his pants and missed."

Russ glowered at Grout. "Other witnesses verify that Patterson shot it twice . . ."

"Impossible." Grout glared at Russ.

". . . and we have several reports," Russ continued, unperturbed, "that Leta plugged him once, too."

Chief Watson held up his hand as Grout opened his mouth to speak again. "Amazing. I'm willing to accept the veracity of the reports. But why wasn't the werewolf killed? Evidently, it wasn't even scratched. How can this be?"

"It can't be," Grout snapped. "Proves my point that they all missed."

"All of them?" Russ demanded.

"Sure," Grout stated, shrugging his shoulders. "Why not?"

"If the witnesses didn't agree with him," Chief Watson interrupted their argument, "I might suspect the rookie missed. But Patterson is a seasoned professional and I doubt he'd develop a case of nerves. Officer Ballinger proved herself the last time she was attacked by the werewolf. I believe all three shot at the thing and hit it."

"Why wasn't it killed?" Grout wanted to know.

"I wish I knew." Chief Watson stretched.

"I mean"—Grout couldn't leave well enough alone— "a three fifty-seven isn't a peashooter. You hit someone with it and the son-of-a-bitch is going down whether he wants to or not. Am I right?"

"Unfortunately, you are," Chief Watson conceded. "So we can add another element to the mystery concerning our werewolf. It's bulletproof."

"Nothing is bulletproof," Grout stated with certainty.

"This werewolf appears to be," Russ said, then turned

to Chief Watson. "The press is clamoring for a statement. The major television networks have sent crews here. Have you seen outside lately? The building is surrounded by reporters and the curious."

"I know." Chief Watson rubbed a cramp in the calf of his leg. "The governor has been trying to reach me, our senator has been calling, Perkins has been on my case, the switchboard has been swamped with calls . . ." He let the sentence trail off.

"I sure as hell hope Earl pulls through," Russ mused aloud.

"I sure as hell hope we make an arrest in this case before another week goes by." Chief Watson frowned. "I had a nightmare the other night that we weren't able to catch this madman and he went on killing and killing and killing."

"He could, you know," Grout observed.

"What?" Chief Watson stood and performed a knee bend to alleviate the pain in his leg.

"Sure. Look at that Ripper guy recently in England. Didn't he get away with murder, literally, for five years? What about that case in Atlanta? And remember the original Jack the Ripper? He was never caught."

Chief Watson walked up to Grout, bent over, and positioned his face an inch from the startled captain's. "You know, Bob, you've missed your calling. With your perennial optimistic attitude on life, your cheery disposition, you should have been a circus clown." He straightened, sadly shook his head, and exited the office.

"What'd I say?" Grout asked Russ.

July 11

"I SAID NO AND THAT'S FINAL."

"How come?" Leta demanded. "You have every available person on the case, pulling out all the stops, working around the clock. You have the special task force the governor appointed and all those officers from other agencies, the State Police, and—"

Chief Watson waved his right forefinger in the air and she fell silent. "Officer Ballinger, I'm truly sorry. But I won't assign you to the werewolf squad."

"But you've got to!" she said, persistent.

"I don't have to do anything of the sort." Chief Watson smiled to lessen the sting of his words. "And the answer is no. You're dismissed."

"Why?"

"I beg your pardon?"

"Why won't you assign me?"

"You said it yourself. I have everyone on the werewolf case I can possibly afford to take away from their routine jobs. I can't afford to take you off your regular duty."

"Bullshit."

"What?" Chief Watson leaned on his desk and eyed her quizzically.

"I said bullshit, sir. That's not the reason and you know it." Leta looked down at the floor to hide her hurt expression.

"How is Earl, anyway?" Chief Watson softly inquired.

"Still . . . still . . ." She hesitated, tears brimming in her eyes. "Still in the coma."

"I'm sure he'll recover. Listen, Leta. You know and I know you're too involved with this one. Policy is policy. I'm sorry. Believe me."

"I do. Thanks."

Chief Watson watched her leave, wishing there was something he could do to relieve her distress, adding another reason for despising the werewolf to his already lengthy list.

The intercom buzzed.

Idly, preoccupied, he pressed the *send* switch.

"Yes?"

"Sir," his secretary announced, "there is a Mr. Turk here to see you?"

"A Mr. Turk?" He couldn't place the name.

"Yes. He says that Chief Blair sent him down from Trenton."

"Oh." He remembered now. Why had he agreed to this nonsense? "Okay. Send him in."

Mr. Turk opened the door and stood in the doorway a minute, surveying the room. He was a small man, not much over five feet tall, and quite portly. His thin hair was thinning on the center of his head, gray on the sides.

"Mr. Turk." Chief Watson stood. "Come on in and have a seat. I'm glad you could come."

Mr. Turk settled into the chair indicated.

Chief Watson sat back down. As Blair had advised him,

he didn't offer to shake Turk's hand. Something about disrupting the aura. He studied Turk. The man was well dressed in a three-piece suit, with a gold watch and a gold bracelet displayed on the right and left wrist, respectively. Turk's fingernails were rather long and manicured. Interesting. The chief smiled and waited for Turk to speak.

"I hope I'm not disturbing you." Mr. Turk grinned, and Chief Watson marveled at how trim, even, and white the man's teeth were.

"Not at all. I understand there is a possibility you can aid us in our search for the werewolf."

"Hopefully. I've rendered assistance to law enforcement agencies in the past with some positive results."

"I know. That's why Chief Blair contacted me. I want to tell you, up front, that I don't expect too much from you."

"Oh?" Mr. Turk chuckled. "You doubt my ability?"

"I just don't believe in psychics," Chief Watson admitted.

Mr. Turk slapped his knee and laughed.

"What's so funny?"

"A personal joke."

"Oh?" Chief Watson leaned back in his chair, wondering what manner of nutcase Blair had sent him.

"Let me explain. Last night, after Chief Blair called me and requested that I see you, I bet myself a bottle of Chablis that you'd be a nonbeliever. Looks like I treat myself the next time I dine out." Mr. Turk laughed again.

Chief Watson smiled amicably. He was tempted to tell Turk his services wouldn't be needed. Werewolves. Psychics. They could all be included in the same category: mumbo jumbo. "So what's your first step?" he asked. "Gaze into your crystal ball?" He kept his features fixed in

254

a friendly smile to indicate he wasn't being sarcastic.

Turk stopped laughing. "I do not specialize in scrying."

"Scrying?"

"Crystal ball gazing. You mentioned it, remember?"

For a moment their eyes met in silent confrontation, then each man grinned.

"Touché." Chief Watson nodded once at Turk. "What exactly do you specialize in?"

"My realm of expertise is in psychometry."

"You got me again."

"Allow me to elaborate." Turk crossed his legs and settled into his chair. "I translate impressions, Chief Watson. To put it concisely, without any technical jargon, I serve as a conduit for images garnered from inanimate objects."

"I understand, Mr. Turk," Chief Watson said, and paused. "I think."

"Call me Elton, please."

"Okay, Elton."

"You see, Chief Watson, I can hold anything in my hands and receive vibrations from whatever I'm holding. Give me a ring belonging to someone, and I'll provide you with a character sketch of the owner. Let me sit in a chair someone has sat in for any length of time, and I'll supply a picture of the previous occupant. I was of service to Chief Blair once about a year ago, I think it was, when the only clue he had concerning a certain suspect was a button the suspect lost at the scene of the crime. From that small brown button, and nothing else, I was able to give Chief Blair information which eventually resulted in an arrest and conviction. I might be able to do the same thing for you with this werewolf."

"I don't have a button," Chief Watson commented.

"What do you have, if I may inquire?"

"You may. And the answer"—Chief Watson sighed—"is zero."

"I see," Turk said. "Unfortunate."

"Extremely. Oh, we know this werewolf is a man, approximately six feet two inches or so, registering on the scales in the vicinity of two hundred or two-ten. We know he's using a werewolf costume made with genuine wolf hair. At least, we hope it's a costume. You don't believe in werewolves, do you?"

"Of course not." Turk shook his head. "Superstitious drivel, that's all it is."

"Then we're in agreement there. We also have a possible blood type."

"That's all?" Turk was obviously surprised by the lack of evidence.

"That's it."

"Now I know why you consented to see me. You're desperate."

"I wouldn't say . . ." Chief Watson began.

"No need to apologize," Turk stated. "It's obvious. I only pray I can lend you a hand."

"What's the first step?"

"Waiting."

"Waiting?"

"If any object I'm touching has been owned by any one person for a considerable length of time, then the images I receive are clear and precise. If the object wasn't owned by any individual for any period, but was very recently in contact with someone, say, for instance, a tree someone has just leaned against, and if I arrive at the site quickly, then I can often pick up fleeting impressions. But if the contact was fleeting, and if more than a few hours elapse between the time the object was touched and the time when I handle it, then my chances of an accurate reading diminish. Psychometrists define the effect as clouding, an obscuring of the images. In other words, to be of use to you, I must touch whatever the werewolf has touched within hours after he's touched it."

"In other words"—Chief Watson frowned as comprehension dawned—"the werewolf has to strike again before you can do a thing?"

"Exactly."

"Shit. And I was getting my hopes up."

"Sorry."

"It's not your fault. Shit." Chief Watson half-heartedly grinned and added an afterthought. "Pardon my language."

"No problem."

July 14

"DID YOU SEE THE MORNING PAPER?" Don Baxter asked his son.

"No," Allan answered. "Why?" They were in the living room, watching the Phillies on television. His mother was in the back yard tending her garden.

"There was another story on that werewolf in Ocean City."

"So?" Allan responded indifferently.

"They've called in a psychic to help find the thing."

"That's nice." Allan glued his eyes to the game. It was the top of the ninth, the Phils were only one measly run ahead, and the other team had two outs with the bases loaded.

"Think he'll be able to do it?"

"Do what?" Allan shot his father an annoyed glance.

"Do you think this psychic will find the werewolf?"

"Who cares?"

The batter swung and missed for his first strike.

"You didn't answer my question," Don persisted.

Allan tore his eyes away from the TV. "I don't know, Dad. What does it matter?"

"I thought you might be interested."

The batter swung again. Strike two.

"What does it matter to me?" Allan demanded. "I couldn't care less."

The Philly pitcher was taking his time. The strain was showing.

"Really? Are you sure?"

Allan glanced at his father, surprised to note he was smiling broadly. "What are you getting at, Dad?"

"Oh, nothing."

Another pitch. Ball one.

"I thought you might be following this werewolf thing very closely," Don told his son.

Ball two.

Allan faced his father. "Will you quit beating around the bush? Why should I be interested in this werewolf?"

"The police haven't been able to locate it."

Ball three.

"So?"

The Philly pitcher went into his windup.

"We'll be in Ocean City on August first."

The batter swung for all he was worth and missed. The game was over. The Phillies won.

"Oh, wow!" Allan exclaimed, suddenly understanding.

Don Baxter grinned. "I knew you weren't as dumb as you look."

July 17

BERT TAPPENDICK HEFTED HIS METAL DETECTOR and swept
the gleaming arm in an arc across the sand, hoping for a
positive reading on his meter, disappointed when the nee-
dle remained still. What had happened to this beach? At
one time the sand would yield over a hundred dollars a
day in coins, an occasional watch, and other valuables.
He stopped and gazed over his shoulder at the almost
empty beach. There weren't more than a dozen or so people in sight, a dismal turnout for a summer afternoon. Bert
knew who to blame for the lack of tourists in Ocean City.
It was all the fault of that damned werewolf! Ever since the
boardwalk attack on the Fourth of July, the tourists were
avoiding Ocean City like the plague. No vacationers
cramming the beach, no dropped coins or lost watches,
and no extra source of income for a retired mechanic, a
widower, who subsisted on a small pension and lived in a
cottage located south of Ocean City. Just his luck the
werewolf selected Ocean City to hit!

Bert sighed and wearily trudged to the top of the nearest
dune. The sun was several hours above the western horizon. Gulls were winging overhead. He sat down and
rested his tired legs. A yacht, plying the waves a half-mile

distant, attracted his attention. How could anyone live anywhere except near the ocean? How could anyone afford to miss all this beauty? He placed the metal detector to one side and reclined, using his hands, entwined behind his head, as a pillow. Several clouds were floating out to sea, and he lazily watched them, soothed by the breeze and the sound of the waves gently breaking on the beach. He closed his eyes.

"Chief," his secretary alerted him via the intercom, "call for you on line seven."

Chief Watson punched the appropriate button and lifted the receiver. "Chief Watson here."

"Hello, Chief. Elton Turk here. How are you?"

"Fine, Mr. Turk." He placed a report he'd been studying on his desk. "We haven't had another attack or a sighting yet. I've still got your number in case we do."

"Good. You might need it sooner than you think."

"How's that?" he asked, all ears, detecting an urgency in Turk's voice.

"I'm going to pass on some information to you. You can take it for what it's worth. I know how you feel about paranormal phenomena, but I thought you should hear this."

"What have you got for me?"

"Well, I've been consulting with some of my associates in related fields, and earlier this evening one of my friends called me. She specializes in precognition, in foreseeing future events. Do you want to hear what she told me?"

"You wouldn't have called if you didn't think it was important."

"Okay. She believes the werewolf will strike again

261

tonight."

"Tonight?"

"Tonight."

Chief Watson reflected a minute. "How reliable is your source?"

"I said she's my friend."

"Thanks, Elton. I appreciate this."

"What will you do?"

"Not much I can do except place my men on increased guard and step up our patrols. Did your friend foresee any additional details?"

"One other thing, but I can't say how significant it is."

"Let me be the judge."

"She saw metal."

"Metal? What type of metal?"

"Sorry, Chief. That was all she could tell me. I realize it's not much, but like I said, I thought you'd like to know."

"Thanks. I'll call you if anything does develop."

"Take care, Chief."

" 'Bye."

Bert opened his eyes and for a moment was uncertain of where he was. He could see stars and hear the surging ocean and he sat up, confused. The metal detector was lying beside him. At the sight of it he remembered; he had been combing the beach, had stopped to rest, and had fallen asleep. He rose to his feet and stretched.

What time was it? He wondered. He checked his watch and was surprised to see that the luminous dial indicated ten o'clock. On a normal day he'd be home by seven.

Bert picked up his metal detector and walked down the

dune to the beach and headed north toward Ocean City and a hearty meal. He was hungry, and he mentally ran through a list of possible suppers. Chicken and dumplings appealed to him the most. And some wine. He smacked his lips, envisioning the repast.

That was when he heard the footsteps.

Bert halted in his tracks, listening, positive he'd detected the padding of feet on the sand, like the sound a dog would make as it ran along the beach.

Silence.

Bert continued on his course. He took several steps and, abruptly, there was the noise again, behind him. He looked over his shoulder.

There was no sign of a dog, of anything.

He shrugged his shoulders. The nearest lights were only a quarter mile away and he made in their direction.

Again, the footsteps.

Bert didn't stop. If the thing following him was only a dog, what did he have to worry about? What else could it be? The answer hit him then, and he hurried, walking as fast as he could. Impossible, he told himself. Couldn't be. No way.

The padding was louder.

Bert considered dropping the metal detector and breaking into a run, but the detector was vital to his income. He couldn't . . . *wouldn't* . . . leave it behind. Besides, maybe it was only a dog.

Something growled.

What should he do? He knew that the thing knew *he* knew it was following him. Why didn't it attack? What was it waiting for?

The stealthy tread was right on his heels.

Bert felt the small hairs on the back of his neck rise, and he instinctively sensed the thing following him was ready to attack. If he was going to act, now was the time.

The thing hissed.

Bert spun, gripping the metal detector by the arm, swinging for all he was worth.

The werewolf was in midair.

The metal detector caught the werewolf on the temple, knocking it aside, and it sprawled to the ground. The impact jarred Bert and he dropped the detector and gawked at the stunned werewolf, unable to accept the reality of his situation. It *was* the werewolf!

Snarling, the thing began to rise.

Bert broke his temporary shock and ran. Those lights were close now, and he could discern people walking along a street. If he reached them maybe he'd be safe. He regretted leaving the metal detector, but he could always return for it the next morning.

The footsteps were behind him again.

Bert pumped his legs as rapidly as he could. He thought of his late wife, his beloved Ann, and vividly remembered the scene at her deathbed. That detestable cancer! He'd hated to see her suffer so, to watch as she lingered on and on. God, how he missed her!

The werewolf was almost on him, pounding steps immediately to his rear.

Bert felt a stabbing pain in his chest. His body wasn't conditioned to this type of rigorous exertion. Maybe he wouldn't retrieve that metal detector tomorrow. Maybe he'd be with Ann tomorrow.

The werewolf shrieked with fury and pounced.

July 18

THE PATROL CAR SCREECHED TO A stop and the officer driving alighted. He opened the rear door and waited. The passenger stepped out and glanced up at the early morning sun.

"I haven't been awake to view a dawn in ages," the stout civilian commented.

"This way, sir," the officer directed, indicating a path to the beach. He led the way.

The two men reached the edge of the beach, the boundary where a field ended and the fine sand began. More officers appeared; some were scouring the field, others searching the beach, several making a plaster cast of a series of footprints, and a group of them clustered around a blanket-covered body, engaged in heated dialogue.

The officer led his charge up to the men near the deceased. "Sir," he said to his superior, "I have him here."

The older man turned and smiled. "Thank you, Higgins. That will be all." He started to extend his hand and thought better of the move. "Good morning, Elton," he stated his welcome instead. "Thank you for coming."

"No problem," Elton Turk replied good-naturedly. "I was expecting your call, Chief."

"Yes." Chief Watson frowned. "I don't know how your friend did it, but her prediction was accurate, gruesomely accurate." He stared at the blue blanket draped over the corpse.

"I'm sorry," Turk offered his sympathy. "I wish she could have been wrong."

"So do I. That's water over the bridge. Let's concentrate on the here and now."

"Okay."

"What do you want to do first? View the body?" Chief Watson grimaced. "Personally, I don't recommend it. The bastard really outdid himself this time. Tore the throat to a pulp. I can't release the identity of the victim as yet. We are still attempting to contact the next of kin. Legal procedure, you know."

"I understand." Turk noticed a hand, the left one, protruding from under the blanket. "That won't be necessary. The victim isn't the one we're interested in, is he?"

"Right." Chief Watson nodded wearily. "So what is the first step?"

Turk didn't answer. He walked around the body and knelt in the sand near the exposed hand.

"What the hell are you doing?" one of the men standing alongside Chief Watson demanded.

"Be quiet, Bob," Chief Watson ordered.

Turk reached out and gingerly touched the hand, softly at first, and then gripped it and held on tightly. "What I'm about to do," he explained to the surrounding officers, "is extremely difficult. This man is dead and his aura is diminished. I am praying enough lingers to permit a reading."

"What is this. . ." Grout began, and Chief Watson

266

poked him in the ribs.

Turk clutched the hand and closed his eyes. He knelt there a minute, immobile. The officers waited expectantly.

Grout glanced at Russ Gilson, arched his eyebrows, and shook his head, silently signaling his opinion of the entire operation.

"I see. . ." Turk began. "I see fear, great fear. I see violence . . . run . . . run . . . I see . . . I see . . . I don't understand . . . I see peace . . . happiness . . . I see . . . I see . . ." Turk opened his eyes and sadly gazed up at Chief Watson. "I'm sorry. I see nothing of the werewolf. Nothing."

"That's okay. You tried." Chief Watson raised his arm and snapped his fingers and one of the nearby officers ran over. He handed something wrapped in a handkerchief over, spun on his heels, and rejoined his fellow officers who were involved in examining the beach for clues.

"I remembered what you told me the other day," Chief Watson mentioned as he unfolded the white handkerchief. "About needing to touch something the werewolf had touched. Maybe this will help you. We found it clenched in the victim's right hand."

Chief Watson carefully handed the handkerchief to Turk. On top of the cloth was a small clump of hair.

"What is it?" Turk inquired.

"We haven't tested it yet," Chief Watson answered. "But I suspect it's genuine wolf hair, torn from the werewolf in the victim's death throes. We're still looking, but I don't expect we'll find anything else the werewolf has touched, unless you can count footprints. Can you do anything with footprints?"

"No," Turk admitted.

"What about the hair, then?" Chief Watson asked hopefully. "Is it any good for your purpose?"

"We shall shortly see." Turk rose. He held the hair in his left palm. Slowly, cautiously, he pressed his right palm on top of the hair. He closed his eyes.

The assembled officers could detect the degree of his concentration. They watched, fascinated.

"There is some clouding. . . ." Turk said in a low tone at last. "I can see some images . . . I see . . . I see . . . a police uniform . . . I see . . . the moon . . . and a pile of something . . . books . . . No! . . . magazines, I think . . . and comics . . . and something on a wall . . . I can't make it . . . Yes! . . . I see a huge, hairy face . . . leering . . . and I see sand . . ." Turk stopped. He began to sway, and sweat beaded on his furrowed brow.

Those around him were scarcely breathing, hanging on his every word.

"I see . . ." Turk inhaled deeply. "A casket . . . shiny . . . sitting in a hole in the damp earth . . . I see tears . . . many, many, tears . . . There is more clouding . . . I can not . . . Wait! . . . What is this? . . . Something . . . primitive . . . savage . . . teeth and claws . . . a hunger . . . a hunger. . ."

Sweat was streaming from Turk and his eyelids were fluttering rapidly.

"I see . . . there is much . . . garble . . . confusion . . . I see the night . . . and . . . and . . . is it a bicep? . . . What? . . . I am losing it . . . losing it . . . yet . . . one more thing . . . I do not understand at all . . . the shield that protects . . . is that it? . . . So tired . . . can't tell much . . . can't . . . ."

Turk collapsed, and Russ and Grout caught him by his

elbows before he could topple onto his face.

Chief Watson took Turk by the shoulder and shook him. "Elton! Elton! Are you all right? Can you hear me?"

Turk opened his eyes and smiled at them. "Yes, thank you. I'm just . . . weak . . . Just weak." He tried to rise, and Russ and Grout had to brace him to prevent another fall.

"Are you sure you're okay?" Chief Watson persisted.

Turk nodded. He was breathing deeply.

Chief Watson pointed at a neatly folded brown blanket on the ground six feet from the victim. "Place him on that," he directed Russ and Grout.

"What?" Grout asked. His attention had been riveted on Turk's face.

"Let him rest on that extra blanket," Chief Watson repeated.

Russ and Grout eased Turk down to a sitting position on the blanket.

Chief Watson knelt alongside the apparently exhausted man and placed his hand on his shoulder. "Can you talk yet, Elton? Can you tell me about it?"

Turk was breathing easier. "I'm fine. Really." He wiped his forehead with the back of his hand. "Just a wee bit pooped."

"Anything I can get you?" Chief Watson inquired.

"Nope. Appreciate the solicitude. Don't worry, though. After I've engaged in a psychometric reading, I'm invariably drained of all physical and psychic energy. Take a while to recover." Turk wiped his brow again.

"I want to thank you for what you just did," Chief Watson said. "I was very impressed."

"Do you mean converted? You?" Turk smiled.

Chief Watson laughed. "Not quite," he confessed. "I don't understand what just transpired, and the things you saw are a bit confusing. Can you explain them?"

"I wish I could," Turk acknowledged. "But I only see them. I can't interpret the visions any better than you could. And since detective work is your profession, I'll gladly leave the deducing up to you while I go home and luxuriate in a long, hot bath."

"Well, again, let me thank you for all you've done."

"I just pray I've been of some assistance."

Chief Watson stood and motioned to two officers standing nearby. They came on the double. "Give Mr. Turk a hand to a patrol car," he ordered. "One of you will drive him to his car—"

"I parked my car at the station," Turk broke in. "Then that other young officer brought me here as you'd directed."

"Think you can make it back to Trenton?" Chief Watson helped Turk to his feet. "I could have a man drive you."

"That won't be necessary," Turk stated. "I'm okay enough to drive. Besides, you need every available man you've got to work on your werewolf case."

"All right. You take care."

Turk offered his right hand and Chief Watson, after a second of surprised delay, shook. Turk smiled warmly, turned, and walked off, flanked on either side by one of the officers.

Chief Watson watched until Turk rounded a dune and was out of sight. He heard someone come up behind him.

"He was sure a big help!" Grout scoffed. "What the hell was that all about?"

Chief Watson spun, glaring, a thin smile on his face.

"Hey!" Grout backed away a step. "What'd I say?"

"Déjà vu." Russ joined them, smirking at Grout. "Make anything of what that psychic said, Chief?"

"I'm not sure," Chief Watson stated, gazing at the blanket-covered corpse. "Turk was able to help Chief Blair in Trenton. We can't discount his legitimacy. Let's consider his reading point by point. What did he see?"

"Well,"—Grout extended a finger as he rattled off the list—"I remember a police uniform, a moon, magazines and comics, a hairy face, and . . ." he stopped, mentally organizing the sequence. "Then came sand, a coffin, some sucker with teeth, a bicep, and the last thing he mentioned was something called the shield that protects. If you ask me, it's all a bunch of nonsense."

"I didn't ask you," Chief Watson reminded Grout. "Let's break it down further. A police uniform . . ."

"The officers that the thing's attacked," Grout suggested.

"Or Charlene, the one it killed," Russ interjected.

"Possibly," Chief Watson concurred. "What about the moon?"

"That's obvious," Grout said, beaming. "The moon brings out the werewolf."

"He's been seen on moonless nights, too," Russ remembered.

"True. What do you make of the magazines and comics?" Chief Watson asked.

"Beats me." Grout shook his head. "Maybe the werewolf is the literate type. Maybe it refers to his past. We all go through a phase where we read comics and the like, don't we?"

"I did." Chief Watson smiled. "Keep rolling, Bob. You're on a hot streak. A hairy face?"

"Got to be the bastard himself," Grout answered.

Russ nodded his agreement.

"The sand?" Chief Watson prompted.

"The beach. The Dunes. The thing has a habit of sticking near the ocean. Maybe it's the romantic sort." Grout snorted.

"And the coffin?" Chief Watson continued.

"Charlene Winslow," Russ responded this time, erasing their momentary mirth.

"The sucker with teeth," Chief Watson said, then added quickly, "another obvious one. Then there's the bicep?"

"We already know the son-of-a-bitch is strong as a bull," Grout declared.

"That leaves us with the final item." Chief Watson stroked his chin thoughtfully. "The shield that protects."

"Beats me," Grout said. "Possibly there's some kind of mystic or occult significance to it."

"Russ?" Chief Watson urged.

"I honestly don't know," Russ declared. "But this thing has some kind of protection. It's bulletproof."

"Here we go again," Grout snapped.

"That's the entire list," Chief Watson concluded.

"Seems to me the psychic didn't tell us a hell of a lot," Grout summed up his feelings.

"Unfortunately, Bob, I think you're right." Chief Watson sighed, conveying his disappointment. "So we're back to square one."

272

July 28

"HERE YOU GO, LIEUTENANT." OFFICER DOYLE handed Russ a
manila folder. "The latest batch."

"Thanks." Russ placed the folder on his desk.

"Anything else?" Doyle wanted to know.

"No. Thanks a lot."

"You bet."

Doyle departed, and Russ turned his attention to the reports. Ever since the boardwalk attack the department received several dozen calls daily from concerned citizens
who swore they'd seen the werewolf or knew his identity.
None of the leads bore any fruit.

Russ yawned. His window faced the western horizon.
He could see the sun about to sink from view. God, how
he'd love to take a week off and go camping, or fly out to
visit his brother in Colorado. That man had the life! A
cushy job. The mountains. No fucking werewolves frolicking over the landscape, tearing the natives to shreds.
Why bother dreaming about the good life, though? He'd
chosen his career years ago. It was too late to go back
now.

Hell.

Russ flipped open the folder. All of the leads deemed

273

worthwhile were selected by the task force for them to follow up. The rest, those dubbed the "crazies," were passed to him. Chief Watson had placed him in charge of checking and verifying the less promising leads. Brother, were there a lot of dingbats in the world! He studied the individual reports.

There was one from a vagrant who claimed he was attacked as he was rummaging through some garbage cans. He told the officers who discovered him inebriated in an alley that he fought the werewolf off with a broken wine bottle.

Russ chuckled.

There was another report, testified to by five members of a yachting party, that the werewolf was seen swimming in the ocean a mile from the shore.

Jesus!

The third report was from a woman who called the station every day, alleging the werewolf was entering her bedroom each night at the stroke of midnight and ravishing her.

Where did these people come from? Russ laughed.

The fourth report was from an elderly woman living on Palmer. She asserted she'd spotted the werewolf, on two separate occasions, jogging on the sidewalk in front of her house.

What next? He started to grin, then stopped, his mind troubled. What was it about the old lady's report? He reread it slowly. Something about it was nagging at him, and he couldn't determine the reason. He opened the top desk drawer and removed a map of Ocean City. Palmer Street. There was something about Palmer Street. He spread the map open and located Palmer on the map.

Nothing unusual about it. A residential area. He placed his right index finger on the block the old lady lived on and traced the length of Palmer with the index finger of his left hand, noting the intersections.

Iron Avenue.

Ash Avenue.

Court Circle.

Wilkinson Avenue.

Newton Avenue.

Powell Avenue . . . Wait a minute!

Russ hunched over the map and studied the discovery intently. Newton Avenue. That was where they'd found the body of that reporter, McKeen. Interesting. Coincidence? He resumed his examination.

Powell Avenue.

Avalon Avenue.

Avalon? Gretchen and Harvey lived on Avalon. He sat back, surprised, realizing he hadn't heard from them in weeks. In months! When was the last time he'd visited them? It was back in April sometime, before all this werewolf business began. Strange that Gretchen would allow so much time to pass without inviting him over. Highly unusual.

Russ grabbed the phone and dialed the Painter number. He let it ring a dozen times before he hung up.

The sun was gone, stars in the sky.

Russ stood and began to pace, his hands folded behind his back, his thoughts racing. What the hell was bothering him? He had the distinct feeling he was missing an aspect to the case, some element was pricking his subconscious, and he was annoyed. Angrily, he picked up the report from the elderly woman and placed it in his jacket pocket.

Fresh air might clear the cobwebs.

A drive along Palmer, perhaps.

Russ switched off his lights, closed his door, and walked in the direction of the parking lot.

"Lieutenant Gilson!"

Russ stopped and turned.

Officer Doyle was approaching him.

"What is it?"

"Chief Watson is meeting with Mayor Perkins in an hour and he'd like you to be there."

"In his office?"

"Yes, sir."

"Okay. Tell him I'll be there. Why didn't he just call me?" Russ asked.

"I don't know, sir. He was on his way out the door with that man from the governor's office when he saw me and requested I relay his message."

"Okay. Thanks."

Doyle spun and walked off.

What was in the works now? Russ wondered. He hurried to his car. An hour wouldn't give him much time. He wanted to visit the woman on Palmer and swing by and see Gretchen and Harvey. Wouldn't Gretchen be amazed! Him dropping in without an invitation—she'd think he was sick.

He sure hoped the shock wouldn't drive her to drink.

Not funny, he criticized himself. Definitely not funny.

921 South Palmer Street.

He casually strolled up the walk, his eyes taking in the white picket fence, the verdant lawn, a flowery garden, the light showing at the edges of drawn shades in the three windows at the front of the house. As he stepped onto a wooden porch he detected the harsh sound of a small dog yapping like crazy inside the house.

He reached for the doorbell.

The front door swung open several inches and the twin barrels of a shotgun poked out, inches from his face.

"Hold it right there, sucker," a raspy feminine voice demanded. "I'll air-condition your head if you don't."

He froze.

"Raise them hands, buster!"

He raised them.

"Okay. Now you can open your mouth. What the hell do you want? Make it good."

He flashed his widest, brightest smile. "I'm sorry to disturb you, ma'am."

"Then what are you doing here, sneaking up on an old lady, scaring her half out of her wits?"

He laughed. "Sorry, ma'am, but I seriously doubt you're the scaredy-cat type."

"Perceptive, ain't you? You still haven't answered my question."

"I'm Lieutenant Gilson. I'm here about the report you filed with the police."

"You are, huh? Got any identification on you?"

"Sure do." He started to reach into his inner jacket pocket.

"Slowly, mister! I've got an itchy trigger finger."

Very carefully, he withdrew his badge and presented it to the partially open door. "There you go. Are you satisfied now?"

The shotgun was pulled from view and the door opened all the way.

"I'm really sorry, officer, but a girl can't play it too safe these days."

She wasn't more than five feet tall, thickset, with grey hair swept up in a bun. Her eyes were brown and she wore glasses.

"Are you Ethel Baumgartner?" he asked.

"Yes, sir, I am." She held the shotgun in her right hand and fussed with the wide collar to her red dress with her right. "I'm happy to see you. Won't you come in?"

"I'd like to," he admitted. "But I don't have much time. I want to ask you some questions about the report you called in."

"About that hairy son-of-a-bitch?"

He grinned at her selection of words. "Yes, ma'am. About the werewolf."

"Well, I tell you I saw him and I don't care what Phyllis says."

"Phyllis?"

"My best friend, one of the few still kicking. When you reach my age, young man, you'll thank the Lord for every friend He hasn't called into the great beyond. Know what I mean?"

"I think so," he answered, wondering if it would be difficult to keep her on the subject of their conversation.

"Anyway, Phyllis insists my eyes are starting to go. But I know better and—"

He could see it would be. "Excuse me, Ethel, but you were going to tell me about the werewolf?"

"I was? About who?"

"The hairy son-of-a-bitch."

"Oh. Him. Not much to tell."

"I'd like to hear it."

"Oh. Well, it's like I told the officer I talked with on the phone. Two times I've seen him go trotting by."

"Where?"

"Right there." She pointed at the sidewalk in front of her property.

"And what was he doing?"

"Maybe you need your ears checked. I just told you. He was just running."

"Where were you when you saw him?" he inquired.

"Right inside. I look out my front window a lot. Like to keep my eye on the neighborhood. You never can tell. Why, once, about ten years ago, or was it twelve, I was mugged—"

"Excuse me, ma'am," he interrupted her digression. "But the werewolf."

"What about him?"

"You said he was running. . . ."

She twisted her neck and watched him, frowning.

"Is something wrong?" He couldn't decide if she was telling the truth or just another dingaling.

"I've told you, and I don't know how many times, that I saw the werewolf go running by my place. How many times are you going to ask me the same stupid question? Would you like to come in and have some tea?"

"No, thanks."

"You sure?"

"Yes, ma'am."

"Then what do you want?"

"You saw the werewolf running. . . ."

"Here we go again!" She sighed and looked at him sadly.

Maybe the department could put her in charge of prisoner interrogations, he mused, grinning. She'd break down any criminal in minutes.

"What's so funny?" she wanted to know.

"Nothing. Can you tell me which direction the werewolf was heading when you spotted him?"

"No problem. I'm not senile, you know," she snapped angrily.

"Okay, then."

"Okay, what?"

"Which direction?"

"Oh." She raised her left arm and pointed.

North. Toward Newton Avenue. He smiled. "Thank you, Ethel. You've been a great help." He turned to leave.

"Sure you wouldn't like to come in and enjoy some hot tea?" she asked.

"I've got to run." He took three steps, then remembered another question he wanted to pose. A crucial one. He faced her.

"Change your mind?" she entreated him eagerly.

"Wish I could. But I do have one more question."

"It figures."

"What time?"

"Time? Oh, I don't know." She glanced over her shoulder. "I can't see the clock from here."

"No. No. I'd like to know the time you saw the werewolf run past your house. What time was it?"

"Oh." She considered for a minute. "I'm not positive, but I'd say around five in the morning."

"Five?" he repeated, surprised.

"Sure. I usually wake up at four. You don't sleep much when you get to my age, young man. You're afraid to miss one precious moment. Understand?"

"Yes, I do," he said sincerely, liking her, regretting he didn't have the time for that tea.

"Well, you're welcome to come back and visit me anytime. You have nice manners." She grinned. "That's rare, nowadays."

"Thank you, Ethel. I'll take you up on that offer someday." He waved and walked to his car.

Christ!

His damn job never permitted a second for relaxation. He was getting fed up with the long hours spent on the werewolf case and he was way overdue for a vacation. If they didn't apprehend that bastard soon . . . he might start baying at the moon himself.

Russ drove north on Palmer. He slowed as he passed the intersection with Newton and craned his neck to view the church. That poor reporter! What a way to go. He drove on, passed the junction with Powell, and reached Avalon. There were still twenty minutes remaining before he had to meet with Chief Watson. Plenty of time to see how Gretchen was doing. He turned left on Avalon. Why hadn't she called him? Had she finally tired of rubbing his nose in his guilt? No. No, that was unfair, he chided himself. She didn't blame him for Brian's death.

He parked in front of the Painter house and got out of the car.

Odd.

All the lights in the house were out except one upstairs. Ordinarily, Gretchen would keep all the lights in the place blazing. She wouldn't be in bed this early. Was she sick? Was that why she hadn't called?

Russ walked toward the front door. He saw a huge shadow pass across the shade on the upstairs window.

281

Must be Harvey. At least he was home.

Wait a minute.

He paused, noticing another unusual item. Despite the darkness, he could see the lawn was unkempt, the grass over six inches high. Had their lawnmower gone on the bilnk? Gretchen prided herself on her neatness, and she made Harvey keep the lawn mowed and the borders trimmed.

She had to be sick.

Or possibly Harvey was the sick one.

Russ walked up to the door and rang the bell.

No one responded to the chimes.

He pressed the button again.

Minutes passed.

"Gretchen!" he called to attract their attention. "Gretchen! It's me, Russ!"

Another minute elapsed and no one opened the door to greet him.

Christ!

What a waste! He took the time from his busy schedule to pay them a visit and they didn't have the courtesy to acknowledge his presence. Maybe they didn't want to see him.

Suited him fine.

He would head for the station and the meeting with Chief Watson.

Screw them!

Russ looked up at the window and spotted the shadow again.

What the hell was going on here?

Angry, he pounded on the door. "Gretchen! Open your door. It's Russ."

Harvey obviously was home. Why didn't he answer the door? Was he too engrossed in building up those biceps of his or reading his comics?

Russ raised his fist to knock on the door again. He'd break the—

Biceps?

Comics?

Christ!

He froze.

Christ!

It couldn't be.

What else had the psychic seen? Think, Gilson, think! What else? A police uniform. A casket. Tears.

Oh, dear God in heaven!

What else? Think! A hairy face. Teeth. The shield that protected. No, those didn't apply. But the others?

He gazed at the lighted window. No sign of the shadow. He rapped on the door, determined not to depart until his suspicions were allayed. But were they justified? Could Harvey be the . . . be the . . . he *couldn't* be! The very idea was stupid. Or was it?

Face it, Gilson! You've definitely been working on the damn werewolf case too long. Suspecting Harvey Painter?

He sighed, convinced he was overwrought, his nerves frazzled. Now he was building mountains out of mole-hills. Besides, Chief Watson would be waiting.

Russ took a step in the direction of his car.

"Uncle Russ?" someone inside the house yelled. "Come on in." It sounded like Harvey.

"Harvey? Is that you?"

"Yeah. Come on in. We've been expecting you."

"Oh."

Russ opened the front door and hesitated before entering. Why were all the downstairs lights out?

"Harvey?"

Harvey didn't answer.

"Harvey? Why are all the lights out?"

Harvey didn't answer.

"Harvey!" Russ shouted, impatient. "Why are all the lights out? Where are you? Where's your mother?"

There was still no response.

"Harvey! Damn it! Answer me, boy!"

Somewhere in the depths of the pitch-black house a floorboard creaked.

Russ drew his service revolver.

"Harvey! I'm coming in. Where are you?"

Russ warily moved along the hall, his back against the wall, listening intently. He didn't like this. He didn't like this one bit. Something was drastically wrong. He stopped in the living room doorway and used his free hand to grope for the light switch. His fingers closed on it, and he snapped it up.

The lights didn't come on.

Christ.

"Harvey!"

He wasn't surprised when Harvey didn't give an answer. This entire setup stunk. In fact, the *house* stunk, as though the garbage hadn't been taken out in weeks.

"Gretchen!"

He cautiously moved to the base of the stairs. The shadow had been on Harvey's window. Harvey must be in his room. What the hell kind of game was the boy playing?

"Harvey! You'd better answer me, if you know what's good for you!"

There was a swishing sound upstairs, ending as abruptly as it began.

"Harvey!"

He could call in for a backup. But what if he was wrong and there was a perfectly logical explanation for all of this?

Something squeaked.

Russ tightened his grip on his gun and stepped up the stairs, one at a time, pausing frequently to listen. He edged to the top and peered around the corner. One door, evidently Harvey's, was open and light was pouring into the hall. The only other door was closed.

The rotten odor in the air was much stronger now.

He crouched and sidled the length of the hall until he reached the open door.

What *was* that smell? He knew he should recognize the source of it, but he couldn't. Decayed meat, maybe?

Russ stood and spun, extending his arms, pointing the revolver into the room, alert for any movement or noise.

"Christ!" he blurted, not believing what he was seeing. Posters everywhere. One wall was pasted over with werewolf posters. Hairy face after hairy face. Gleaming teeth. On top of a dresser was a stack of magazines and comics.

Every piece fit.

The puzzle was complete.

Russ cocked his Magnum and walked to the other door. He glanced down at the bottom edge. There was no light showing. He clasped the doorknob and slowly twisted. The door swung open easily. He found the switch and flooded the interior with light.

The room was empty, but the odor was stronger here than anywhere else in the house.

Strange.

The bed was neatly made. Imprinted in the center of the bedspread was the impression of a body, as if someone had lain there for a considerable length of time.

Where was Gretchen?

Russ moved to the top of the stairs. If the lights upstairs worked, and the lights downstairs didn't, then someone had pulled a fuse or tripped a breaker. Deliberately.

Harvey was playing games.

Russ stepped down the stairs, his eyes probing the darkness below.

Where was Harvey?

The lights upstairs abruptly blinked out, casting the entire house into gloomy blackness.

It was time to leave and call in that backup.

Russ cautiously walked to the front door. He reached for the knob, then froze, remembering.

He'd left the door open!

What the hell! He gripped the doorknob and turned, but the door wouldn't open. Someone had locked it while he was upstairs; locked it with a key, and he couldn't get out.

Russ faced the living room, his senses primed, ready. Harvey must think he had him trapped. Well, that son-of-a-bitch was in for one big shock! He silently tiptoed to the living room. His eyes were beginning to adjust to the lack of illumination and he could discern furniture and other, unfamiliar, configurations. He could distinguish the sofa, the television set, and the shape of the rocker.

Where was Harvey? Had he hauled ass? Or was he hiding somewhere in the house? In the kitchen? Did Gretchen have a basement? Finding him would be hopeless without any lights.

A slight creaking sound, almost at his elbow, startled him.

Russ crouched and scanned the room and the hall, seeking the cause.

Something moved, a fluctuation of the shadows to his left, and he squinted, forcing his eyes to focus. There was the television and the rocking chair . . .

The rocking chair! The contour was too bulky, too pronounced for an empty chair!

Russ swept his gun up, bringing the Magnum to bear, yet even as he did the ink-black mass leaped, and he knew the thing would be on top of him before he could get off a shot.

It was lightning fast.

A heavy form crashed into him, smashing him against the wall, and his service revolver hurtled from his fingers. An agonizing pain lanced through his back as he struck the floor. Hairy hands closed on his throat and squeezed.

Russ rose to his knees, exerting all his strength in an attempt to dislodge the vise around his throat. He pounded on the steely arms holding him down, but they wouldn't budge.

The thing . . . *the werewolf* . . . hissed.

Russ couldn't see clearly, he didn't know exactly how the werewolf was positioned, and he wasn't certain at which points the werewolf would be most vulnerable. He didn't have much time to consider the issue, either. He balled his right hand into a fist and struck at where he thought the werewolf's face would be.

He missed.

Russ drew back his fist and punched again.

This time, he connected with a furry, yielding ear.

The werewolf snarled and increased its pressure on its victim.

Russ felt excruciating anguish pierce his neck, and he swung again.

No reaction.

Russ hit the werewolf a third time.

Still no effect.

In desperation, Russ brought both of his fists around, boxing the werewolf on its ears, realizing that if he wasn't able to break free soon, he never would.

The werewolf shrieked and backed away.

Russ lunged to his feet, gagging, wondering what had happened to his gun, knowing he had to get out of the house. The werewolf had the edge in the murky surroundings. There wasn't time to try and bust through the door. A window would be his best bet. There was one located on the far side of the living room. He girded himself, inhaled deeply, and ran toward the window.

Midway across the room a hard object collided with his shins and he went down, tumbling against the sofa.

Russ involuntarily groaned as he quickly stumbled to his feet. His left ankle was throbbing and would barely support his weight.

Christ!

Howling, the werewolf rammed into its prey.

Russ was knocked sideways, unable to retain his footing. His body collided with the rocking chair and he fell, carrying the chair with him, his arm entangled in the horizontal rungs. He landed on his back, dazed.

The werewolf was growling.

Russ shoved the rocking chair aside and scrambled to his feet one more time. He spotted the werewolf, crouched near the sofa, just as it screeched and bounded straight at him.

The werewolf impacted violently with its quarry and they toppled to the floor, the werewolf on top. The victim went momentarily limp, and the werewolf, glimpsing a white patch of exposed throat, tore at the neck with claws and teeth, rending and gouging, slicing and goring, exulting in a surge of primal fury, spattering the area with blood and chunks of flesh.

Russ was vaguely conscious of pain, of a moist sensation on his chest, and of the werewolf pinning him to the floor. He wanted to rise and run, to break free, but he felt so very tired. His limbs were becoming weaker by the second. What was the matter with him? Why was it becoming so difficult to think? Was he dying? Was that it? Funny, the way he seemed so detached about it all. Funny, too, that Harvey was the one killing him. Harvey, of all people. But maybe it was appropriate. A balancing of the scales, an atonement for Brian.

His body convulsed and his sentience faded.

A werewolf!

Murdered by a fucking werewolf!

Christ—

Save me!

"AND YOU'RE SURE IT'S HIS?"

"Yes, sir. We verified it with the motor pool. No doubt about it. It's his."

"Bob, I don't like this."

"Me either, Chief. We argued a lot, but I liked Russ."

Chief Watson glanced up at Captain Grout. "You're a bit premature with the past tense, aren't you?"

Grout paled. He was standing at attention in front of the desk. "Sorry. But the blood we found on the steering wheel, and those pieces of skin . . ."

Chief Watson held up his hand. "Okay. Okay. Where was the car found?"

"On Surf Avenue. About halfway between Ocean City and the Dunes. It was parked by the side of the road, the lights on, the radio blaring, and the driver's door wide open. A motorist passed it and called us from a service station."

"Any prints?" Chief Watson asked.

"None yet. The boys are still dusting it. The lab techs are analyzing the blood and some hair found clinging to the seat."

"I want it gone over with a fine-tooth comb," Chief

Watson ordered.

"Don't worry about that. It will be."

"Have a seat." Chief Watson indicated one of the chairs for Grout to sit in, then spun his own so he could gaze out his window at the traffic below.

Grout patiently waited several minutes for Chief Watson to speak. Finally, he decided to break the silence himself. "Maybe we'll discover a clue, a big one, and we'll be able to break this damn case," he offered optimistically.

"I pray you're right." Chief Watson sighed. "This one has me close."

"Close?"

"To the edge. You know how some cases get to you, how you live them, breathe them, until they're solved. I've been immersed in this werewolf case since Officer Winslow was killed, I've taken it personally, and the strain is beginning to take a toll. I looked in the mirror last night and saw wrinkles I never had before, worry lines that weren't there six months ago. With each attack I feel worse inside. I've started to lose sleep. Not just one night at a time, either. Two. Three, all in a row. And after Mckeen got it, I felt worse. I find myself speculating on how our werewolf conducted his day. Where did he eat? What kind of social life did he have? How many times a day did he shit? See what I mean?"

"I think so," Grout said softly.

"After the Fourth of July massacre, as the press so quaintly dubbed it, I thought I was going nuts. All those poor bastards killed or injured. How is Officer Patterson, by the way?"

"Still comatose."

"Have you seen Officer Ballinger? All her life, all her

spirit is gone. She spends all her off-duty time sitting in the hospital beside Patterson."

"I've seen her," Grout stated sadly when Chief Watson paused.

"And now this. Russ Gilson! How the hell did the werewolf get Russ?"

"I don't know, sir."

"Who was the last one to see him alive?"

"Officer Doyle, as far as we know."

"And Russ gave no indication of where he was going?" Chief Watson inquired.

"None. He told Doyle he'd meet with you in an hour, as you'd requested," Grout replied.

"And we both know he never arrived at that meeting. We've had no idea where he was until that car was discovered this morning. And now . . ." Chief Watson stood and leaned against the window frame.

"Would you like some coffee?" Grout asked, perceiving his superior's turmoil, wanting to change the subject.

"No." Chief Watson shook his head. "I want that hairy son-of-a-bitch! I want his hide nailed right there!" He pointed at his east wall. "I want to gloat over his dead body, and jump for joy when the bastard is dead. Do you realize what this means?" He looked at Grout.

"I'm not sure."

"It means I'm involved, damn it! Subjectively, emotionally involved with this case. The very thing I accused Leta Ballinger of being and the very reason I wouldn't allow her to work on the case."

"Don't be so hard on yourself," Grout tried to soothe him. "By now, we're all involved with this one. Every officer on the force wants to be the one to blow this fucker to pieces."

Chief Watson whirled. "And don't you see, Bob? Don't you see?"

"See what?" Grout blurted, confused.

"That attitude violates every legal principle we're obligated to uphold! We're a police force, not a bunch of fanatic vigilantes! Understand what I'm trying to say?"

"Yes. But I don't agree."

"What?"

"We're only human, Scott. I've heard you say a dozen times that you'd like to blow the werewolf away. We can't help but get involved in this one. One of our officers has been attacked. This thing has probably killed Russ now, too, and you want us to remain the objective, detached, professionals we're ideally supposed to be? Come on! Be serious. At least be realistic." Grout stopped, surprised at his own eloquence.

Chief Watson smiled. "Thanks, Bob. I needed that."

Grout grinned. "No problem, Chief."

Chief Watson sat in his chair. "The press will go crazy with this one. Our tourist trade will dry to a trickle. The governor already has me on his shit list. Now he'll probably demand that I be beheaded."

"Can we keep it from the media for a while? Buy us some time?" Grout suggested.

"As far as is legally possible, I think we'll put the lid on this one. Damn!" Chief Watson frowned, downcast. "Poor Russ. I can't believe the werewolf got him."

"Me neither," Grout agreed.

"I want every available person on this," Chief Watson directed.

"We've already got every available person on this,"

Grout reminded him.

"See if you can pull two or three officers from regular duty and add them to the werewolf task force."

"We're already operating on a skeleton regular shift," Grout protested.

"I know. But see what you can do."

"Yes, sir," Grout conceded, wondering where in the world he could dig up two additional bodies.

"I want you, personally, to go through Russ's desk and see if you can find something."

"Something that might give us an indication of where he went that night before the meeting?"

"Exactly. Maybe he had a clue he didn't inform me about," Chief Watson speculated.

"Doesn't sound like the Russ I know," Grout observed.

"Yeah. If he had something, he'd let me in on it. Russ wasn't the whimsical type." Chief Watson sat back in his chair, reflecting.

"Hey."

"What?"

Grout was grinning. "You're a bit premature with the past tense, aren't you?"

"Bob," Chief Watson smiled. "I ever mention to you that you're a pain in the ass?"

"Hundreds of times."

They laughed.

August 1

CHIEF WATSON WAS SITTING IN THE lounge, morosely munching on a peanut-butter-and-jelly sandwich, when he heard his name called. He looked up and saw Grout approaching. Two others were with the captain. Walking on his right was Officer Ballinger. On his left was a tall young man wearing jeans and a green T-shirt. The young man had an intelligent, inquisitive air about him. He had black hair and brown eyes.

"Chief," Grout said, grinning impishly, "I've got someone here for you to meet."

"Oh?"

"Yep. Officer Ballinger ran into him as she was leaving the station and she brought him to me. We have a guy who came all the way from . . ." Grout paused. "Where was that again?" he asked the young man, smirking.

"Bethlehem," the newcomer answered.

Chief Watson could tell the boy didn't appreciate Grout's sarcastic attitude one bit.

"That's it," Grout continued. "All the way from Bethlehem, Pennsylvania, to tell us how we can catch the werewolf. . ."

"I never said that," the young man spoke up.

"What's your name?" Chief Watson asked the boy, not enjoying Grout's derision himself.

"Allan Baxter, sir," he nervously responded. "With an A."

"And what might I do for you, Allen Baxter, with an A?" Chief Watson placed the remainder of his sandwich on the table.

"I'm here to offer my services, if you can use them," Allan replied.

Chief Watson studied the boy, measuring his character. "And what services might those be?"

"I'm a tracker, sir."

"A tracker?"

"Yes, sir."

Grout laughed. "Sure your name isn't Tarzan Baxter, sonny boy?"

"Captain Grout." Chief Watson indicated his annoyance with the formal tone he employed. "I thought you were engaged in important task force activities this afternoon, were you not?"

"Yes, sir."

"Then tend to them," Chief Watson commanded.

Grout departed, and Chief Watson noticed Officer Ballinger was doing her best to suppress a smile. He turned his attention to the boy again. "Now, you say you're a tracker?"

"Yes, sir."

"How do you think you can help us?"

"If you can show me some fresh tracks made by this werewolf, I can track him for you," Allan confidently stated.

"Oh? Just like that?" Chief Watson snapped his fingers.

296

"Not just like that," Allan said. "I can do it because I've spent years tracking. I've helped the police and park rangers before. I have a letter from the chief ranger in Nockamixol State Park testifying to my ability." He pulled an envelope from his back pocket and handed it to Chief Watson.

Chief Watson opened the envelope and slowly read the one-page letter enclosed. Finished, he set the letter on the table and eyed the boy. "You saved that girl's life," he observed.

"I did what any man would have done," Allan rejoined.

"Not many men have your evident skill. If a veteran ranger says you're one of the best damn trackers he's ever met, than you've got talent." Chief Watson considered a moment. "You think you can help me, do you?"

"I'd like to try," Allan admitted. "I've read about this werewolf in the papers and heard about him on the radio and the television. . . ."

"Killers are always big news," Chief Watson philosophized. "Says a lot for the mentality of our society, doesn't it?"

"Sir?"

"Nothing. Go on."

"Well, like I was saying, I've heard you're having a hard time catching this guy."

"The understatement of the century." Chief Watson grinned wearily.

"Have you tried tracking him?" Allan questioned him.

"Have you ever tried tracking in soft, dry sand?" Chief Watson retorted. "Believe me, it's not easy. Yes, some of our officers have tried to track the thing, but they always lost the trail. Once, after he killed a retired mechanic, we used dogs. They lost the scent. You think you can do better than them?"

"I'd try my best," Allan promised.

"Yes, I bet you would." Chief Watson thought for a minute. "Where are you staying, Allan?"

"My famiy has a cottage on Davenport Street. We're down here for the family vacation."

"Son, you might just be the answer to my prayers. I've utilized every law enforcement agency and every scientific technique conceivable and this werewolf has continued to elude us. I even used a psychic, although the information he supplied hasn't been of much assistance. Tell you what I'll do . . ." He glanced at Leta.

"Officer Ballinger?"

"Yes, sir.'

"Are you still on regular duty?"

"Yes, sir." Her mouth creased downward.

"Well, I can't afford to take you off it just at this moment." Chief Watson saw her evident disappointment. "But I am appointing you as our official department liaison."

"Liaison?" She was puzzled. "With what?"

"With our official consultant expert tracker." He pointed at Allan. "What about it, son?"

"That's the reason I came to see you." Allan beamed.

"I wish you'd come on your vacation sooner. Give Officer Ballinger your telephone number. If the werewolf attacks again I'll notify her and she will contact you. Fair enough?"

"Yes, sir."

"Fine." Chief Watson was hit by an afterthought. "Allan, how long is your family on vacation?"

"We'll be here for two weeks," Allan answered.

"Any chance you can stay longer?"

"Why?"

"Sometimes weeks elapse between attacks. I'd hate to think the werewolf won't strike while we have an opportunity to avail ourselves of your services." Chief Watson bit his lower lip, disturbed by the possibility.

"I could stay until the last week of August," Allan offered. "I start a new job in September, and I won't be able to stay after that."

"I can understand," Chief Watson said. "Okay. We're settled. Officer Ballanger, do you have any objections?"

"None, sir."

"I didn't think you would," Chief Watson cracked. "Now all we need do is wait for the werewolf to show himself again." He paused, then pounded the table in irritation. "Damn!"

"Something wrong?" Allan asked.

"Nothing much." Chief Watson stood up. "Except all these past months I've been dreading each new werewolf attack, and now I find myself looking forward to the next one with the fervent hope that we'll finally apprehend the son-of-a-bitch." He grinned. "Pardon my French."

"I think I understand," Allan said.

"Good." Chief Watson held out his right hand. "I'm glad one of us does."

They shook, and Chief Watson left, carrying the letter of recommendation and his partially eaten sandwich.

"I like him," Allan acknowledged.

"We all do." Leta was watching the Chief leave.

"Well, suppose I give you my phone number so you can reach me if the werewolf is spotted again." Allan drew a pen from his pocket, bent over, and extracted a napkin from one of the holders on the table.

Leta scrutinized him while he jotted down the number. He smiled and handed the paper napkin to her.

"Thanks," she said.

"Thank you for helping me find my way around here."

"I hope you can do it," she stated.

"Find the werewolf?"

They began walking toward the main doors.

"Yes," she answered. "I want him."

"Seems like everyone wants to find this werewolf." Allan grinned.

"I can only speak for myself." Leta placed her right hand on her revolver butt. "I have a personal reason for wanting to get him. He hurt someone very dear to me. Now that person is in a coma, has been since July fourth, and the doctors can't say for certain when he'll be normal again. Yes, I want that werewolf."

Allan was surprised by her intensity. "Well, Officer Ballinger, like I told Chief Watson, I'll do my best to track him down."

"Call me Leta. I hope you get the chance, Allan."

They reached the main doors and Allan held one open so Leta could pass through first. Outside, they paused before separating.

"It was nice meeting you," she said. "Hope I see you again, real soon."

"Mind if I ask you a question?" He was staring into her eyes, attempting to gauge her motivation.

"So long as it's not too personal." She grinned.

"What do you intend to do if we do find the werewolf?"

Her pretty face broke into a broad smile. "Be near you

phone, Allan. My intuition tells me you'll be hearing from me shortly. 'Bye." She walked off.

Allan, troubled, gazed up at the blue sky and asked himself a question: Do I know what I'm letting myself in for?

August 6

DAISY LARSON FINISHED TOTALING THE DAILY receipts, wrapped the bills in a rubber band, and carried her tally over to Curt West.

"Here you go, Curt." She deposited her collection on top of the counter Curt was working behind. He stopped his inventory of golf balls, looked up, and smiled. "Thanks, again, for covering for me," she added.

"No problem. I wouldn't want to stand in the way of your big date." Curt chuckled and waved at the door to the pro shop. "Enjoy yourself."

"Thanks, you adorable hunk, you!" she bubbled.

"Don't I wish."

Daisy whirled and hurried toward the back room and her locker.

Grinning, Curt resumed his inventory count. The zest of youth, he told himself. He could vividly remember when his veins would burn with anticipation. He sure would be depressed when Daisy quit the shop at the end of the summer. She was a breath of fresh air in the stuck-up environment of the Muncipal Golf Course. The majority of those who came to play their daily eighteen were somber, stodgy types, determined to improve their game at the expense of their humor, their humanity. Wasn't golf designed to be a relaxing pastime? Why was it, then, that so few of the people he saw on the course each day were laughing and having fun?

Curt paused, listening.

There was a faint scratching sound coming from the front of the shop, an area hidden from his view by the counter.

"Daisy?"

The scraping stopped.

"Daisy, is that you?" Curt asked.

"Did you say something, Curt?" she yelled from the back room. "I didn't catch it."

Curt stood up and surveyed the shop. The night was warm and they had the front door propped open with a putter. All of the items they sold and rented were neatly stacked on the appropriate shelves. The clubs were organized and arranged in their stacks. There was no sign of anyone else.

"What did you say?" Daisy called.

"Never mind!" he shouted. He glanced at the large clock over the door. Nearly ten. He looked through the bay window and glimpsed several stars.

"I still didn't hear what you said." Daisy came into the room. She had freshened her appearance and brushed her shiny red hair.

"I was talking to myself." He smiled, admiring her beauty.

"Did you answer yourself?" she asked.

"Yeah, why?"

"They say that's when you know you're off the deep end," she joked, and laughed.

303

"I've known I was crazy for years," he rejoined. "You'd better get going. I thought your date was for ten."

She shot a look at the clock. "Oh my God!" She walked behind the cash register and grabbed her brown leather purse. "I've got to get going. Thanks again, Curt. I'll see you tomorrow morning." She was halfway to the door.

"Yo!"

She stopped and faced him. "What?"

"Don't you stay out too late!" He winked and grinned.

"Yes, Daddy." Daisy gave a small wave and headed for her car, parked in the lot on the west side of the shop. Her clogs smacked on the pavement as she crossed the intervening twenty feet and reached for her car door.

That was when something growled.

Daisy paused and scanned the nearby green and the closest stand of trees. Was that a dog she'd heard? There was nothing in sight. She shrugged her slender shoulders and took hold of the chrome handle.

Something snarled.

Daisy shivered, suddenly petrified, recalling the howl they had heard back in June, remembering all the warnings the papers and the radio had given concerning the werewolf and the necessity of not being outside, at night, alone. If the growler wasn't someone playing a practical joke—and the only other person within a mile was Curt and he was still inside the pro shop; and if it wasn't a dog—and strays were rare this far from the city; then there was only one thing it could be . . . and she trembled at the idea . . . the werewolf!

It abruptly appeared out of the night, bounding onto the top of her Pinto, landing on all fours and hissing.

Daisy gaped, speechless, at the bristling figure, her

muscles frozen.

The werewolf leaned forward and glared into her eyes. Its right hand reached out and stroked her hair.

The contact broke her spell. She stepped backward and screamed.

The werewolf pounced, its greater bulk forcing her to the macadam, bruising her back and legs, tearing her green skirt, its claws closing on her neck.

Daisy kneed it and shrieked.

The werewolf reared up, grabbed her by the shoulders, and heaved her into the air.

Daisy stumbled a dozen feet and sprawled on the pavement, scraping her arms and elbows. Before she could rise the werewolf was on her again.

The werewolf howled, clamped its hands on her throat, and squeezed.

Daisy struggled, striking at its face.

"Me, you bastard! Try me!"

Suddenly Curt was there, swinging a putter, smashing the werewolf on the back of its head.

The werewolf released Daisy and staggered to one side, dropping to its knees.

"Run, Daisy, run!" Curt roughly yanked her to her feet. "Get into the shop and lock the door! Move, girl!" He shoved her to hasten her along, then faced the werewolf, the putter raised over his head.

Daisy ran, reaching the shop door. She looked back. The werewolf was standing now, hunched over, and snarling. It slowly circled Curt, seeking an opening.

"Curt!" she shouted. "Get inside with me!"

"Don't worry about me!" He didn't bother to glance at her. He kept his eyes on the werewolf. "Use the phone.

Call the cops!"

"Okay!" She rushed inside and pulled the phone from its cradle on the wall. Her hand was shaking, her fingers unsteady. She concentrated, striving to calm her frayed nerves. What was that damn emergency number? What was it? Nine . . . what?

Outside, the werewolf was howling.

The number came to her and she frantically dialed nine-one-one.

"Ocean City Police Department," a male voice answered.

"Help!" she shouted, the words coming in a rush. "Help us! This is Daisy Larson out at the Municipal Golf Course! The werewolf is here! The werewolf is here! Help us, please!"

"Calm down, Daisy, please," the officer said softly, but firmly. "Tell me exactly where you are."

"In the pro shop."

"Okay. Where is the werewolf?"

"He's outside. He's fighting Curt West. Please! Help us!"

"Just a second." The officer said something to someone else, but Daisy couldn't hear what it was.

Through the open door came the noise of the conflict in the parking lot. Curt was cursing, and the werewolf was snarling.

"All right, Daisy." The officer had returned to the line. "We've dispatched help. We estimate the first patrol car should arrive there in eight minutes. Can you hold out for that long?"

The fight was reaching a crescendo of frenzied ferocity.

"We'll try. Please," she begged, "please hurry! The thing is horrible! It's trying to kill us!"

"Our men are on their way," the officer assured her. "Leave this line open," he directed her. "We want to maintain contact."

The commotion outside unexpectedly ceased.

Daisy groaned.

"What's the matter?" the officer urgently asked. "Why'd you do that?"

Daisy kept her eyes riveted on the doorway.

"What is the matter?" he repeated his question.

"I don't know," she answered, quaking. "Curt and the thing were fighting. Now it's real quiet. I don't know what happened. Maybe I should look outside?" she suggested.

"No!" the policeman almost screamed. "Stay where you are! Daisy, is the door to the shop locked?"

"No."

"No? Why didn't you tell me?"

"I didn't—" she began.

"Never mind!" he cut her off. "Can you get to the door and lock it?"

"I think so," she said bravely.

"Better yet," he quickly added, "is there somewhere you can hide and protect yourself? A sturdy closet, maybe? Anything?" His concern was straining his voice.

"We've got a back room, but I've got to check on Curt."

"No!" he shouted. "No! Lock yourself in the back room. Our units are five or six minutes away and closing fast. If you can stay safe until then . . ." His voice trailed off.

"But what about Curt?" she demanded.

"We'll check on Curt. We've got to think of you now. Can you lock yourself in the back room until we arrive?"

"I think so."

"Don't think. Do it!" he ordered.

"All right, but please hurry!"

"Five minutes," he reminded her.

Daisy glanced up at the clock, then at the doorway. "Oh, my God!" she exclaimed, panicked.

"What's the matter?" the officer shouted. "Daisy, are you there? Daisy? Daisy?"

"I'm here," she whispered, so faintly he could barely hear her.

"What's wrong?"

"It's him."

"The werewolf?"

"Yes," she replied timidly.

"Where?"

"He's . . . he's . . . standing in the doorway." Daisy inched toward the back room, her wide eyes glued to the menacing dark form.

"Get in that back room!" the officer urged her. "Move, girl, move!"

"Okay. She placed the receiver on the nearest counter and backed toward the security of the rear room. If she could close and lock the heavy door . . .

The werewolf dropped to all fours and growled, an ominous, low rumbling in his chest.

Daisy darted for her goal.

Howling, the werewolf charged.

August 7

"THAT GIRL SURE WAS A SCRAPPER, wasn't she?"

"She put up a good fight."

"I'm glad she'll survive, Chief."

"So am I, Bob. So am I. Wish we could say the same for the poor slob in the parking lot." Chief Watson gazed at the blanket-covered form lying in a wide pool of blood. How many more times must he go through this, he wondered, before they stopped the werewolf once and for all?

"Yeah," Grout agreed. They were standing outside the pro shop, in front of the large bay window. "Fractured skull, broken neck, and a throat like spaghetti. At least he managed to put up a good fight. The girl says he saved her life."

"Has someone obtained her report or is she still hysterical?" Chief Watson asked.

"The boys who followed the ambulance to the hospital are waiting for permission from the attending physician before taking her story. We have bits and pieces, though. The werewolf jumped her in the parking lot, this Curt West went after it with a putter, it killed him and attacked her in the shop. If she hadn't been able to knock over that club stand, she never would have made it to that back locker room."

"Her guardian angel was watching over her," Chief Watson commented.

"Yeah. When the son-of-a-bitch tripped, she was lucky. Good thing that door withstood his assault until our units arrived and scared him off."

"What time is it now?" Chief Watson wanted to know. He began buttoning his overcoat. The late night breeze was chilling him.

"Sometime after one," Grout answered after consulting his watch. "The lab boys will be here all night."

An officer emerged from the shop and walked over to them.

"Were you able to get hold of him?" Chief Watson inquire hopefully.

"Yes, sir."

"Good. What'd he say, Officer Ballinger?"

"He said he would be waiting for me to pick him up at five and he'd be able to begin tracking at the first light of dawn."

"Good. Good." Chief Watson rubbed his cold fingers together. "This might be the break we need."

"You think this Baxter boy can actually do it?" Grout asked skeptically.

"Do we have any viable recourse?" Chief Watson countered. "We have no fingerprints, no clear footprints, no description except hair and teeth, and no idea of what the bastard looks like without the werewolf mask. We are no closer to apprehending this guy than we were the day after his first attack. If Allan Baxter can track the werewolf to his daytime lair, I'll kiss his feet."

"Sure hope he bathes regularly," Grout joked.

"Do I accompany him?" Leta broke in.

"Are you crazy?" Grout retorted.

"Yes, you will," Chief Watson said.

"What?" Grout exploded impetuously, incredulous. "Why don't we send two dozen men along with our great white hunter?"

"Because"—Chief Watson sighed—"we don't want an army following Baxter and possibly erasing some clue vital to his tracking. We send two officers, Ballinger and one other, to trail some distance behind Baxter, always keeping him in sight. That way Baxter can track undisturbed. Ballinger will carry a radio and maintain contact with us. Even I know enough about animals and men to know they sometimes backtrack themselves to confuse and elude pursuers. Too many officers with Baxter might obliterate some of the tracks. No, I think my way is the best way."

"I think so too," Leta eagerly agreed.

"You seem happier than usual tonight," Grout observed.

"Haven't you heard the news?" She glanced at both of them.

"What news?" Grout looked at Chief Watson and they shrugged their shoulders in unison.

"About Earl!" she replied, excited.

"Good news, I trust," Chief Watson stated.

"Yep. The doctor called me this evening and said Earl came out of his coma late this afternoon. He's still in serious condition, but the doctor says his chances of total recovery are now tremendously improved. Isn't that good news?" She beamed.

"The best I've heard since I don't know when," Chief Watson admitted.

"Damn good news," Grout added.

"I'm so happy!" Leta laughed. "I'm on cloud nine."

"Well, Officer Ballinger." Chief Watson was smiling. "I think you'd best float on home and get some rest. I know it might be hard, but try. Pick up Baxter at five and immediately bring him out here. We'll have everything cleared up here by then."

"Might toss his cookies if he saw that mess." Grout pointed at the corpse.

"I wonder if that poor girl will ever recover from tonight," Leta speculated, gazing at the puddle of glistening blood surrounding the body of Curt West, revealed in the lights from the half-dozen police cruisers encircling his torn and bleeding torso.

"Do any of us ever recover from senseless atrocities?" Chief Watson said, frowning. "I wonder."

"Are you ready to begin, son?"

"Yes, sir, I am."

"Good."

Allan watched Chief Watson walk over to a group of task force personnel and begin conversing with them. He saw Captain Grout appear from inside the pro shop and approach Chief Watson. The early morning sun was just visible above the eastern horizon, rays of bright sunshine gleaming off the dew coating the lush green grass of the golf course. He glanced at the two officers who were slated to follow him. One was Leta Ballinger, the other a policeman named Doyle. Leta held a walkie-talkie, Doyle carried a shotgun.

"Any time you're ready"—Chief Watson was back— "so are we."

"I'm all set," Allan said.

"Okay. Now listen carefully and we'll cover this again. Those two"—Chief Watson indicated Ballinger and Doyle—"are assigned to follow a prudent distance behind you. Officer Ballinger will maintain constant contact with us. Officer Doyle will cover you with the shotgun. I will monitor your progress from my car. Captain Grout and I will be in the lead cruiser and six other patrol cars are following us. We will keep as close to your actual position as the roads and highways permit. A dozen extra cars are parked at strategic intervals between this point and Ocean City. We have every reason to believe the trail will lead into the city, if we're lucky and can follow it that far. Remember, at no point will you be more than a minute from additional help. These two officers will be with you all the time. I want to impress upon you that your life will not be in any danger. We've organized this hunt so you will be as safe and protected as is humanly possible."

"I'll be fine," Allan assured him.

"We want to insure that you remain that way," Chief Watson reiterated, then stopped, listening.

Allan heard the noise at the same moment. A loud *whump-whump-whump*, growing louder, coming from the north. He looked up and saw it closing in, a swift helicopter swooping over the nearest trees.

"Oh, yes, I nearly forgot." Chief Watson was smiling. "As added insurance, I've called in the State Police helicopter to assume aerial surveillance for as long as its fuel lasts."

The helicopter hovered one hundred feet over their heads and the pilot waved.

Chief Watson returned the gesture, then faced Allan.

313

"Well, son, the rest is all up to you."

"Then I guess I'd better get this show on the road." Allan grinned, feeling his stomach muscles tense up.

"I was a bit surprised your parents didn't come with you," Chief Watson observed.

"What could they do?" Allan stooped over and tightened the white laces on his sneakers. He was wearing old jeans and a faded denim shirt. "I'm the tracker in the family. Besides, they felt they'd just get in the way."

"What's holding us up?" Captain Grout said as he joined them.

"Nothing," Chief Watson answered. He extended his hand to Allan. "Good luck, son."

Allan shook. "Thanks."

"We're ready," Leta stated.

Allan moved away, across the parking lot and onto the golf course. The pro shop was located south of the course itself, flanking the fairway between holes one and two. He jogged to a point fifty yards from the shop. Chief Watson had told him that the officers who arrived first last night and chased the werewolf off saw it cut across the course in this direction. He walked slowly, examining the grass, searching for any sign that the werewolf had passed on a northerly bearing.

Almost immediately, he found what he was looking for.

Evidently, the werewolf had departed in extreme haste last night, not bothering to hide its tracks. Whoever it was, it was tall, well over six feet, and heavy, at least two hundred pounds, if its footprints were any adequate representation. Six tracks were discernible in a narrow strip of thin grass. Thankfully, whoever tended the course didn't do a perfect job.

314

Allan knelt, closely scrutinized the impressions, and gazed in the direction they were heading—due north toward a cluster of trees a half mile away. The werewolf was making for cover.

Allan calculated. Time was crucial. He could hear the helicopter overhead. How long would their fuel last? He still had twelve to fourteen hours of daylight remaining, but if the trail proved difficult he could run out of sunlight before pinpointing the werewolf's lair. That wouldn't do. The werewolf would have another night to kill some innocent person. If time was critical, shortcuts were necessary. Put your mind in the werewolf's head, he directed himself. Try and think like the werewolf would. The werewolf didn't want to confront the police last night. It desired escape, and concealment, and accordingly ran for those trees.

Smiling, Allan stood and continued jogging in the direction of the timber. What if I'm wrong? he thought. What if the werewolf changed its course at midpoint on the fairway? Then the trail would have to be backtracked until he rediscovered the turning angle.

I've got to be right, Allan told himself. I can't waste precious time seeking each individual track. I've got to anticipate and accommodate. If the werewolf made a direct beeline for the trees, then he would discover more tracks at the entrance spot into the timber. He had to be right!

He was.

Ten feet from the trees the grass ended, replaced by soft red earth. Clearly imprinted where it must have bounded into the woods were more werewolf tracks.

Allan dropped to his knees and bent over the tracks. These were clearer than the ones on the fairway, the con-

315

tours and shadings more precise. He was impressed by the strength of the leg muscles which made the tracks. The feet were jammed into the earth with powerful force. If the werewolf kept this up, tracking him would be a breeze.

The helicopter was poised above the trees, the pilot waiting.

Allan looked over his shoulder. Leta and the one called Doyle were twenty yards behind him and running his way. Good. He rose and hiked into the woods, grateful for the loose ground, easily following the trail, marveling at the manner in which the werewolf bulled its way through the brush. Why hadn't the werewolf attempted to hide its passage? Was it that contemptuous of the police and their limited ability to follow it? Was it really that difficult to track in sand, as Chief Watson maintained? Maybe some day he would find out for himself.

Suddenly he stopped, upset. The tracks were gone! That would teach him! He knew better. Never think when you're tracking, just track. The first basic rule.

Allan spun and reversed direction.

The werewolf had abruptly altered its course and was now moving due east, keeping to the timber.

Good.

Allan followed the tracks for forty minutes until they broke from the trees and hit—a highway.

Six police cars were stopped in the southbound lane. Two officers were directing traffic around the cruisers. Chief Watson and Captain Grout were standing by the side of the road, engaged in conversation.

Allan ran up a small bank and stood alongside them. "I'm a bit surprised to see you here," he said, grinning.

"Officer Ballinger kept us posted on your progress,"

Chief Watson explained. "It wasn't hard for us to determine where you would come out."

"Where are we?" Allan asked.

"Bay Avenue," Grout replied.

"Is this one of his tracks?" Chief Watson pointed at a smudged track in the gravel bordering the highway.

Allan studied it. "Yeah," he responded.

"Then here we go again." Chief Watson patted Allan on the shoulder.

Allan ran, jogging south now, adhering to the tracks. The werewolf had reached the highway and bore south, not bothering to run on the tarmac, running on the softer gravel instead. The prints were not as defined as in the woods, but they were unmistakably the mark of the werewolf.

The sun ascended well above the horizon.

The helicopter slowly circled above him.

Leta and Doyle were forty yards behind him.

Chief Watson and his police motorcade were fifty yards back and creeping after him.

Allan checked his watch. Eight thirty. Where was the werewolf heading? It appeared to be skirting Ocean City and bearing due south. He could see the city to his left, a row of quaint cottages several hundred yards distant on the far side of a field marking the outer limits of habitation.

The sun climbed higher.

Allan walked now, his body fatigued. The temperature was rising rapidly. He could imagine how hot it would be by late afternoon. He hoped he would locate the werewolf by then.

An hour elapsed, and still the werewolf stuck to

the gravel.

Allan's mind drifted. So his coming to Ocean City wasn't a complete washout this year. His vacation was actually exciting, in a perverse sort of way. Who would have ever imagined he'd be tracking a werewolf? Most likely it was some insane person who thought he was a werewolf. He remembered the cute Klien girl. This tracking was even more important than hers had been. This time more than one life was at stake. How many had the werewolf killed to date? He didn't know. But he knew the werewolf would continue killing until stopped, permanently. Behind bars for life would be his guess.

The tracks stopped.

Allan halted and stooped low.

The final track was twisted, inclined towards the east and the tarmac.

No! If the werewolf traveled any distance on the highway the tracks could be lost. Or, at the very least, it would require hours before he located the point where the werewolf had left the road.

Allan glanced both ways, made sure no traffic was near him, and ran across the highway. Maybe fortune would smile on him. Maybe the werewolf had simply crossed the road and resumed its southerly course.

Yes and no.

Yes, the werewolf had crossed the tarmac, but the huge tracks, instead of continuing south, headed east toward Ocean City.

Allan paused and studied the terrain ahead. A field five hundred yards wide, covered with brush and choked with tall grass and reeds, separated the highway from the nearest homes.

The tracks led across the field.

Allan resumed tracking, the going tedious, laborious, because the earth was firmer and covered with assorted weeds. One factor in his favor was the spacing of the tracks. They were closer together, as if the werewolf had deliberately slowed. Why? The werewolf was suddenly cautious, here in the middle of a deserted field. It made no sense. Why?

The tracks became less defined. The werewolf had been treading lightly now, stealthily. What was the reason? Had it seen someone? A dog, maybe?

There was a small but steep thicket-cluttered hill in front of him.

Allan spotted hand prints now and realized the werewolf had dropped to all fours.

What the blazes was it up to?

He pushed his way through the brush and reached the crest of the hill. Suddenly there were flies everywhere and a repugnant, acrid odor. He gagged, his lungs heaving, the stench nauseating, overpowering. He glanced around, seeking the cause.

That was when he saw her.

She had been a small child of eight or ten. Her curly hair, once blond, was caked with blood and dirt. Grime covered her face. One of her blue eyes was protruding from the socket. Her neck was ripped open, exposing ragged tendons, ruptured blood vessels, and white bone. One of her arms was wrenched at an unnatural angle. The remains of a tattered pink dress were clinging to her tender body. Her abdomen was gouged open, her intestines draped over her thin legs.

Allan hastily backed away from the corpse, tripped,

319

and tumbled down the hill. He struggled to his knees and the reaction set in, doubling him over as he vomited, his senses swirling.

"Allan?" he heard someone call.

He tried to rise, but his limbs were weak, faintness overwhelming him.

"Allan? Where are you?" It was Leta.

He opened his mouth to shout an answer and fell forward, blacking out.

"I'm so embarrassed."

"No need to be."

"But I fainted!"

"Had you ever seen anything like that before?"

"No, Leta. Thank God."

"Then don't blame yourself, Allan," she soothed him.

"How long was I out?" he asked.

"Two hours."

"What?" he couldn't believe it.

"There was no need to bring you around sooner. We had to settle this first." She gazed sadly at the hill in the field, currently swarming with police investigators and members of the task force. "They took her away about fifteen minutes ago."

"Who was she?"

"Leslie Unger. Her mother reported her missing thirty minutes before you discovered the body. Leslie was supposed to have spent the night with a girl friend. Her mother didn't realize she never showed up at the girl friend's, and the girl friend assumed she wasn't able to come. It wasn't until this morning that the mother called the girl friend and learned Leslie never arrived." Leta frowned. "And now the werewolf has another victim to add to his string," she stated coldly.

"Dear God."

"Here comes Chief Watson."

Allan followed her gaze and saw Chief Watson and Captain Grout approaching from the hill. He stood, rising from the stretcher they'd place him on. Leta, who'd been sitting beside him, also rose.

"How's Tarzan feeling?" Grout quipped when they were three feet away.

Chief Watson stopped and shot a withering glance at Grout. "Not now. Get back there and supervise the search."

"Yes, sir." Grout was gone.

"How are you feeling, Allan?" Chief Watson's concern showed.

"Fine."

"You sure?"

"I'm feeling fine," Allan assured him. "I'm ready to track again."

"I'm gratified to hear that," Chief Watson said as he mopped beads of perspiration from his brow with his jacket sleeve. "Especially in light of the latest."

"What's happened?" Allan anxiously inquired. "Did you lose the trail?"

"No." Chief Watson shook his head. "I've got my men searching for the place where the werewolf left the field. We have another, bigger problem."

"What is it?" Allan could see a dozen officers fanning across the field, seeking the tracks.

"That," Chief Watson replied, raising his hand and pointing at the western horizon.

Allan turned. "Oh, no!" he blurted.

Completely filling the western sky was a gigantic bank of roiling black clouds. Flashes of lightning periodically punctured the dark mass.

"I've called the National Weather Service," Chief Watson stated, frowning. "Initially, they didn't expect this storm front to arrive until late this evening. Unfortunately, low pressure systems aren't very predictable. This one picked up speed and is now expected to arrive in less than two hours."

"Two hours?" Allan glanced at Chief Watson and Leta. "But we're so close!"

"I know," Chief Watson lamented morosely. "I know."

"Maybe we've still got time," Leta optimistically interjected.

"I don't see how," Chief Watson commented.

"She's right," Allan agreed. "If I can trace the werewolf to his lair before the storm hits, we have a chance."

"It's worth a try," Chief Watson admitted thoughtfully. "What have we got to lose? If you can't do it, the storm will obliterate every track it made last night and we'll need to wait until the son-of-a-bitch strikes again."

"So it's a go?" Leta eagerly questioned.

Chief Watson smiled. "It's a go," he conceded.

Suddenly there was a loud commotion from the field. One of the officers was yelling and waving.

"I think this is an omen." Chief Watson grinned.

"How do you mean?" Allan wanted to know.

"I believe that young officer flapping his arms like a bird in flight has just found what we need."

Chief Watson led them to the northeast corner of the field.

322

"Is this what you wanted to find?" the officer asked Chief Watson as they neared him.

"Here's the man who can tell us," Chief Watson indicated Allan. "Go to it, son."

Allan knelt and examined the ground. The officer had, indeed, located exactly what he needed. Four clear footprints, heading northeast.

"It's the werewolf, all right," Allan told them.

"Terrific!" Chief Watson gazed over the field. "Captain Grout!" he shouted. "Officer Doyle! On the double!"

They were there in ten seconds.

"Allan is going to try and track the bastard before the front hits. Officer Ballinger and Officer Doyle will follow him, as before. Bob, stay here and coordinate the cleanup with the task force. I'll take three cruisers with me as the backup." He looked up at the blue sky still overhead. "Too bad the helicopter ran low on fuel and had to leave."

"Good luck, Tarzan." Grout smiled warmly. He rejoined the officers clustered around the small hill.

Allan glanced at the approaching storm system. Less than two hours, the Chief had said. There was no time for any more small talk. He stooped over and began tracking again, steeling himself against a residual queasy sensation in his stomach. After the grisly sight he'd seen, there was no possible way he would turn back now. The werewolf had to be caught, and it had to be done today!

The trail led across the backyards of a row of cottages, then bore east. It passed between two of the cottages and over a front lawn. Fortunately, the grass was relatively sparse and there were many areas of exposed earth. He wasn't surprised the lawns were poorly attended. Who came to the shore to grow grass?

Allan reached a curb. Which way to go? They were in the outskirts of Ocean City, the cottages and houses becoming closer and closer together. There would be less natural space for tracking and more concrete walks and streets to confuse the spoor. With the storm on the way he couldn't afford to delay. He had to intuitively guess correctly the first time, each time. On the far side of the street was a row of houses interspersed with cottages. Two houses to his left was a small hedgerow. That had to be it.

Leta and Doyle were catching up with him.

Allan ran to the hedge and studied the ground at the base. There they were, as he'd anticipated, bearing east again. The werewolf was moving quickly, using the hedgerow for a cover. The thing didn't miss a trick.

The wind was gathering strength, testifying to the proximity of the converging storm front.

Allan hurried as fast as the conditions permitted, crossing the lawns and gardens he encountered quickly, slowing when the werewolf reached a street, carefully scouring the opposite yards until he discovered the trail again.

Twenty minutes passed.

Often, on harder ground, the prints would be obscured, the werewolf's passage exposed by scattered traces of a heel or the faintly imbedded outline of claws.

Allan was perturbed by the claws. Even on the fresh, detailed tracks the claws were thin, indistinct lines. But claws on his feet? Artificial werewolf feet? Did they make such an outfit? What kind of nut would wear such a bizarre thing? He grinned, amused at himself. What kind of idiot would ask such a stupid question? The remains of that unfortunate child was proof positive, as if any were needed, of the extent of the werewolf's lunacy.

Another twenty minutes elapsed.

The gusty winds were steadily increasing in intensity and the atmosphere felt moisture-laden.

Allan looked over his right shoulder. Leta and Doyle were thirty yards behind him, engaged in conversation with the owner of a yard they had cut across. They were explaining to the man, as they'd done to three others so far, the reason his property was being traversed.

The storm system arrested his attention. The sun was obscured from view. The sky immediately over his head was covered with gray clouds, the huge, darker cloud mass rapidly arriving from the west. He estimated another thirty minutes, or less, before the first rain would descend.

Perturbed, he vigorously renewed his tracking. The werewolf was still bearing generally in an easterly direction. Was it making for its home base or merely romping through the city? The footprints crossed yet another lawn and entered an alley. They turned south, and the spacing indicated the werewolf was running at full speed, hastening, perhaps, to an intended destination.

Allan felt a drop of moisture strike the back of his neck. Then another.

Oh no!

The rain was beginning sooner than he'd expected!

Allan ran, alarmed, straining to discern the tracks in the packed gravel of the alley. If the precipitation should drop in a steady volume—the prints would be erased!

Five minutes went by. Only intermittent drops continued to fall.

The alley intersected with several streets, and each time the trail would resume on the other side of the roadway.

Five more minutes.

The werewolf was keeping to the center of the alley.

Lightning pierced the clouds, and for the first time thunder rumbled from the heavens.

The rain picked up.

No!

Allan ran bent over at the waist, his eyes alertly scanning the alley, detecting an entire track here, a smudged print there, all heading south.

The rain was now a drizzle.

Allan lurched forward recklessly, ignoring the few people he passed, not bothering to check the streets he crossed for oncoming traffic. Once he heard brakes squeal and someone curse.

The wind and the rain tingled his body, invigorating him.

Allan abruptly stopped, the sign gone. Where were the tracks? He backed up several feet and found them. The werewolf had turned left and entered a backyard.

Thunder boomed, lightning crackled, and the downpour began, instantly blotting out the spoor and limiting his vision.

If only he'd had five more minutes!

Allan faced the house in the center of the yard, squinting, the drops lashing his face. It appeared to be a white frame home, two stories high. Was it the werewolf's hiding place, or had he simply cut through the plot?

The thunder crashed nonstop as the full brunt of the storm engulfed Ocean City.

A hand gripped his left shoulder and Allan involuntarily jumped, startled.

"It's only me!" Leta yelled so she could be heard over the raging elemental fury. Doyle was beside her. "Did you

326

find anything?"

"Not much!" Allan shouted back. "The tracks enter this yard. He was probably just—"

A bolt of lightning rent the sky, not a quarter mile distant, and the ensuing erupting thunder drowned out his voice.

Leta pulled his left ear closer to her red lips. "Allan, you stay here and wait for Chief Watson. He should be along any minute. The atmospheric conditions are preventing me from contacting him with my radio. Doyle and I will check out this house. You wait here! Do you understand?"

Allan nodded, not bothering to attempt a verbal answer; the thunder was deafening.

Leta and Doyle ran toward the Painter house. The rain was falling in sheets. They were lost to view within twenty feet.

Allan patiently waited, the drops pelting his skin, drenching his clothes. God! He hoped Chief Watson would come along soon.

Several minutes passed.

Where were they? How long did it take to check a house? Allan walked onto the lawn and paused, attempting to see through the watery gloom. He'd give them five minutes more, and that was all.

The rainstorm gave no sign of abating, but for several seconds the lightning ceased and the thunder hushed.

In the lull he heard the shotgun.

Allan froze, listening. He was certain he'd heard the sound of the shotgun being fired. Once. What did it mean? He glanced down the alley, hoping, but there was no sign of Chief Watson and his backup. What should he do? Wait some more or see if Leta and Doyle required assistance?

The lightning and thunder broke loose again.

Well, at least inside he could dry off! He jogged around to the front of the house and found the front door.

It was wide open.

Allan slowly walked to the doorway and peered inside. Every light in the house was off and the interior was cast into deep shadow, highlighted by the recurrent flashes of lightning.

"Leta!" he screamed. "Leta! Are you in here?"

How could he expect her to hear him over the thunder?

Allan moved inside, glad to be out of the rain.

"Leta!"

No one responded.

Allan headed for a room at the end of a hall. The bright bursts of lightning revealed a living room; he spied a rocking chair, a sofa, and a television.

Someone groaned.

Allan was turning to leave and he stopped, hunting the source. Had his ears played tricks on—

"Leta!"

They were lying in the center of the living room floor, Doyle face down, a tiny pool of blood near his left cheek, his shotgun, the stock shattered, inches from his outstretched fingers. The next flash of lightning illuminated Leta, prone on her right side.

"Leta!"

Allan started to go to them, to aid them, when strong hands grabbed him by the shoulders, lifted him bodily from the floor, and flung him backward. He caught a glimpse of a leering, hairy face, and he slammed to the floor, dazed, groping, struggling to regain his footing.

The werewolf towered over him.

Allan kicked, his foot striking the werewolf's left shin, and the thing howled and backed off a step. His mind clearing, he scrambled away from the wicked monstrosity, gaining valuable distance. If the werewolf cornered him, he was done for! His only hope was to get outside and find help!

Snarling, the werewolf pounced.

Allan was astonished at its speed. The thing was on him before he could react, iron claws lunging for his neck. He tried to poke the werewolf in the eyes, to blind it. They rolled back and forth, neither gaining a decided edge, the werewolf shrieking.

A lightning streak revealed the werewolf's face; glinting eyes, lips curled, teeth glistening, saliva dripping over the bristling chin.

Allan sensed he was losing the battle. The thing possessed fantastic strength and stamina. Why hadn't he stayed in the alley?

They crashed into the hall wall, the werewolf bearing the main force of the jarring impact, and Allan knew his opportunity was now or never! He shoved and broke free, heaved to his feet, and ran for the door.

He almost made it.

A foot from the doorway the werewolf tackled him and they sprawled onto the porch, the rain promptly whipping them. They tumbled off the porch and fell onto the concrete walk. Allan felt an excruciating pain in his right elbow and his arm abruptly went limp.

The werewolf growled and finally locked his fingers, encircling his victim's throat.

Allan surged his body upward, bucked and heaved, but

the thing was too heavy, too immensely powerful.

Howling, the werewolf sadistically squeezed.

Allan could feel his consciousness slipping.

No!

The werewolf was trying to bite his neck!

"You son-of-a-bitch!"

Someone else was there. Allan could see a hand, clutching a revolver, hitting the werewolf on the back of the head again and again.

"Leave him alone!" someone shouted, and Allan recognized the voice of Leta Ballinger.

The werewolf twisted, releasing its primary prey, facing this new challenge, hissing.

Leta swung her Magnum, catching the thing on the temple. Enraged, it backhanded her, knocking her to the grass.

The werewolf rose, raised its claws to the thundering sky, and shrieked its primal fury.

Stunned, unable to assist Leta, Allan gaped, watching the eerie tableau.

The howling werewolf closed on its new target.

Leta aimed the .357 and, at point blank range, pulled the trigger.

The impact of the slug hurled the thing to the ground and it convulsed for several seconds, then lay still.

"Good shot," Allan muttered, smiling, realizing he could hear his voice and noticing that Leta heard him too. The lightning and thunder had ceased and the rain was now a drizzle.

"Are you okay?" Leta asked, rising to her knees.

"I think so," he answered, observing her shaky condition, her trembling hands. He couldn't blame her. Not after what they had just experienced. "How about you?" he inquired, surprised at the shocked expression on her white face. "What's the matter?" He glanced in the direction she was gazing and felt goosebumps prickle his skin.

The werewolf was rising!

"Dear God, no!" Allan mumbled.

The werewolf was erect, snarling, hunched over.

Allan looked at Leta, expecting her to shoot.

The werewolf shuffled forward.

Leta held the Magnum limply at her side.

The werewolf advanced on her.

She appeared to be thoroughly petrified.

Growling, the werewolf closed in. It was three feet from her and still she hadn't budged.

"Leta!" Allan tried to attract her attention.

The werewolf was two feet away and its paws were coming up toward her neck.

"Leta!" Allan screamed.

One foot.

Allan pushed himself to his hands and knees. "Leta, use your gun!"

The werewolf stood inches from its victim and placed its hands around her throat, slowly, disdainfully, savoring victory.

"*Leta!*"

Leta, incredibly, smiled. Coolly, swiftly, she brought the .357 up, pressed the tip of the barrel against the werewolf's forehead, and fired.

Allan gawked, fascinated, mesmerized, as the top of the werewolf's head exploded, blood and flesh showering outward.

The werewolf's body swayed, but it would not collapse.

331

Leta aimed her magnum at the remainder of the hairy face and shot one more time.

The massive form silently crumpled to the wet grass.

"Dear God!" Allan heard sirens clamoring, getting louder.

Leta Ballinger looked up at the sky, rain drops spattering her face, and laughed.

"I'LL NEVER BE ABLE TO THANK you enough, son."

"No thanks are necessary, Chief."

They were standing in the sunshine on the steps of Seacrest Hospital.

"Are those your parents down there?" Chief Watson asked.

"Yeah. I told them I wanted a minute with you alone."

"I never did get to meet them," Chief Watson said.

"You'll get your chance next year."

"You mean you're coming back?" Chief Watson chuckled.

Allan smiled. "I've discovered the shore isn't as boring a place as I always believed it was."

Chief Watson laughed. "I'm really sorry about that." He pointed at the cast and sling on Allan's right arm.

Allan shrugged. "A broken arm isn't the end of the world."

"I hope it doesn't interfere with your new job," Chief Watson stated sincerely.

"No problem." Allan glanced at his parents, standing in the parking lot below. "Say, I wanted to thank you for keeping my name out of the papers."

"You missed a chance to be famous," Chief Watson observed.

"I think I've outgrown that urge," Allan retorted. "I've had enough adventure and excitement to last me years."

"You know, Allan, we never could have caught Painter without your help."

"Oh, in time you would have." Allan adjusted his sling to a more comfortable position.

"And how many lives would have been lost before then?"

"Point made." Allan offered his left hand.

Chief Watson clasped Allan's fingers and held them. "I'm also sorry your vacation was cut short."

"That's my parents for you. They want me home where they can fuss over me and be sure I rest and eat my chicken soup." Allan grinned.

Chief Watson released Allan's hand. "When you come back next year will you stop and visit me?"

"You bet, Chief."

"Oh." The Chief suddenly remembered a message. "Leta wanted me to relay her apologies that she couldn't be here. She's tending to her fiancé, Earl Patterson."

"They got engaged?"

"In his hospital room. She wanted me to wish you the best."

"Tell her the same from me. It's been a pleasure knowing all of you. Even Captain Grout. I read in the paper about your friend they found buried in Painter's basement. His mother, too. Why is it I feel like I'll never get over what happened here?"

"That's normal. Just when you think you've adjusted to it, it will happen again."

334

"What?" Allan's eyebrows rose an inch.

"Oh, not here, not to you personally. But you can bet that somewhere, sometime soon, another mass murderer will indulge in a killing spree and the cycle will begin all over again."

Allan grimaced. "Sad, isn't it?"

"Nothing we can do about it until we find a way to weed out the degenerates and the defectives, until we find a method of detecting and controlling them. You're right. It's a crying shame."

"Well"—Allan started down the steps—"I'd best be going. We have a long drive ahead of us." He glanced fondly at his newfound friend. "I've got your address. I'll keep in touch."

"Keep up the tracking. You're the best I've ever seen. Maybe someday you'll teach me a few tricks of the trade?"

"Someday." Allan smiled and waved. "Take care, Chief."

"You bet." Chief Watson grinned and watched Allan walk to the bottom of the steps.

Allan stopped, looked up, and waved one final time. "Remember, watch out for the weirdos!"

EPILOGUE

It was satiated.

It was tired.

The vessel had developed nicely.

A rest was called for.

Rest.

Then it would feed again.

There was no rush.

The vessels would still be below, involved in their narrow little lives, no wiser, no closer to the truth.

There was no rush.

They could not destroy him until they all saw the light, and so few knew even the meaning of the light.

There was no rush.

It was timeless.